Praise for the authors of
Turn Up the Heat

New York Times bestselling author
LORI FOSTER

"Foster hits every note (or power chord)
of the true alpha male hero."
—*Publishers Weekly* on *Bare It All*

"A sexy, believable roller coaster of action and romance."
—*Kirkus Reviews* on *Run the Risk*

USA TODAY bestselling author
CHRISTIE RIDGWAY

"Emotional and powerful…
everything a romance reader could hope for."
—*Publishers Weekly* (starred review) on *Bungalow Nights*

"Sexy and addictive—Ridgway will keep you up all night!"
—*New York Times* bestselling author Susan Andersen
on *Beach House No. 9*

USA TODAY bestselling author
VICTORIA DAHL

"Victoria Dahl never fails to bring the heat."
—*RT Book Reviews* on *Too Hot to Handle*

"Rising romance star Dahl delivers
with this sizzling contemporary romance."
—*Kirkus Reviews* on *Close Enough to Touch*

LORI FOSTER

turn up
the heat

CHRISTIE RIDGWAY
VICTORIA DAHL

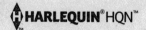

ISBN-13: 978-0-373-77838-6

TURN UP THE HEAT

Copyright © 2014 by Harlequin Books S.A.

The publisher acknowledges the copyright holders of the individual works as follows:

LOVE WON'T WAIT
Copyright © 2014 by Lori Foster

BEACH HOUSE BEGINNINGS
Copyright © 2013 by Christie Ridgway

STRONG ENOUGH TO LOVE
Copyright © 2013 by Victoria Dahl

Recycling programs for this product may not exist in your area.

Printed in U.S.A.

www.Harlequin.com

CONTENTS

LOVE WON'T WAIT

Lori Foster

Dear Reader,

After the *Love Bites* anthology was released with my story "Love Unleashed," about Evan Carlisle and his love, Cinder Bratt, many of you wrote to me asking about Evan's brother, Brick. Yes, Brick. What a name, right?

Well, now you get to find out how he got that name, and so much more! I very much hope you enjoy his consuming romance. I found it lots of fun to write.

If you haven't yet read *Love Bites,* rest assured each story stands alone. It's just a matter of which brother you meet first.

You can always see related books, their covers and a brief description of how they're related on my website under the "Connected Books" link.

Happy reading!

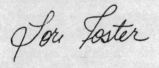

www.LoriFoster.com

CHAPTER ONE

RUMOR HAD IT, she was a virgin. As in, had never had sex.

Ever.

Looking at her now, Brendan Carlisle—Brick to those who knew him well—found that hard to believe.

Young, sure.

But not so young she hadn't had time and opportunity to get busy. He figured her to be in her mid-twenties, which would put her at a few years younger than him. Plenty old enough for just about anything. Actually, for everything. Like all those things now crowding his brain and making him twitchy.

Shifting in the booth seat, Brick settled back a little more and continued to study her.

Sweet? Oh, yeah, she was super sweet. Just look at that smile. And the dimples in her velvety cheeks were so damned cute. He'd almost swear her big green eyes sparkled as she spoke to customers and took orders. Polite but engaging. And yeah, really, *really* sweet.

But sweet enough to remain untouched? *Pfft.* He'd known plenty of sweet women who loved sex. Sometimes they dragged him off to the bedroom. He'd always adored sexually aggressive women. It was a big turn-on.

But the idea of sexual innocence teased him. He'd never before realized how exciting it might be to be…the first.

Until now. Until he looked at Merrily Loveland.

From the get-go, he'd been drawn to her. For nearly a month he'd been flirting, chatting her up and teasing while keeping things superficial—the way he preferred his relationships to be. He liked to sit back and let women make the first move. Then he would inform them of his intent to stay single, and take it from there.

Merrily hadn't made a move.

She was friendly enough, always gifting him with those dimples and smiles and bright green eyes.

But then, she gifted everyone the same way.

Why would an attractive, lusciously built, friendly woman have remained a virgin?

Lack of interest from guys? No way.

Merrily—God, he loved her name—looked like a stacked elf. Curvy, but still petite. Adorable, but

with a sensual heat lurking in her gaze. Bubbly...
and yet somehow a little reserved.

Religious convictions?

He didn't think so. Not that he'd know how to
tell just by engaging in occasional casual conversation with her while ordering lunch. But she had
such a ripe look about her that it seemed at odds
with any deep religious affiliation.

Waiting for marriage?

If so, then maybe he could convince her that
experiencing life was better than waiting.

She finished taking an order and turned to head
back to the kitchen. Her silky brown hair, held in a
high ponytail, swished back and forth between her
shoulder blades with each hurried step she took.

A plain sky-blue T-shirt hugged her upper body,
while snug jeans showed off her curvy backside.

Brick shifted again. In the weeks he'd known
her, he hadn't pressed her beyond friendly greet-
ings and putting in his lunch order. But how much
time could he spend hanging out at the diner before she caught on to his interest?

Was she a virgin? He wanted to find out. He
would find out.

And with that decision made, he felt himself
stir.

Damn it, around her, he had to constantly fight
off a boner. Insane. At twenty-eight, he didn't lack
control. But she affected him—and that was rea-

son number one why he'd hesitated to ask her out. A woman with that much influence on his libido could only be trouble. He *liked* being free of commitments and took great pleasure in answering to no one for anything, being accountable only to himself.

A clingy, marriage-minded woman could put a kink in his lifestyle.

But he could be her first...

Brick shook himself because reason number two—her supposed innocence—was a biggie.

If she was waiting for Mr. Right, or if she had some strong reasons for avoiding intimacy, well... he'd be as wrong for her as wrong could be. He'd ensure she enjoyed herself while in the sack, but afterward, when the spark faded and he walked away...

Yeah, much as he relished the idea of her innocence, he didn't relish the idea of breaking her heart.

Unfortunately, he wasn't into self-torture, and *not* having her would be pretty torturous, so to hell with it. He'd just have to figure out a way to have it all, and if—

"Hey, Brick. What's up?"

Guilty over the carnality of his thoughts, Brick jumped a good foot. "Damn it," he complained when diners at nearby tables glanced at him. He scowled over the appearance of his good friend, Jesse Baker. "I didn't see you come in."

As he sat opposite Brick in the booth, Jesse scrutinized him. Then he looked back at where Brick had been staring. He saw Merrily bent over a table as she served an older couple, turned back to Brick and grinned. "Taking in the view?"

"I was—but you shouldn't."

"Ho! Are you warning me off? Seriously?"

Brick hated to admit it, but… "Yeah, I am."

"Huh." Jesse eyed him with humor and great interest. "Well, in case you missed it, every guy with a pulse is also taking in the view. Why should I be the only one not to look?"

Brick didn't have to answer because Merrily joined their table, menus in hand. As she leaned over to place a menu in front of him, she said, "I'm so sorry for the wait. What can I get you guys to drink?"

Brick inhaled the scent of her hair and skin and froze as his pulse rushed and a slow heat unfurled. Her nearness affected him like a full-body caress, leaving him in a lust-inspired stupor.

Straightening, she struck a casual stance, one slim brow lifted, a half smile on her mouth, her eyes inquisitive…and Brick knew he was going to get hard.

Jesse eyed him again, snickered at his obvious condition and said, "I'll take a Coke."

"Yeah." His voice was so thick, Brick cleared his throat. Fighting the urge to study her body, he locked his gaze on her face. "Coke, light ice."

"Sure thing, guys. Be right back."

As she sashayed off, he released a pent-up breath.

And Jesse let loose a big guffaw. "What the hell, Brick?"

"Shut up." He tugged at the leg of his jeans, but it didn't help with the restriction of the denim.

"She's hot," Jesse agreed, as if he'd invited comment. "For a virgin, that is."

Eyes closing, Brick fought off the wash of automatic anger. He had no claim on Merrily—and he didn't want a claim.

He just wanted to be first.

So why should Jesse's taunt bother him so much? Easy answer: it shouldn't.

When he felt calm enough, he stared at Jesse and spoke in what he hoped sounded like mere curiosity. "You heard that, too, huh?"

"Yeah." Jesse studied him with tempered humor. "It's an intriguing concept, right? Initiation and all that."

Oh, yeah. Brick shook his head in denial. "You're an ass, Jesse."

"Just being honest. What red-blooded guy wouldn't be drawn to the idea of a woman who looks like she does but is still untouched?"

"Who says she's untouched?" The croak was back in his voice, but he pretended not to hear it. "There're all sorts of things to do that could leave a woman a technical virgin but not really inexperienced." And thinking about those things wouldn't help to cool his engines.

Merrily returned. She set the drinks down and pulled out a notepad and pen from her apron pocket.

And damn it, even that rumpled apron seemed somehow sexy, which was absurd given it was plain old sturdy white cotton.

"What's it gonna be, guys?"

God, such a loaded question.

Jesse, obviously enjoying his predicament, looked at Brick and waited for him to order.

Without touching the menu, Brick said, "Burger, loaded. Fries. And some hot sauce, please."

Her dimples appeared. "I should have known. That's a regular order for you. Maybe I can start using that old clichéd line."

The things her smile did to him... "What line is that?"

She struck a pose, then asked, "The usual?"

"Ah." She was *so* cute. "Could be. I've been eating here forever, but you've worked here for... what? A month now?"

"Just about."

He already knew that, of course. Hell, he could

tell her how many days, and if he thought about it, probably how many hours. He'd been a little obsessed since the first day he saw her, and once he heard that virgin business, he'd been lost. "Time flies when you're having fun."

Jesse kicked him under the table. Yeah, that was pretty lame, deserving of a kick.

But she didn't seem to notice. "I like it here. Everyone is so nice. And they've been great about working with me on my hours."

This was the first time she'd deliberately lingered to talk and Brick wanted to take advantage of it. "Meaning?"

She was always there for lunch but barely for the start of the dinner crowd and almost never for breakfast.

"I have classes." The smile widened. "I'm going to be a physical therapist—that is, if I ever get done. It's been slow going so far."

"Yeah?" His elbows on the booth top, absurdly charmed for no apparent reason, Brick leaned forward. "Why the delay?"

"I relocated, and that threw me off for a while, getting settled in and everything. It wasn't easy finding a place that'd take my pets. And the pets, of course, take up some of my time."

"Pets, plural?" So she was an animal lover, too? Nice.

"Two dogs and three cats."

He liked animals, so that didn't faze him. "A regular menagerie."

She laughed, and it was like getting French-kissed by a really hot chick.

"They have very different personalities, and I love them all. They've gotten me through some rough times." Suddenly catching herself, she shook her head—still smiling—and turned to Jesse. "I'm sorry for going on and on. What can I get you?"

As if waking up, Jesse said, "Hmm? Oh. I'll take a BLT and chips, and throw some pickles on the side, will you?"

"You've got it. I'll get this right out to you."

Off she went, with Brick staring after her... until Jesse grabbed his heart and feigned a swoon.

Damn it, it rankled that Jesse had reason to harass him. "Go screw yourself."

Jesse laughed. "You look like a lovesick pup! What the hell, Brick? Mooning over her? Hanging on her every word? I half expected you to slide out of your seat and onto your knees before her."

"I repeat, go screw yourself." But he knew it was true. Even now he had to consciously fight the urge to track her every movement in the restaurant. He didn't do things like that. He didn't get all hung up on a woman. Ever.

Not even a hot little virgin.

And that reminded him... "So where did you hear that virgin stuff?"

With a knowing smile, Jesse shrugged. "I overheard some of the other waitresses talking, and one of them said she heard it from a past boyfriend of hers."

"Probably jealous," Brick muttered.

"Probably," Jesse agreed. "She's getting more than her fair share of attention."

Something he'd already noticed—and didn't like. "Tips, too." In the small town where they all lived and worked, everyone knew everyone. Brick ran the family-owned hardware store, and Jesse was a carpenter with his own shop. Brick's brother, Evan, worked for the elementary school as a gym teacher, and Evan's wife, Cinder, was a nurse.

Most days, Brick and Jesse met for lunch at the diner because it was just across the street from Brick's store. It served good, homemade food, it was affordable, and it catered to locals by celebrating high school sports and supporting the other businesses.

When Ms. Merrily Loveland started working at the restaurant, everyone noticed, especially everyone male—and the gossip started.

"Where did you hear it?" Jesse asked.

"Couple of bozos came in a few weeks ago to buy paint. One guy said he'd asked her out and was turned down flat. The other said he used to live in the same town with her back in college, only a couple of hours from here."

"Same with the waitress." Jesse shrugged. "I think maybe they were in college at the same time."

"One of the guys claimed she used to be engaged, but when she wouldn't give it up, the guy left her."

"And told everyone about it?" Jesse snorted. "What an ass."

"Yeah." Brick took a big drink of his cola. "The talk went downhill from there." He wouldn't repeat it all because it hadn't been kind, but there'd been insults claiming her to be cold, asexual, even deliberately manipulative, as if she used her innocence as a tool.

"And you didn't throw them both out? Huh. Good for you, Brick." Jesse reached across the booth to slap his shoulder. "I mean, I can see you're pissed about it, so the fact that you actually kept your temper in check—"

As Merrily returned to them, Brick gave a quick shake of his head. But not in time.

While setting their food on the table, she teased, "You have a temper? No way. You're always so nice."

"He would never show that temper to you," Jesse assured her. "But yeah, when warranted, it makes an appearance."

Brick gave him a dirty look. Was he trying to scare her off?

Intrigued, Merrily asked, "Is that why they call you Brick?"

She knew his nickname? Nice. Though they'd chatted casually many times, they hadn't been formally introduced. He'd seen her name on her name tag and used it as most would. Apparently she'd been paying attention when others spoke to him.

"Actually," Jesse said, now on a roll, "he got that name ages ago when he fell off a roof onto his head and was still able to laugh about it."

"Ohmigosh." She stared at Brick in disbelief. "You're serious?"

"Yeah, but it's not as bad as it sounds." He'd strangle Jesse later for bringing that up. "The house was half-built into a hill, so the roof at one end was pretty close to the ground."

"Still…"

"I only dropped around ten feet."

"Ten feet?" Her eyes widened again. "And you weren't hurt?"

"Just bruised my pride." He gave a slight grin. "That is, as much pride as a nine-year-old boy can have."

"If you guys were that young, what in the world were you doing on the roof?"

Brick felt his neck getting hot.

Jesse, of course, launched into details. "He was pretending to be Batman. His brother, Evan, who's a year younger, was Robin."

She smiled, and this time, the smile was unlike any other—softer, gentler. "Aww. That's so sweet."

He snorted. "No it's not. After I fell, Evan ran home to tell our mom and she grounded us for a week." A week that had felt like a month.

"I can't say I blame her." Looking a little wistful, Merrily tipped her head to study him. "Did you and your brother wear costumes?"

"Masks and capes." He grinned despite his efforts not to. "Looking back on my misspent youth, I think it's a wonder I survived."

"Your poor mother," she agreed. Another customer called to her, so after a quick touch to his shoulder, she slipped away.

That touch—on the freaking shoulder, for crying out loud—brought his temperature up a few degrees more.

"Pathetic," Jesse said. "Get a grip, will you?"

"She likes me."

"Yeah? And you drew that conclusion...why?"

He shrugged. "She touched my shoulder."

Jesse grabbed his heart again. "Your shoulder? Damn. That brazen hussy. I guess it must be love."

Ignoring that, Brick said, "I'm going to ask her out."

That seemed to surprise Jesse but not because of his intent. "You haven't already?"

"No."

"Why not? I figured you'd hit on her from day one and just got shot down."

"No." Why he hadn't yet asked her out, he couldn't say. He'd known her plenty long enough. And he'd only recently heard that virgin business. But there was something about her that made him not want to rush things—

"Never knew you to be insecure, Brick. There go my illusions."

He snorted. "I'm not insecure." And Jesse knew it. Hell, he didn't have an insecure bone in his entire body. But speaking of bones… He shifted again. "I'll ask her out today."

"Yeah? So?"

"So I want you to stuff that food down your throat and then get out of here."

"This is my lunch break! And it's not like she's going anywhere. If you've already waited a month, why can't you wait until I finish eating?"

Yeah…he supposed he could. He didn't want to, but it made more sense than throwing Jesse out of the restaurant and rushing things. "Fine." He liberally poured hot sauce on his food. "But don't linger."

For an answer, Jesse took an enormous bite of his sandwich.

For the next twenty minutes, Merrily stayed pretty busy. Brick noticed that she chatted with everyone. He wasn't special in that regard.

Except that she didn't touch anyone else, so regardless of what Jesse thought, her fleeting touch to his shoulder did mean something.

What, exactly, he didn't yet know.

By all accounts, she'd turned down dates. Not that it mattered. He wasn't an insecure schoolboy who quailed in the face of possible rejection.

If she turned him down, he'd just have to figure out a way to change her mind.

Without seeming pushy. Or stalkerish.

Coming out of the kitchen with a loaded tray, she moved around her seating area, dropping off food, refreshing cups of coffee, taking new orders and seeing that everyone had everything they wanted.

Finally, while digging a bill out of her pocket, she approached again.

"You guys need anything else? More to drink? Dessert?"

Jesse said, "I'm good, thanks."

"Same here."

She placed respective bills on the booth top before them, clasped her hands together and faced Brick again. "If you're all done, mind if I ask you something?"

After a stifled grin, Jesse did him a solid by saying, "It's your turn to pay, Brick, and I'm running late. So if you don't mind...." He pushed his bill toward Brick and slid out of his seat.

Merrily sent him a smile. "Thank you for stopping by. Come see us again."

"Will do." Whistling under his breath, Jesse sauntered out.

In the middle of a busy restaurant, at the tail end of the lunch crowd, Brick relished the moment of relative privacy. "Got a second to sit down?"

"Oh, yes. Thank you." She untied her apron and took Jesse's seat opposite him. "I'm actually off early today."

So now might be a good time to get to know her better.

She wrinkled her pert little upturned nose. "I can't stay long, though. I have a ton of stuff to get done."

"Classes?"

"Those are in the morning. But the animals have been closed up since this morning, I have laundry piling up, and I'm hoping to put in a doggy door."

"You have your own house?" He'd love to find out where she lived.

She shook her head. "I'm renting a duplex, but my landlord is okay with it—for a small fee, of course—and I know my pets would appreciate it. I hate leaving them cooped up while I'm away, so…" She shrugged. "That's what I wanted to ask you. I know you own the hardware store. Do you sell whatever I'll need?"

He had what she needed, all right. "Actually, it's a family business. Mom and Dad retired early, and Evan wasn't interested in it, so I run it. In a couple more years, I'll buy them out."

"That's nice. You're close with your family?"

"Real close. You?"

Avoiding his gaze, she moved aside Jesse's plate. "Dad died in a car wreck when I was seventeen. Mom was disabled. But last year she passed away, too."

Wow. His heart clenched over such devastating losses. "Siblings?"

She shook her head. "It was just Mom and me." With a cheerless smile, she added, "And our menagerie."

So she'd inherited the animals? Drawn to her, needing the contact, he touched her slender fingers, hesitated, and when she didn't pull away, he held her hand. "You said your mom was disabled?"

"Except for doctor appointments, she preferred not to venture out much. It was too difficult for her, and she felt conspicuous."

"Did she need full-time care?" He couldn't imagine that type of responsibility being dumped on someone so young.

Merrily shook her head. "I kept meals ready for her, and we cleared the house enough that she could get around pretty well in her powered wheelchair. When I had to be away, for school and grocery shopping and stuff like that, I kept a cell phone on me for any emergency calls. She loved our animals, and they loved her. They kept her company when I couldn't be with her."

Damn. "I'm sorry, Merrily."

"We managed okay. I mean, until she worsened." Slowly she freed herself from his touch. "After she passed away, the animals had a hard time adjusting. I figured a change of scenery would be nice, so here I am. *With* the animals, who, like I said, are family to me."

"But you need that doggy door."

"Yes. They're happier now, but they were used to her being there. Now they're alone..." She blew out a breath. "I think they'll enjoy it more if they can get outside and play a little or even just lay in the sun."

He considered her, wondering how much her mother's health might have played into her broken engagement. Not many men would sign on for that type of responsibility. "Are you handy around the house?"

She laughed. "Not really, no. But I can read directions."

Man, she had a nice laugh. Not too girly, not at all fake. Just...nice. "Do you have a good tool set?"

"I have a hammer and a screwdriver." She bit her bottom lip but ended up shaking her head. "Will I need a lot of other stuff?"

Perfect opening. If it hadn't been for the heart-breaking story she'd just shared, he'd have grinned in anticipation. But given her reasons for relocating, he managed to hold it together. "Tell you what. Why don't I put in the doggy door for you?"

He waited for objections, for excuses, or a flat-out no.

She dropped back in her seat. "Seriously? You'd do that? I mean, I'll pay you, of course, but I—"

"Neighbor to neighbor," he said, cutting her off. Given what he wanted from her, no way could he let money change hands. "I'm happy to help out."

Still surprised, she said, "But we're not neighbors."

No, but he wanted her bad. "In this town, everyone is a neighbor."

"You're sure?"

"It'll be my pleasure." He'd find out where she lived, make himself useful and in the end…he'd have her under him, where they'd both have some fun.

Even to him, that sounded like a Grade-A prick move.

But she forestalled any opportunity for him to retrench when she said with heartfelt gratitude, "Thank you. I appreciate it more than I can say."

CHAPTER TWO

MERRILY LOOKED AROUND the duplex again, saw everything was in order and tried not to listen for Brick's knock at her front door. The laundry would have to wait for another day. She'd tidied the space as much as she could with five pets underfoot. Like toddlers, they had toys everywhere. And though she'd just vacuumed, fur was a never-ending issue.

Dundee, an Australian shepherd and border collie mix, knew something was happening. He watched her with ears perked up, expression alert. "It's okay, Dundee. Just be on your best behavior, please." Because Dundee was always a happy fellow, eager to please, that wasn't asking too much of him.

Dolly, a smaller bearded collie mix, didn't really care enough about any visitor to skip her nap. Merrily could hear her low snores and, as always, it made her smile.

The cats kept vigil in different windows, with Union Tom and Stan the Man sticking together against Eloise, who tended to run the show. Ellie was a lovely lady, but as the only female cat, she ruled the dogs and the male cats with little more than a look.

Merrily ran a hand over her loose hair and again wondered if she should contain it in a ponytail. For the longest time, her regimen had included washing, dressing and restraining her hair. She almost felt pretentious for letting it hang loose.

As for her lip gloss, she'd already chewed that off, so it had been a complete waste of time. At least her jeans and yellow T-shirt weren't much different from what she wore at work.

Chaos erupted with Brick's first tap on her door. The cats shot off the windows, Dundee started dancing and Dolly awoke with such a barking start she almost fell off the couch. Merrily could barely hear herself as she urged them all to hush, to heel, to try not to appear quite so much like wild animals.

She opened the door and found Brick standing there with a smile.

"I hear them," he said with amusement. He leaned around her to peek in, and the smile widened to devastating impact.

Oh, God, Merrily thought. If he was an animal lover on top of being so gorgeous and funny and...*attentive* to her, she'd be a goner in no time.

"Come on in."

He got one foot in the door and Dundee was on

him, his paws on Brick's chest as he tried to lick his face, pelting him with doggy breath.

Brick laughed outright. He set aside a large toolbox that looked like it weighed a ton and went to one knee.

Big mistake.

Dundee all but took him to the floor. But Brick was stronger than her so he didn't end up on his tight muscled butt. Instead he seemed to enjoy Dundee's attention.

With high-pitched maniacal barking, Dolly vied for her own share of notice.

Sitting on the floor, Brick laughed some more and struggled to give both dogs the pets they craved.

"Really," Merrily told them. "You guys will have him thinking you're neglected, that I'm a terrible pet owner who leaves you starved for crumbs of attention."

"Nah," Brick said around his chuckles. "They're terrific."

Terrific? Seriously? Maybe he hadn't noticed the cats yet. Or how dog hair already clung to his dark T-shirt. Or the...oh, no...doggy drool on his shoulder.

She covered her mouth and asked in a horrified whisper, "Should I call them off?"

"Why? I like the enthusiastic greeting."

Dolly got into his lap, and he let her. Dundee

kept snuffling his neck and chest—which was something Merrily wouldn't mind trying if given half a chance.

Unsure what else to do, she seated herself on the couch. Eloise immediately joined her to watch the display with disdain.

Tom and Stan strode into the fray and with little more than a meow had the dogs backing off enough to sit beside Brick instead of on him.

"Names?" he asked Merrily, as if being accosted by an animal horde was just fine and dandy.

She cleared her throat. "Dundee is the bigger dog, Dolly the smaller. That yellow fellow with the round face is Tom, better known as Union Tom because he was found by Union Terminal. That's Stan the Man with the adorable yellow eyes. And here in my lap is Eloise."

"She has beautiful coloring."

Merrily wanted to melt. "She's a dilute tortoiseshell, and yes, very beautiful."

"You said Tom was found by Union Terminal?"

"They've all been adopted from shelters. Dolly was…not treated well."

Brows coming down, Brick reached out to the little dog again.

"Her shaggy gray fur needs a lot of work and her previous owners just didn't care. They kept her outside, and she was dirty, matted… I'm sure she was miserable."

Brick said nothing, but his jaw tightened and he cuddled Dolly a little closer.

Well. A telling move, that. So he was breathtakingly gorgeous *and* kind.

No wonder he had such an amazing reputation with the ladies.

She swallowed back her sigh of longing. "Dundee is seven years old but still acts like a pup. As you already found out, he loves to give doggy kisses."

In an absurd voice, he said to Dundee, "Yes he does. Don't you boy? You do. Lots of doggy kisses."

Merrily gaped at him. And wanted to melt again.

Returning his attention to her, and his voice now normal, Brick said, "I'll be stopping by my brother's later. He and his wife have a dog and cat who'll think I've been out cheating on them when they smell your pets on me." He laughed. "Doug and Cate can be very possessive."

"Those are the pets?"

"Yeah. Doug the dog and Cate the cat. Love the names, right? They were shelter pets, too. Evan and Cinder weren't a couple then, just neighbors." He smiled. "Though Evan had it for her bad, I don't mind telling you. Anyway, they went to the shelter together. She got Doug, and he got Cate, and later they got married, and now they're a happy family."

Her heart swelled. "That sounds like a lovely fairy tale."

Brick shot her a puzzled look. "Nah. Just real-life love. Happens all the time." Putting the animals aside, he came back to his feet.

He was so big that it prompted her to stand, too, so he wouldn't be towering over her. At least not as much as when she sat. Since he stood well over six feet tall, and she was less than five and a half feet, there'd be some towering going on no matter what she did.

But with Brick, she sort of liked it.

The cat squirmed in her arms, so Merrily started to set her down. Eloise had other ideas. She held on while staring at Brick in something akin to challenge.

A small, sexy smile tilted his mouth. He touched Eloise under her chin, and the cat closed her eyes in bliss. "So you're the boss, huh?"

How did he know that? "It seems the cats are naturally bossier than dogs. And she's the only female cat, so…"

"Nature's way, I guess." His hand went from Eloise's chin to Merrily's hair, tucking it behind her ear, then grazing her cheek. "You look nice with your hair loose."

Her tongue stuck to the roof of her mouth so all she could do was stare at him. The combo of a casual touch and a compliment packed a wallop to her starved senses.

"But I like the ponytail you usually wear, too."

"Oh…um…"

That knowing smile of his widened. He ran his big thumb along her jaw…then dropped his hand and looked around her home. "You have a nice place."

"Thank you."

He looked up at the cove ceiling. "There's so much character in an old house like this."

"I like it." In a very short time, it had become her *home,* not just her residence. "The landlord, Tonya Bloom, did a great job in dividing it up for a duplex. In most of the rooms, you can't even tell that it used to be one house."

"Who lives next door?"

"She does. The landlord, I mean." Merrily really didn't want to talk about Tonya.

"She's nice?"

"Very nice." As well as beautiful, incredibly built, smart and successful. The comparisons could depress her, except that Tonya was one of those people who treated everyone like a cherished friend.

She did *not* want Tonya treating Brick that way.

Time to get him thinking about a different topic. "I was hoping the doggy door could open to the backyard." Eloise still refused to be put aside, so

Merrily carried her in her arms as she went into the kitchen.

Along the way, Brick held silent, and she assumed he was taking in the original high baseboards and the sloping wooden floors. But when she looked back, it was her behind he stared at. She faced forward again and tried not to put any more swing in her walk than necessary.

"Right here would be the ideal spot." She indicated the thick wooden door that opened to the small fenced yard.

When she turned, Brick was right there, crowded in close behind her in the small confines of the galley kitchen. He was so close, in fact, that Eloise could lean out and rub her head against his shoulder.

A little dumbfounded, Merrily stared up at him while breathing in the amazing scent of hot, hunky male. She'd been around other men and never noticed their scent. Did he smell different? Or just better?

Brick glanced at her with a raised brow and a barely there smile.

She *had* to get it together or he'd start to wonder at her motives, which, yes, included the desire for more than a doggy door to accommodate her pets.

Sidling around him, Merrily tried to gather her wits. "Would you like anything to eat? Or drink?"

He knelt down to examine the base of the door.

His dark T-shirt stretched tight across his broad back and solid shoulders and the denim of his jeans hugged his flexed thighs. "I'll take a drink, thanks."

Lord, have mercy. Stalling, Merrily lifted a hand and fanned her face, but it didn't help with the flash flood of heat.

Maybe she should have started this plan with someone just a little less...everything.

Less macho, less gorgeous, less overwhelming.

Problem was, no one else had appealed to her.

He glanced back. "Merrily?"

Having a big sexy guy around was an aberration and she knew she was bound to trip up occasionally, but still, she wanted to be just a little smoother. "I, ah, don't have anything alcoholic. I'm sorry. I didn't even think about it or I could have picked up some beer or something—"

Releasing her from the snare of his dark gaze, he opened the door and asked, "What do you have?"

"Iced tea or coffee. Cola. Maybe some juice..."

"Tea would be great, thanks." He glanced back at her again, then all over her, before returning his attention to her face. "I'm not a big drinker."

"Oh. Okay." Merrily bit her lip at that lame reply. What did *okay* even mean? Should she admit she wasn't much of a drinker either? No. Not yet.

Not when so many social relationships relied on casual drinking.

After a ridiculous smile, she spun around and almost tripped over Dolly and Dundee. They sat there, staring at Brick with the same fascination she felt.

She put Eloise in a kitchen chair and opened the fridge.

By the time she'd finished filling a glass with ice and pouring the tea, Brick was standing again, his hands on his hips, expression pensive.

She handed him the tea. "Is there a problem?"

"Not a problem, exactly. I can do it. It's just that I kind of hate to."

He drank deeply, and she watched the way his throat worked. This late in the day, he had a dark beard shadow. She wanted to touch his throat, to feel the rasp of his stubble, maybe brush over it with her lips…

After finishing half the drink, he frowned at the door. "Your landlord actually agreed to let us do this?"

Merrily had no idea what he was getting at. "I talked with her about it before making any real plans."

"Well…" He rubbed the back of his neck. "Before I do anything, I'd like to talk to her, too. Do you know when she'll be around?"

No, no, no. She didn't want Brick and Tonya in

the same room together—with good reason. "You don't believe me?"

"Sure I do. But I'm guessing neither of you realize the value of that door. Before I start cutting on it, I want to talk to her myself."

The idea of him meeting Tonya disheartened her, but what could she do? Merrily shrugged. "She's usually home by now, actually." Tom stretched up to her leg, so she lifted him. "I don't understand your concern."

"That's one hell of a vintage door to chop up. Solid, probably original to the house, and still in great shape. They don't make them like that anymore, not unless someone wants to spend a small fortune. People refurbishing old homes would go nuts over it. Seems a shame to mess it up. Once I cut it for the pet door, it'll never be the same, and replacing it later with another door like it wouldn't be easy."

"Oh." Merrily looked at the door, but to her, it was just…a door. "So I guess a pet entry is out."

"No, we can still do it. But if your landlord agrees, I'd rather take that door down and store it so it can be put back in if you ever move. In the meantime we can throw up a cheaper door and use it for the pet entry. It'd still look nice, and it'd be plenty secure. What do you think?"

"Won't that be more work for you?"

"Not a lot. As long as you don't mind having me around an extra day or so, it's not a big deal."

Mind having him around? He had to be joking. "There's a shed out back where you could store it or maybe in the basement or attic." She hated to sound unsympathetic to the old house, and she loved the idea of prolonging his visit, but… "How much would a new door cost me?"

"Nothing. Jesse probably has something lying around that would fit."

"Jesse?"

"My friend from lunch today." He tipped his head. "You don't remember him?"

"I do." Jesse had an engaging smile, blond hair and green eyes, but sitting across from Brick, he'd been almost invisible—at least to her. Without thinking it through, she admitted, "I heard a few of the other waitresses talking about him."

"Yeah? Saying what?"

She cleared her throat. "Just…girl talk."

At her show of discomfort, his gaze brightened and a smile played over his mouth. "Tell me."

"No." She shook her head. "I couldn't."

He set his drink aside and, with teasing intent, stalked closer. "C'mon, Merrily. Out with it."

She back-stepped until her backside bumped into the counter. Heat rushed into her face. This was a new game to her, but she didn't want him to know that.

He got so close that her heart hammered and a strange tingling spread out to her limbs.

It wasn't at all an unpleasant feeling. Not with Brick.

"Now don't faint on me."

"No. I won't." She might jump him, but she wouldn't pass out and miss any of this. She cleared her throat. "They, ah, said that Jesse was so sexy, he…"

"He what?"

To get it over with, she blurted, "Made panties drop."

Brick didn't put any space between them. In fact, he brushed her cheek with the backs of his knuckles. "And what about you?"

"What about me?"

"You think Jesse is all that?"

"What? No." She shook her head hard. "I mean, I'm sure he's nice enough."

"He is."

But he wasn't Brick. She shrugged. "That's it. He's nice."

Brick's slow smile said a whole lot of stuff—but she wasn't sure what exactly. "He's a carpenter, so he always has extra materials on hand. If he doesn't have a door that fits exactly, he can cut it down to make it work. Piece of cake for him."

He was still too darned close for coherent

thought, but she muddled through. "I'd have to insist on paying him."

Slowly, his gaze warm and intimate, Brick tucked her hair behind her ear—and finally gave her some space. "You can take that up with Jesse, but either way, it wouldn't be much. So what do you say? Why don't we go discuss it with the landlord right now so I can get to work on this for you?"

Darn it. She didn't want to. If she had her way, Tonya Bloom would never be within smiling distance of Brick. Tonya smiled and men went stupid—she was *that* beautiful. But with Tonya living next door, the idea of them never running into each other was unrealistic and she knew it. "I could just talk with her and then let you know what she says."

Brick studied her. She *knew* he studied her, that he wondered at her motives, and it made her want to squirm.

After a few nerve-racking seconds of scrutiny, he seemed to come to a conclusion. He nodded at her kitchen table. "Mind if I sit down while I finish my tea?"

Oh. "That'd be fine." She followed him to the table, but when Brick pulled out a chair, he found Eloise curled up in it. The cat gave him a "do not disturb" look and settled again.

"Sorry, old girl." He pulled out another chair, and there was Tom draped over the seat. In the next chair was Stan, one leg in the air while he "groomed" himself.

Feeling foolish, she explained, "They like to be where I am."

"Can't say as I blame them." Instead of acting put out, he smiled at the cats. "The couch, then?"

"I could move them." It was a lame, unenthusiastic offer. She hated to disturb her pets when they slept. So often, she would inconvenience herself first.

Brick curved his big, warm hand around her upper arm. "The couch works." He led her back through to the living room, Dolly and Dundee following hot on their heels. He sat and urged her down close to him.

But rather than finish off his tea, he set it aside and turned to her, his gaze moving slowly over her face. "So."

So...*what?* She waited, uncertain what to say or do, not knowing what he intended.

"Why don't you want me to meet the landlord?"

Wow, intuitive and straight to the point. She wasn't used to guys being so up-front.

Actually, she wasn't all that used to guys, period. But the ones she had known weren't exactly straight shooters. More like vague with hidden agendas.

By way of an answer, she asked her own question. "What makes you think I don't?"

His gaze softened in understanding. "Not to brag, Merrily, but I know women."

She was sort of counting on that.

Casually, he put an arm up along the back of the couch—behind her shoulders. "And I see it in your expression."

Dolly jumped up to the couch and went into his lap, circled twice, then plopped down with a sigh. As if he barely noticed, Brick scratched the dog's ears with his free hand and continued to stare at Merrily, waiting for her reaction.

Even after Dundee sat on his foot and leaned into his leg, Brick didn't pull that unwavering gaze from her face.

A multitude of reasonable excuses tripped through her mind, but she'd always been a terrible fibber. If he could be up-front, maybe she should be, too.

"Tonya is…really pretty." Lame. Tonya was well beyond merely pretty.

"So?"

"So…" Her face went hot, but she lifted her chin. "I do want a doggy door. As you can see, I need one."

"Agreed."

"But I was also hoping…that is…" How did one spell out carnal intent? She met his gaze and went for broke. "I like you."

The corner of his mouth tilted in a crooked smile. "I'm listening."

He was, very intently, and it rattled her composure big-time. She cleared her throat. "You know I'm still kind of new to the area. Between school and work, I haven't had a chance to get to know that many people." She didn't really know him either, but not only did she enjoy talking to him at the restaurant, she also found him oh-so physically appealing.

And the other waitresses didn't talk only about Jesse. They'd had plenty to say about Brick, as well. He had quite a reputation, and it was so scintillating, so exciting, she couldn't resist the idea of a daring sensual adventure.

That is, if Brick cooperated.

"I was hoping…that is…" For crying out loud, she sounded idiotic. "I don't want to scare you off or anything. I'm not trying to rope you in. But I think you're…sexy."

His smile warmed.

"And you're nice. And there's just something about you…" *Something raw and appealing and exhilarating.* Merrily put her shoulders back. "I'd like to sleep with you."

Surprise chased off his smile. His eyes widened a little, then narrowed.

Just in case she hadn't been clear enough, she stated, "For sex."

There. She'd said it. Not the smoothest come-on, for sure, but under her extenuating circumstances, it would have to do.

She waited on pins and needles to see how the oh-so-awesome Brick Carlisle would react.

WOMEN RARELY THREW him for a loop, but Brick had to admit that Merrily did it when she wasn't even trying.

A hungry look, a nervous smile, and he missed a beat. She was just so open, so unguarded in her desire.

It made sense that when she *did* try—with a straight-shot, spell-it-out confession, no less—he was guaranteed to falter.

No way had he expected her to make it so easy for him. No way had he expected a supposed virgin to state her case so bluntly.

Out of necessity, he lifted the dog away from his lap and set her on the couch between them. He shifted and stretched out one leg, but it didn't help.

"Well?" Probably as much for comfort as out of habit, Merrily scooped up the dog and hugged her close.

He was saved from trying to reply coherently by a knock on her door.

Looking a little stricken, she closed her eyes and blew out a breath.

"You expecting someone?" Brick asked.

"No." She opened her eyes to show churning un-
certainty. "The only one who visits me is Tonya."

No guys visiting, then. Good to know.

She'd claimed to like the landlord, so why so
glum now? "That's a problem...because?"

Again she lifted her chin. "I want you."

"Yeah. Heard that the first time." If she kept
saying it, how the hell did she expect him to show
any finesse at all? "I'm on board, honey, trust me.
So why don't we talk to the landlord to clear up
the door situation, then we can discuss..." He gestured between them. "You having me."

She blinked at him.

Yeah, way to be romantic, Brick. Way to se-
duce her.

Way to encourage her. He snorted at himself,
then forced a smile. "Are you going to ignore the
knocking?"

"No, I suppose not." She put Dolly onto the
couch and stalked off to answer.

Curious, Brick stood, did a quick adjustment
with his jeans, then followed her. So did Dolly and
Dundee. Luckily the cats slept on in the kitchen.

Merrily opened the door and— Holy hell, her
landlord was a knockout. She stood damn near as
tall as Brick, with long, pale blond hair and longer legs well displayed in a short suit skirt and
fashionable high heels. Heavy lashes framed light
blue eyes.

The vision said, "Hi, Merrily! I was wondering how…" Her voice trailed off when she spotted Brick. The smile changed, going from real warmth to mere formality. She extended her hand. "Hello. I'm Merrily's neighbor and landlord, Tonya Bloom."

"Pleasure." Brick took her hand in a brief greeting. "Brick Carlisle."

In a silent, almost funereal invitation, Merrily held the door wide.

Suit jacket open to reveal a feminine blouse and perfect curves, Tonya stepped inside. Dundee and Dolly ran up to her, but they didn't jump. In fact, they had impeccable manners, stopping before her, waiting patiently for the expected pats she gave.

"Hello, babies, how are you?" She made kissing noises at them, scratched their chins, and they stared back at her in blind canine adoration. "Where are the kitties?"

"Kitchen," Merrily said. "Sleeping."

Brick wondered at her short replies, but Tonya forged into the kitchen, asking, "Is the doggy door in yet?"

"I wanted to talk to you about that." He took Merrily's hand and tugged her along with him as he followed in the wake of Tonya's subtle and seductive perfume. He explained about the value of the door and made his suggestions for trading it out with something less vintage.

Tonya listened as she greeted each cat in turn. Bending from the waist—offering a tantalizing view of a heart-shaped ass—she rubbed Tom's ears, tickled under Eloise's chin and stroked along Stan's back. The combined purrs set the kitchen humming.

The woman had killer looks and a luscious body to go with the face; what she did for a suit would make most men stammer. Brick imagined she had a hard time fending off the attention.

He caught Merrily's tortured expression. He didn't entirely understand it, but he squeezed her hand in quick encouragement. "We can put in a door that still goes with everything but won't be as valuable."

"That's so nice of you." She eyed the door with new insight. "Of course you're right. I don't know why I didn't think of it. And yes, as much as I love it, someday I'll sell this property."

Because holding her hand didn't suffice, Brick pulled Merrily into his side and put his arm over her shoulders. She stood frozen beside him, stiff and unyielding.

Yet minutes ago, she'd claimed to want him.

Tonya's knowing smile touched on them both. "Well, I don't want to intrude."

"You're not," Merrily said.

Brick spoke over her, saying, "Thank you." The sooner he got the landlord on her way, the sooner he could decide how to proceed with Merrily. "I'll get with my friend, Jesse, and pick out a door that matches close enough. If it works for Merrily, we'll get it installed tomorrow."

"Tomorrow?" Merrily asked, and damned if she didn't look surprised. "Really?"

"Yeah, why?" No matter what happened today, they were far from finished with one another. "You busy?"

She shook her head.

"Good." He recalled her exact words—that she didn't plan to rope him in. What exactly did that mean? Did she want sex only once?

Like hell! Once wouldn't cut it. A dozen times might not suffice. He intended to get his fill—but he'd make it good for her, too.

"I'm free, you're free. Might as well get it taken care of, right?"

She nodded fast. "Okay."

He hugged her a little closer before turning back to Tonya. "Where did you want to store this one?"

"My basement would be best. Do you suppose you or your friend could bring it over?"

"Not a problem. You'll be around tomorrow?"

"After two o'clock, I will be."

He tried to head her toward the living room. "That works. Guess I'll see you then."

Tonya said her goodbyes to the cats and then to each of the dogs. They hung on her every word, adoring her. It made Brick smile. "You're good with the animals." There was something very appealing about a gorgeous woman who was also kind.

And that gave him an idea.

Tonya paused at the front door. "And I take it you're good with your hands?"

Clever, too. He grinned. "Very."

"His family has a hardware store," Merrily rushed to explain. "Brick runs it."

He had no idea why she sounded so proud about that. "And I'm very handy."

"Wonderful." Tonya stepped into the hall. "I don't want to take advantage, but do you suppose you could also check the fence to make sure it's secure? I don't want the doggies to get loose."

"I could do that," Merrily said.

At the same time, Brick replied, "Be glad to." Damn it, was she already trying to get rid of him?

Tonya laughed. She looked at Merrily and laughed again. "Thank you both. Brick, if I need to do any repairs to the fence, just let me know." Still smiling, she turned to go next door to her half of the house. "Have fun, you two!"

Tension arced between them as Brick closed the door. He felt Merrily's gaze on his back, felt her interest. Slowly, bracing himself for the impact of her appeal, he turned toward her.

Damn, but she did it for him. Everything about

her seemed specifically designed to push his buttons; the way her wide green eyes watched him, how she shifted her feet, even how she breathed a little fast and low as if she expected him to rush her off to bed right this very second.

He'd disappoint her on that score. They'd get to the bed but not until he cleared up a few other things first.

Until then, he needed to taste her.

Reaching for her, Brick muttered low, "Come here, Merrily."

CHAPTER THREE

As HE PULLED her in close to his chest, Merrily wondered what would happen. Did he plan to take her to bed right *now?*

She wanted to, she really did, but she'd assumed he'd be working on the door and that they'd have more time to talk first, to get more familiar with each other, to get more...comfortable.

If he meant to do this now, she really needed to give the dogs a quick trip outside first. And she should probably freshen up. Maybe turn down the bed.

It was still light out and while she wasn't exactly shy, she didn't know that she wanted to do this in broad daylight—

Brick paused with his mouth very near to hers. "Merrily?"

"Hmm?" Oh, God, the anticipation nearly did her in.

"Tell me what's wrong."

Was she that obvious? Should she give him more honesty, or should she brazen it out?

He touched his mouth to hers in a brief, barely-there kiss that had her swaying toward him in a silent plea for more.

"You can tell me anything, okay?" He kissed her jaw, then curled her toes with a soft, damp kiss to her throat. "I want you to know that."

Surely that wasn't true. He couldn't want to hear of her reservations, or the past that had stalled her sexual curiosity, or the broken engagement that had left her humiliated and defeated—

"Tell me," he insisted while still tasting her skin.

Knowing she had to say something, Merrily drew a breath. "I'm not quite ready yet."

Leaning back to see her, he asked gently, "For a kiss?"

Was he mocking her? Oh, he'd said that seriously enough, but something close to amusement showed in his dark eyes, and a secret little smile played with the corners of his sexy mouth.

"A kiss is okay," she assured him. "Great even. It's just that I—"

"Thank God." He put his mouth to hers again, this time more firmly, lingering, moving.

Her heart thundered even as he eased away again.

"Okay?"

She nodded fast.

"How about this?" He turned his head a little,

moved his lips over hers until he'd nudged them apart, then touched with his tongue.

A rush of heat stole through her. "Yes." She clutched at his shirt and, lips parted, went to her tiptoes to make that amazing contact with his tongue again. He tasted so good, smelled delicious and felt...amazing.

Suddenly everything moved, and then her back was to the door, Brick pressed up against her, his hands holding her face, his fingers in her hair.

"And this?" he asked in a husky whisper that brushed her damp lips.

She barely had time to note the rough rasp of his voice before he took her mouth in a deep, hot, tongue-twining kiss that left her knees weak and her body taut. Against her breasts, she felt the pounding of his heartbeat, and against her belly... Oh. Hello.

He ended the kiss as if it took a great effort. "Damn."

She couldn't seem to get enough oxygen into her starved lungs. She'd known other men—but none like him.

She'd been kissed before—but never like that.

Hands still knotted in his shirt, she whispered, "What's wrong?" It startled her, hearing that breathy little wisp of sound in place of her own voice.

"Around you, I'm trigger happy." He kissed her

again, short and sweet, then put another kiss to her cheekbone, one to her temple. "What is it about you, Merrily?"

Not understanding, she shook her head. "Trigger happy?"

His half laugh turned into a short groan. "I think about you, and I get a boner. Kissing you damn near puts me over the edge. It's insane."

Her heart skipped a beat as she assimilated the meaning behind the words. She'd felt the...boner, of course. No missing that. Was he saying that was unusual for him?

Pressing into him, Merrily relished the feel of his excitement. *For her.* "Brick..."

Breathing roughly, he caught her hips in his big hands, briefly caressed them, and then held her still. "Sorry, honey, but I think we're moving too fast."

No way. That was not something men said. Sure, *she'd* thought it—at first—but now...

"I don't want to take advantage."

"You're not!"

"And," he said, stressing the word, "given the way Dundee's jumping against my ass, I think he either wants out, or he wants you to reassure him that you're kissing me willingly, not under duress."

Oh, no. Maintaining her hold on Brick's shoulders, she leaned to look around his side and saw Dundee on his hind legs, his front paws up on

Brick. Her mind went blank. "He, ah, isn't used to guys being here."

"Doing this to you. I know." He gave her a quick kiss and released her. "All the more reason to let up on the gas pedal a little." He turned to the dog. "So what's it to be, my man? You need to go out?"

Dundee barked and turned a quick circle.

Dolly joined him.

"Do you have leashes for them, or do you just let them out?"

Still in a hazy fog of lust, Merrily said, "Out."

"Through the kitchen?"

Why did he have to be so lucid and seemingly unaffected when her legs felt too shaky to support her? "To the backyard, yes."

Reaching out a hand to her, Brick forced her to give up the support of the front door. "Why don't we go along, get a breath of fresh air and maybe talk a little?"

"Okay, sure. Why not?" Not like they had anything more pressing going on.

Trying to get it together, she walked beside him, but even the way he curled his big hot hand around her fingers affected her. She thought of those hands, twice the size of her own, touching other places on her body, and for once she frowned at her sweet pets. "That damned doggy door would have come in real handy right about now."

Brick laughed as he led her and the dogs

through the kitchen, to the door and out into the backyard. "Look at it this way," he said. "If the dogs hadn't interrupted, I might have taken you right there, standing against the front door. And although I'd have loved it, that's not how your first time should be."

He gave her a one-armed hug and, with the dogs dancing around him, continued on into the yard to look around.

Merrily remained where he'd left her, frozen, her heart heavy, her vision narrowing.

So he'd heard the rumors. And believed them.

And now, just like her ex, he wanted to be the first.

Unsure what she should do next, she sank down to sit on the back stoop.

BRICK TRIED TO use the warm, fresh air to clear his head and regain his control, but he wasn't sure a frigid shower would even do the trick. He felt obsessed with lust for her, and the need wouldn't abate until he got his fill.

Damn, but he'd been *that* close to sealing the deal. And like he'd just told her, that wasn't what she needed, and ultimately, it wasn't what he wanted.

Or at least, it wasn't everything he wanted. Not now.

Now…hell, he just didn't know. He wanted time and plenty of it.

Dundee did a quick job of sprinkling a tree, then grabbed a stick in his teeth and loped over to him.

Grinning, Brick took it from him, waited while Dundee watched in eager expectation and then threw it. The dog charged after it, ears back, legs stretching out.

Dolly yapped at him, so Brick bent to pet her. "No running for you, huh?" He glanced back at Merrily, but she sat on the edge of the small stoop, her hands clasped together between her knees, her expression distant as she stared off at nothing in particular.

Sexual frustration would be new to her. He should probably offer to help her with that—but no, he couldn't. Just thinking it—how she'd look while grinding out an orgasm, those sexy little sounds women made, how they smelled and tasted—pushed him dangerously close to the edge.

Tense with desire, he threw the stick for Dundee again, picked up Dolly and joined Merrily in the shade of the overhang.

When she said nothing, he considered how to proceed, but he insisted on honesty always. If he was going to do this—and he most definitely would—then he owed her nothing less.

And if the truth had her backing away? He'd figure it out somehow. "Is it true, then?"

"What? That I'm a virgin?"

Belligerence? Was she touchy about it? He set Dolly down and leaned back on his elbows. Looking out at the yard, Brick took in the fence that would indeed need repairs if the dogs were to be out on their own. He scoped out the rickety wooden privacy wall erected around Tonya's small back porch to divide her property from Merrily's. Shading his eyes, he looked up at the large trees that probably dumped a ton of debris on the roof and into the gutters.

Casual as you please, as if it didn't really matter, he said, "That's what I meant, yeah."

"You couldn't tell?" She made a rude sound. "I'm almost as rare as Bigfoot, you know. In this day and age, there've only been a few sightings."

Brick fought off a grin. "It makes me a little nuts. And it sort of scares me."

That got her attention. "Scares you?" Another rude sound. "Don't worry. It's not contagious."

He laughed aloud. "Yeah, virginity is a long-lost virtue for me. Hell, I was…mmm, sixteen, I think, when our nineteen-year-old neighbor talked me into skinny dipping with her." Ha! He knew exactly how old he was—and the girl hadn't needed persuasion to get him in her pool. "That night, it was almost over for me before it started."

Curious and still somewhat offended, Merrily watched him. "Virtue?"

Huh. He hadn't figured on her latching on to that particular part. "It is, you know. Very few people have the fortitude to wait."

"To wait as long as I have, you mean." She rubbed her face. "It wasn't precisely by choice."

"No?" Hoping to encourage her, Brick put a hand to her narrow back, stroked down her spine and back up again. Through her shirt he felt her warmth and how rigidly she held herself. Trying for subtlety, he nudged her a little closer to him. "I won't believe the guys weren't interested. Not looking the way you look. Not with you so sweet."

She gave a self-deprecating laugh. "My ex-fiancé didn't think I was sweet. Not at the end."

"The end of your engagement?"

"Yes." She dropped her hands and stood, moving away from him. "But you don't want to hear about all that."

Okay, so he'd have to work a little harder now. He didn't mind. On an exaggerated sigh, he stood. "You don't have any lawn furniture."

For three heartbeats she said nothing, then she shrugged. "If I'm out here, it's usually just long enough to let the dogs do their business, and I sit on the stoop."

"A deck would be nice." He glanced around. "Probably for Tonya, too."

Merrily shot him a dirty look. "You should offer to build it for her."

"I was thinking I might." It'd give him an opportunity to hang around more. "You're wrong, you know."

"About?"

"I want to hear everything that concerns you." He watched her and saw her surprise. "So tell me, who dumped who in the engagement?"

She took two steps out to the yard but halted. Shoulders stiffening with defiance, she turned to face him again. Her chin lifted. "He dumped me."

"Seriously? What an idiot." To keep things casual, Brick went to Dundee and again threw the stick for him. Dolly paid little attention; she found a sun-warmed spot in the grass and sprawled out. "Do you let the cats out, too?"

"Yes. They don't go far and they always come right back. When I'm home, it's in and out, in and out. The cats always want to be on the other side of the door."

Brick looked back at the house, and sure enough, all three cats were there looking out the kitchen window. Cute. He went to the house and opened the door. They bolted out as if expecting him to change his mind at any second. And as Merrily had said, they didn't go far.

Stan immediately started eating grass.

"He's like a cow," Merrily complained with a shake of her head. "He'll barf that up later, but I gave up trying to get him to quit."

Eloise joined Dolly in the sun. "Looks like the girls are sticking together."

"They're both sun worshipers."

Tom hung up on the stoop, posture alert as he took in the sight of a few birds in the trees. "Does he ever catch any?"

She shook her head. "So far, no, thank God."

"What hours are you home?"

The quick change of topic surprised her. She rolled a shoulder. "I have classes in the morning, then work at the diner until six or so. I'm usually home by six-thirty, seven at the latest."

"What time do your classes start?"

"7:00 a.m."

Brick whistled low. "Long day."

"I have all day Sunday free," she said, then bit her lip. "I mean… I wasn't suggesting—"

"Good to know." He wanted to spend some time with her, not just rush through hurried sex that she might not even enjoy. "So you're free after six-thirty Monday through Saturday and all day Sunday."

She searched his gaze, wrapped her arms around herself and looked out at the yard again. "He dumped me because I wouldn't have sex with him."

Glad that she'd brought it back up, that she wanted to tell him about it, Brick watched her. "Was there a reason why you wouldn't?"

Nodding, she whispered, "My mother."

"She needed you with her." Made sense to him. It was beyond tragic for her, but he knew there wasn't much he wouldn't give up for his mom.

Then again, no matter what his obligations, he'd find a way to sneak in a quickie here and there.

Brick shook his head at those wayward thoughts. A world of difference stood between him and Merrily. "You had priorities. I get that."

"At times, Mom struggled so badly. There wasn't anyone to help her but me. I was gone enough with school and work. I couldn't see…" She trailed off.

If she'd been experienced, no doubt she'd have found the time for relief, too. When necessary, it didn't take long.

Especially for guys.

But for a young, female virgin? A wham-bam incident wouldn't do, which, again, meant he had to get a handle on his lust. Her first time should be memorable—for the right reasons instead of the wrong ones.

"The timing was off," she explained. "I should never have gotten involved romantically in the first place. I can't really blame Kyle. He was young and healthy and energetic. And at first, he did wait, for months and months."

She sounded far too admiring for Brick's peace of mind. Was she still hung up on the guy? "I'd say he should have kept waiting, but would that have done any good?"

She shook her head. "Maybe because I knew a normal life wasn't in the works for me, I couldn't see getting that intimate."

How intimate *had* she gotten? No, maybe he didn't want to know. "You loved him?"

"Yes."

A little hard to buy because if she'd loved him, wouldn't she have found a way? Or maybe she loved him—but didn't really want him. Was that possible between a man and woman? He adored his sister-in-law, Cinder, but he didn't have sexual thoughts about her.

And any woman that dated Jesse first was automatically off-limits. He didn't go where best friends or brothers had gone before. Period. It had nothing to do with the woman, and it didn't matter how attractive she might be.

"Maybe," Brick ventured, sharing his thoughts, "you loved him more as a friend than anything else."

Merrily frowned, then shook her head. "Actually...I don't know. Maybe I just loved the idea of being in love, the idea of having a marriage and a family and a place of my own."

She deserved all that and more.

But first she deserved the best sex he could possibly give her.

Without her noticing, Brick got closer again. "You wanted a partner to help you carry the burden." His hand slid under her hair to cup around the back of her neck. "That's what he should have been."

His nearness quickened her breath. Nice.

"Without any...*reward* at all?"

"You think your company isn't reward enough?"

"Ha!" She lightly slugged him in the middle. "Like that would be enough for any guy."

"For any guy in love.... Yeah, I don't know." Being in love would only make abstinence more difficult. Hell, Brick wasn't in love with her, and it ate him up to have to wait.

"Understand, Brick, I didn't think of my mother as a burden. I loved her so I wanted to be there with her. But yes, it would have been nice to share that responsibility and worry with someone."

A new thought chewed on his peace of mind. "Do you love him still?"

"No."

The denial came too quickly to satisfy. Brick tipped up her chin. "You sure?"

Without hesitation, she nodded. "Looking back, I'm not certain exactly what I felt for Kyle even then. I know it hurt a lot when he asked for his ring back. He'd said he loved me, that he wanted to be with me, but he couldn't deal with everything as it was." Her mouth twisted. "After he broke things off, he told me that if things ever changed, he wanted to know."

"Meaning what?" Good God, Brick couldn't imagine that sentiment. "He wanted you to get in touch if you walked out on your mom?" Like she would ever do such a thing. Hadn't the guy known her at all?

Lifting one shoulder, Merrily looked away. "Something like that, I guess."

Something like…*when her mother had died?* Damn it, he couldn't help it. He tugged her in closer, tucked her face under his chin and wrapped his arms around her to rock her gently from side to side. "I'm sorry."

She surprised him by clinging to him. "The funniest part is that not long after he said that, he moved in with another woman."

Bastard.

She hid her face against his shoulder. "A few months later…my mother took a turn for the worse and she passed away."

He hugged her tighter still, wishing he could take some of the pain that remained with her.

"Obviously," Merrily choked out, "I did not call him."

"Course not." He kissed the top of her head, her ear. "I'm so damn sorry, honey."

She drew a slow breath. "I didn't know what to do with myself after she died. So much of my life was wrapped up into caring for her. My schedule was set up around her needs. I had a few female friends, but no one superclose, so I decided it'd be best to get a fresh perspective on things. I moved here, found a job and got my credits transferred to the new college."

Brick tangled a hand in her cool, silky hair. "And you decided to lose your virginity." He realized now that it had been a deliberate choice on her part.

He'd been a deliberate choice—and it humbled him.

"Yes." She didn't look at him. "I didn't expect you to know my entire history, though."

"Does it matter?"

"Of course it does. Over and over, Kyle told me he wanted to be the first. I think he probably stayed with me as long as he did just hoping to see the big payoff, you know?"

"You keep underestimating yourself, like you think lack of experience is the only appeal."

A dry, humorless laugh escaped her. "Get real, Brick. For him, at least, it was. That's why even after he broke things off, he still felt like he'd earned the right."

"Tough luck for him, then, huh?" Brick wanted no misunderstandings. "Because I'm here now." And he wasn't about to budge.

Full of resentment, she said, "For the same reason as Kyle."

"Don't compare me to some selfish dick, okay?" He tipped her back so he could see her face. "That's not me."

"Right." Derisive, a little militant, she tried to push away from him. "You're saying it doesn't matter to you?"

"Course it does. Most men are possessive by nature, and virgins factor into fantasies even more than porno stars." He grinned at her. "But aren't you curious why I said you scare me? Because, lady, seriously, I don't scare easily."

Her eyes narrowed. "Okay, not that I'm buying it, but why would I scare you?"

Before he laid it all on her, a bit of forewarning seemed in order. "It's probably going to piss you off a little."

Her expression went taut. "Tell me anyway."

"Promise you'll hear me out?"

"Depends on what you say, now, doesn't it?"

The prickly temper only made her all the more adorable to him. Yeah, he was a Neanderthal, but at least he knew it. "All right." Anticipating her reaction, Brick admitted, "Around you, I have a major loss of control."

Fascination took some of the heat from her annoyance. "What does that mean exactly?"

"Like I said, you look at me, talk to me, or God

forbid you smile, and I react like that testosterone-ridden sixteen-year-old kid again seeing my first naked female. That's not something I'm used to."

She studied him. "Later, I'd like to hear more about your first experience. But for now—"

"For now, you need to understand that I also worried about you getting hung up on me."

"*What?*"

"If you get too involved, I might break your heart. You're so damn sweet, Merrily. I really don't want to put you through that."

It was almost comical, the sweeping emotions passing over her features—emotions that ended in righteous indignation. Intent on freeing herself from his embrace, she gave him a shove, but Brick held on to her, and when he started laughing, he thought she'd slug him.

"Settle down, okay? I already know I'm an ass." He caught her hands and held them behind her back. "Surely you see my dilemma, sweet Merrily."

"No!"

He laughed again. "I'm always up-front with women. I don't want anyone getting ideas. I like my life the way it is. Sex is just that—sex. Not a commitment."

"Don't drive it into the ground, Brick. I get it already."

He gave her a laughing smooch on her pinched

mouth. "The idea of your virginity has been both a lure and a concern."

"Oh, my God. You are so conceited!"

"I know." He nuzzled her in closer, kissing her ear, that special place where her throat met her shoulder. "But I swear, when it comes to sex, I have good reason."

She went still, then soft in his arms. "Lacking in modesty, too."

Yet she sounded intrigued. He hid his smile against her cheek. "So here's what I propose."

She groaned.

"No, not a marriage proposal, so stop all the melodrama." Brick couldn't remember ever being mired in such a powerful combo of lust and humor. It was unique.

She was unique.

He carried her hands back up to his neck and slid his hands down to the small of her back. "For now, why don't I make a strategic retreat? You can have the night to think about things, to decide if you still want me—and if so, I promise you won't regret it. But go into it with your eyes wide open."

"Meaning sex and only sex?"

"Sex and conversation and a few laughs. Some good times." He wanted all that because he didn't want her to have regrets. "I'll make it good for you, Merrily. Better than good. You have my word." Then he rethought that and added, "Well, maybe not the first time. I have a feeling that once I get your panties off, it's going to be a very close thing."

Her mouth fell open, then snapped shut as her face went up in flames.

He remained serious. He wanted her to believe him. "After that, *every time* after that, count on loving it. And that's not an idle brag, okay? I do know what I'm doing."

The heat extended into her gaze. Her lips parted. She nodded. "Okay."

Pretty sure he'd already won her over, Brick added, "But understand that I'm not the type to settle down anytime soon."

"Good."

"Good?"

She nodded. "My life has recently taken a dramatic change. I want to live for a while without serious restrictions—and you already said you're possessive, so you would certainly be a restriction."

"Yeah, probably." He knew himself well enough to know that once he fell in love, he'd probably be nearly unbearable. Luckily, he had no intentions of falling in love, and she didn't want that anyway. Did she? "You're okay with that?"

She nodded. "Once I no longer have that stupid badge of innocence, I won't have to worry what motivates other guys."

Other guys. His good mood slipped. "You're planning ahead, are you?"

"Absolutely."

Damn. He felt…insulted. Hearing her talk about a new life that didn't involve him sort of burned his ass. He hadn't had her yet, so he damn straight didn't want to think about some future bozo getting down and dirty with her.

"So." She smoothed a small hand over his chest. "What do we do now?"

"I'll come by tomorrow with Jesse and we'll switch out the doors." Jesse's help wasn't necessary, but hey, he had a pleasant surprise for his friend and couldn't wait to share it with him. "Sunday I can put in the pet opening. After that, you and I can get busy."

"You're talking *two days* from now?"

She sounded as forlorn as he felt over the wait. But he had to be fair to her even if it killed him. And waiting until Sunday meant she'd then have the whole day free—which meant he'd have all day to really enjoy himself.

"Two days of kissing, maybe a little touching—" God, he'd never survive this "—getting more familiar and after that, after you've had plenty of time to think things over, you can decide what you want."

With any luck, and a little persuasion on his

part, she'd want him, *only* him, for a good long stretch of sexual indulgence.

The way he felt right now, he couldn't accept any other outcome.

CHAPTER FOUR

MERRILY HAD NO real choice but to abide by Brick's bizarre terms—for now.

Why would he encourage her to think it over before making a move if he really wanted her as badly as he claimed? Her only conclusion was that he didn't. She doubted that he'd find sex with her to be a hardship, but all that nonsense about her testing his control? Just that: nonsense.

Seemed to her he had too much control. For sure, far more than she had.

Swallowing back her complaints, she walked him to the front door. Like the Pied Piper, she had both dogs and all three cats following along.

It was pretty nice how Brick accepted them all. He stepped over and around pet toys, picked up a floating tuft of cat fur to throw away and gave attention to each animal before focusing that awesome gaze on her.

She gulped in rising need. "It's not going to be easy, Brick."

"Waiting?" Expression warm and big hands

gentle, he cupped her face. "You're preaching to the choir on that one, honey."

Merrily stared up at him. He was so tall, so broad-shouldered and muscular and sexy. She swayed toward him. "Then maybe—"

He kissed her.

And wow, what a kiss. Firm lips moved over hers until they parted, then his damp tongue stroked in. He was an incredible kisser, teasing and encouraging until she clung to him.

She wasn't inexperienced enough to miss his erection or the way his hands trembled, how his breath hitched.

After freeing her mouth, he hugged her close for a few rib-knocking heartbeats, then stepped back. "I gotta go before I change my mind." He opened the door and stepped out. "Think about me tonight, okay? It's for sure I'm going to be thinking about you."

Holding the doorknob for support, Merrily watched him go in a long-legged, slightly stiff stride. His profile showed the tight way he held his jaw, and after he got into his truck, he sat there a moment, head back, eyes closed.

Okay, so maybe she really did test his control. That made his insistence on giving her time… noble. Considerate.

And so incredibly sweet.

Seeing him struggle for composure made her

want him all the more. Knowing he was so blasted nice really cinched the deal.

Not fall in love with him?

Shoot, she was already halfway there and she knew it. The trick would be making sure Brick never found out. She'd manage because otherwise he might really walk away.

And now that she'd had a small taste, she wanted the whole man.

She wanted Brick Carlisle.

THE NEXT DAY, Merrily hung back as Jesse and Brick discussed her apparently awesome vintage door. If having one big hunk in her small living space was odd, having two there was enough to leave her mute. They took up so much room, had so much presence, and she could almost swear an air of testosterone swirled around them.

They were male with a capital *M*.

It took all her concentration not to drag Brick off somewhere.

When he'd arrived, he'd kissed her hello with warm familiarity, but with his friend standing there, it had been frustratingly brief. And for the fifteen minutes since then, he'd stayed busy introducing her pets, giving them some attention and showing Jesse the door to be replaced.

Last night, the things he'd said and the things he'd done had all conspired to leave her muddled.

After he'd left, she'd spent a sleepless night thinking of him, just as he'd told her to.

Today, she was on pins and needles waiting to see what he'd do.

Brick had bold and outrageous down to a fine art. So much so that she'd accused him of being conceited, but with the way he kissed, she believed him when he said he had reason for boasting.

All those promises of satisfaction left her nerve endings sizzling. And he wanted to give her time to think about his "offer." How could she think of anything else?

What was there to think about anyway? It wasn't like she could summon up the fortitude to turn him away. Like a starving person offered a meal, he tempted her beyond reason.

As far as her falling for him and getting hurt… She'd thought about that a lot last night…and during her classes…and while at work.

Thinking of much else hadn't been possible.

She wasn't a dummy. She knew how their relationship would go. She'd heard the whispers at work, saw the way the other waitresses stared at him.

Already, she was more invested than him. How could she not be?

Yes, she'd wanted to experience life. Specifically she wanted to experience sex. Now…she just wanted to experience Brick Carlisle.

Even in her hottest fantasies, she hadn't dredged up a man even half as appealing as him.

A sexual relationship was, for him, a routine thing.

For her, with Brick, it would be beyond incredible.

She'd rushed home from work, then rushed through a shower. She'd even done some primping for him when there were clearly other things she should have been doing—like laundry, or writing her college papers, or cleaning up all the pet fur that accumulated in a twenty-four-hour period. While she'd hurriedly painted her toenails, the dogs had watched her in fascination, the cats with disdain.

But she didn't care.

Consequences be damned, she wanted him. Sooner rather than later. Somehow she'd convince him that she could stay emotionally detached.

And maybe, if she got lucky, in the process she'd convince herself, as well.

WHILE JESSE PRETENDED great enthusiasm about the door, Brick glanced at Merrily. When he saw her standing there watching him in something of a daze, he smiled to himself. If the flush in her cheeks meant anything, her thoughts ran the same course as his.

She'd spiffed up a little today. Her soft brown

hair hung in loose curls, she wore a pretty sundress and she'd painted her toenails. It was sort of endearing that she thought he needed enticement.

Hell, he wanted her so much, she could probably shave her head and wear burlap and he'd still be panting for her. He had it bad—and only part of it was her innocence. The rest was pure Merrily, the way she smiled, how she watched him so intently.

The idea that she wanted him enough to give up her virginity.

How could any guy be immune to that?

Jesse managed to jab him with his elbow. Low, so that Merrily wouldn't hear, he said, "I feel like an idiot. How long am I supposed to pretend to measure?"

"Long as it takes."

"For what? It's a standard-sized door. The one we brought will fit and you know it. You don't need help with any of this, so tell me again, why am I here?"

As if on cue, a knock sounded on Merrily's front door. Brick almost rubbed his hands together. He couldn't wait for Jesse to see his *surprise*. "Because I have something for you."

"Yeah?" He glanced at Merrily with curiosity.

Brick shoved him in the shoulder, making him stagger. "Not that, so don't even go there."

Jesse laughed as Merrily stepped out of view to greet her guest. "I wasn't thinking that."

"Bullshit."

"Just because you salute every time she looks your way doesn't mean I feel the same."

Damn. His Johnson did do a lot of saluting around her, but luckily, this time Jesse exaggerated.

"She's hot, Brick. I agree."

His teeth locked.

"But I have a rule about these things."

Yeah, he knew that. Jesse felt the same as he did. They shared almost everything—but never women. "Still," he groused. "Don't be ogling her."

"Got it. When she talks to me, I'll stare at the ceiling." He used a shoulder to wipe sweat from his brow. "So what do you have for me? And it better be good since you have me working in this heat, on a Saturday night no less."

Just then, Tonya's husky but feminine voice joined Merrily's in the living room. Jesse perked up, going on the alert. Brick gestured for him to come see.

Intrigued, Jesse stepped over to the doorway and peered into the other room. Awareness settled over him. With obvious appreciation, he gave Tonya a thorough once-over. In an aside to Brick, he asked, "For me?"

"Yeah." The look on Jesse's face was hilarious. "What do you think?"

"Damn, man, thank you."

"All I can promise is an intro. The rest is up to you, but I figured—"

"Yeah, got it." Done listening, Jesse unglued his feet and moved forward with single-minded purpose. "Hello." Hand extended, voice deep, he said, "I'm Jesse."

His sudden intrusion surprised both women.

For her part, Tonya widened her eyes with speculation. She looked at Brick, at Merrily and back at Jesse again. She accepted his hand. "Hello yourself."

Huh. That went even better than Brick had anticipated. He filled in with more proper introductions. "Tonya is Merrily's landlord." To Tonya, he added, "Jesse is going to help me with the door."

"It'll be my pleasure," Jesse told her.

Rolling his eyes, Brick stepped over to Merrily and slipped an arm around her lower back. Beneath the insubstantial sundress he idly explored the pronounced indentation of her waist and the firm swell of her hip.

Her curves were as appealing as everything else. He couldn't wait to touch her bare flesh— and yeah, if he kept thinking that way, he'd embarrass himself.

Because she seemed more than a little confused by the turn of events, Brick said, "Why don't we order a pizza? It'll be my treat. After Jesse and I get the door switched out, we could all sit down to eat."

Merrily firmed her mouth in annoyance. It was so obvious that she wanted to be alone with him, Brick had a hard time sticking to his plan.

While staring at Tonya with palpable heat, Jesse said, "I could eat."

Merrily blushed, but Tonya only smiled in indulgence.

It took a little nudge from Brick, but finally Merrily regained her wits. "Oh, yes, pizza would be great." She lifted her brows. "Tonya, will you join us?"

Tonya held Jesse's gaze while deciding and finally nodded. "That sounds like...fun."

Her smile damn near made Brick blush! Poor Jesse appeared ready to carry her off somewhere.

Time to get back on track. "All right, then. Ladies, if you'll do the ordering, Jesse and I can get to work." He tipped up Merrily's face and gave her a warm kiss. "I like my pizza loaded."

And with that, he dragged Jesse off to the kitchen.

"Nice surprise," Jesse told him under his breath. Then with a curious look, he added, "Can't believe you're passing up the opportunity."

Yeah, his lack of interest had surprised him just a bit, too. He shrugged it off, saying, "She's Merrily's neighbor." But more than that, she wasn't Merrily.

Under Dundee's watchful eye, Jesse got a hammer and screwdriver from the toolbox to tap out the hinge pins. "Used to be a time when that wouldn't have bothered you."

He started to deny it but changed his mind. "Maybe." He glanced back at Merrily again. "Not this time, though." Hell, it seemed when he was around her, he couldn't go more than a minute without looking at her.

Tonya grinned, while Merrily kept a hand to her forehead as if bemused. What were they talking about? "Did you know you're an infamous panty-dropper?"

"Yeah, so?"

Brick laughed. "And Merrily called me conceited."

"Which you are."

He shook his head. "She's heard gossip about you at the diner."

"From the other waitresses?" Jesse moved Dolly out of his way, but the little dog came right back. On the counter behind him, both Stan and Tom leaned in to watch.

Only Eloise remained in the other room with the ladies.

"Yeah." With satisfaction, Brick said, "Merrily barely remembered you, though."

"All things considered, I'm glad to hear it."

YEAH, HE'D been relieved with her lack of interest in Jesse, too. "I'm counting on you to volun-
teer some time," Brick muttered, "for the cause,
you know."

"My cause or yours?"

"Both." But that sounded so mercenary, Brick
had to qualify it. "She seems pretty nice."

"Merrily?"

"No, damn it." He rounded on Jesse, which
fascinated the cats and dog. "Stop thinking about
Merrily."

Jesse snickered. "I wasn't." And then, probably just to be a pain in the ass, he asked, "So she's
not nice?"

"She's more than nice, but she's off-limits to
you. I was talking about Tonya."

"Hey, looking like she looks, I don't care how
nice she might be. As long as she cooperates, count
me in."

"She was already cooperating, and you know
it." Female attention came even easier to Jesse than
it did for Brick—and he had to admit that he'd
never had a problem in that area.

"From what I've seen, there are enough repairs
to keep us both busy for a while."

Jesse nodded back to the living room, where the
women were in close conversation, talking about
God knew what. "Trust me, with her to sweeten
the deal, it'll be my pleasure."

That sentiment should have satisfied Brick, but instead it nettled him. After they removed the door and set it aside, he ensured the women were out of hearing range. "Don't do anything to muck this up for me, okay?"

"Anything like what?" Jesse again sat Dolly out of the way, then started on removing the old hardware. "We're keeping the doorknobs and deadbolt, right?"

"Matches the rest, so yeah." He went to work unscrewing the hinges while answering Jesse's first question. "Like getting on Tonya's bad side."

"So she's a gift with strings attached?"

If the women overheard their very sexist joking, they'd both be thrown out. "I'm just saying—"

"Give it a rest, Brick." He finished dismantling the doorknob. "I can handle things without your input."

Yeah, he knew that, but still… "I don't want any negative associations here."

Jesse sat back on his heels and snorted at Brick. "You're worried about getting tainted by my bad behavior? That's rich, considering your own bad behavior."

Yeah, he sounded like a hypocrite, but so what. His past reputation didn't matter—not with Merrily. "Just watch what you do, okay?"

"Sure thing, Mom." With the door off, the cats went out and a hot breeze blew in. Jesse again moved Dolly out of the way, then stripped off his shirt. When he tossed it aside, Dolly lay down on it.

That made Brick grin. "She likes you."

Jesse shrugged. "Typical female."

"Pizza in forty-five minutes," Merrily said. "Sorry for the long wait, but—" She poked her head into the kitchen—and stared in dumbfounded surprise.

At Jesse. More precisely, at Jesse's upper body.

Brick stepped forward to block her view. "Where'd Tonya go?" Damn it, he needed the other woman around to balance things.

"Home. To change. Back soon." Merrily leaned to see around Brick and cleared her throat. "Are you warm? I have a fan in my bedroom…"

"He's fine." Feeling extremely cross, Brick stripped off his own shirt. "Don't worry about it."

Her gaze shot over to him, then widened. She licked her bottom lip, took a step back. Staring at his abs, she said, "Um, Brick, could I have a word with you, please?"

Enjoying her reaction, he said, "Sure." She could have more than a word. She could have—

He got as far as the doorway before Merrily pulled him around to the hallway, went on tiptoe and plastered herself up against him. Dodging her intent, Brick reversed their positions, with Merrily against the wall and him leading the way into a deep, hot kiss.

Her hands went over his naked chest, up and over his shoulders, then back down again. And damn, but it felt good. Too good.

In a rush, Brick stepped back and, snagging her hand, dragged her farther down the hall.

"Brick." Scandalized, a little excited, she whispered, "We can't do this now, not with Jesse in the kitchen." And then, breathless, "Can we?"

Ah, hell. She made him want to do it when that hadn't even been his thought. He didn't dare step into a bedroom, so instead he stopped at the end of the hall. "No, we can't." Her first time definitely wouldn't be rushed, or awkward. Not if he could help it. "So don't tempt me."

Jesse, being a good friend, found something to hammer on. Sounded like the toolbox, but whatever. It made some background noise, which gave them a modicum of privacy.

"Then what..?"

"I didn't want Jesse to overhear, but, Merrily, honey, you can't kiss me like that and expect me to keep it together."

Perplexed, she stared at him. "Keep it together?"

The way she looked at him wasn't helping. "I told you, around you I'm like a damn jack-in-the-box."

"Oh." Her eyes widened. *"Oh."* When she started to look down, Brick caught her chin.

"Staring definitely won't help." Her curiosity was so cute, he had to kiss her again, this time quick and hard. "Don't ogle Jesse's chest either, all right? I don't like it."

"I wasn't… Well, maybe I was at first. But just out of surprise." She pursed her mouth. "And be-cause…well, he *does* look good."

"Merrily," he warned.

"But not as good as you." She patted his left pec, and the pat turned into a stroke. Before her hot little palm could move over his nipple, he caught her wrist. "Merrily."

Sighing, she pulled her hand away. "If I can't touch, then quit flaunting yourself, okay?" She shooed him away. "Now go on while I compose myself."

"Compose yourself?" She said the funniest things. Things he supposed a virgin might say.

She turned him and gave him a small push. "And put on a shirt, for heaven's sake. Tonya will have a heart attack when she sees you."

Grinning, Brick went back into the kitchen— and he not only put on his shirt, but he also insisted Jesse do the same.

"It's hot as Hades, and the dog has made a bed of my shirt."

"Tough. If I have to wear mine, you definitely have to wear yours, too."

Jesse gave him a look. "You realize how you're acting, right?"

Unfortunately, it wasn't an act. Not even close. "Screw you."

Dolly only grumbled a little when Jesse retrieved his shirt, shook the dog hairs off it, and pulled it back on.

An hour later, with a new door installed, the old door stored in Tonya's basement and warm pizza divided up between them, they sat in Merrily's small kitchen, eating, talking and laughing.

It was nice, comfortable—and it made him nuts.

He loved the way she laughed, how she alternated her attention between playing hostess and coddling the animals and how she occasionally slanted a coy look of interest his way.

She stood to refill glasses of tea, and Brick noticed that she'd left her sandals under the table. Even her feet looked sexy to him—and it had nothing to do with the pink polish on her toes.

He kept thinking how easy it'd be to reach up under that dress, touch her warm thighs, higher—

Tonya laughed at something Jesse said, drawing Brick back from the brink of no return. He blew out a breath.

Time to think about something else. He glanced across the table at Tonya.

Slim-fitting jeans and a worn-in T-shirt replaced her sexy business suit. She'd left her mouth naked of lipstick, her fair hair hanging loose and she looked nothing less than amazing.

In fact, Jesse couldn't keep his gaze off her.

Where Tonya was tall and sleek, Merrily was petite and stacked. Tonya had straight, pale blond hair and light blue eyes, and Merrily had big green eyes and silky, baby-fine brown hair.

Physically the women were as dissimilar as could be, but both were hot. Add in Merrily's sweet personality, her innocence and her curiosity, and Brick knew he was a goner.

Because Dundee and Dolly were only fed healthy dog food and were well-trained, they didn't beg for bites. But they did sit on feet and bark for attention.

"Sorry," Merrily said as she reseated herself. She teased Dolly's chin and patted Dundee's side. "I love them, so they don't bother me. I'm used to them being underfoot. But I can put them out if—"

"They're fine." Brick liked her pets, and he especially liked seeing Merrily with them. He'd never thought about it much before, but a woman who loved animals was somehow more trustworthy and far more likable than a woman who didn't.

Why had he never realized that before?

The pets didn't bother anyone else, either. In fact, Tonya ended up with Eloise on her lap, and

Jesse took turns tossing toys into the living room for the dogs to fetch. Only Stan the Man and Union Tom seemed content to ignore the humans. They both slept atop the back of the couch.

Brick drank the rest of his Coke, then sat back to look at Tonya. "I was thinking about that privacy fence you have out back."

"If you can still call it that." Tonya finished off her third slice of pizza and dabbed a napkin to her mouth. "It's falling down and if it weren't for my hot tub, I'd remove it."

"You have a hot tub?" Jesse asked with interest.

"I don't get a lot of downtime, and I like to relax when I do. The hot tub is new, but the fence is pretty old." She stroked Eloise along her back. "I'm sure Merrily would enjoy it, too, but she has even less free time than I do. Usually when I'm in there, though, one or more of her cats come to sit on the ledge and keep me company."

"Really?" Jesse looked from Merrily to Tonya and back again. Knowing exactly what his friend was thinking, Brick scowled. Maybe if it were any woman other than Merrily, he'd be thinking it as well.

Two good-looking women.

In a hot tub together.

Yeah, there were probably a good dozen male fantasies that sprouted from that exact scenario.

But *not* with Merrily.

Brick leaned forward. "We could put up a new fence for you." One that would ensure Merrily's privacy as much as Tonya's. "Wouldn't take us long."

For only a moment, Tonya looked taken aback. "Thank you, but I can't afford that just yet."

"It'd be less than you think," Jesse told her.

"No it won't, not for what I'd like." Wrinkling her nose, she said, "I have expensive tastes—I know because I already checked out the pricing." She set Eloise aside and stood with her plate and glass. "Hopefully next year, though." She turned to the sink.

Merrily said, "You don't need to do that. I can take care of it after everyone is gone."

Jesse pushed back his own chair. He gathered up the other plates and glasses and plunked them into the sink. "Why don't you show me the fence and let me offer some suggestions? I get supplies wholesale, and better than that, I have a lot of over-run stuff on hand. Can't hurt to just get a price for the supplies, right?"

Considering it, Tonya cast a glance at Brick and Merrily and shrugged. "All right. The dogs can come out with us."

Dolly and Dundee understood and went manic with excitement.

As they all started out the back door, Brick said,

"Take your time," which earned him a grin from Jesse.

Merrily smacked his shoulder. "You're both incorrigible." She stood and went to the sink.

"I've never actually heard anyone use that word before." Watching her backside as she rinsed dishes, Brick stood. The sundress was so soft that it draped her every curve.

She had an amazing ass.

Already his heart beat too hard and fast. It was insane.

And he loved it.

With his hands holding her waist, he leaned down to nuzzle behind her ear. "Damn, but you smell good." He pressed in against that perfect backside to pin her against the sink. It was torture but worth it. "You're awfully hard to resist."

For two heartbeats, she held perfectly still. In rapid order she dried her hands, turned in his narrow hold and held on to his shoulders. "Then don't. Resist, I mean. I'm ready." Her fingers contracted on his shoulders, and she whispered, *"Now."*

CHAPTER FIVE

SHE COULD SEE him wavering, so Merrily pressed her advantage. "If you leave me again, Brick, I won't be able to sleep. I'm already tired from a sleepless night last night. It'd be much better if you—"

Tonya and Jesse strode back in, saw them in a clinch and froze.

Blast their rotten timing. They hadn't been gone very long at all.

Merrily sidled out of Brick's embrace. "So what's the verdict? New fence or not?"

"It might be possible," Tonya said, but she looked uncomfortable at having interrupted. "Maybe Jesse and I should go...talk about it a little more?"

"No." Brick remained facing the sink, too quiet, almost pained. "It's fine."

Merrily frowned at him. It was far from fine, at least from her point of view.

"Why don't you guys go play with the animals in the living room? Merrily and I will pick up the kitchen."

She was starting to feel like a spectacle. "There's

not that much to do." Four plates, four glasses and some napkins to throw away. It hardly required two of them.

Looking at her over his shoulder, his eyes narrowed and direct, Brick disagreed. "Oh, there's plenty for us to do, Merrily. I promise you."

On a whistle, Jesse said, "The living room it is." He called in the dogs and they all filed into the other room. The second they were gone, Brick gave up his pretense of doing dishes.

He turned and stared at her, and there was so much heat in his gaze that she squirmed.

"Come here."

The way he said that left her flustered. It almost sounded like he planned to start something right now.

"Merrily," he said in that deep, compelling voice.

She rushed up to him but forestalled whatever he might say or do. "I want you," she whispered. "Tonight. Right now, in fact." She sucked in a needed breath. "But it has to be exclusive for as long as it lasts."

That threw him. "Come again?"

"You keep... I don't know. Sort of flirting with Tonya."

His face went blank. "No way. Not even."

"You offered to help her with the fence for her hot tub!"

He searched her face—and grinned. "You thought that was so I could spend time with her?"

Suddenly uncertain, she bit her lip. "I don't know."

The grin turned endearing. "Do you know what I did last night, Merrily?"

Imagination in overdrive, she asked in a scandalized whisper, "What?"

He laughed. "I thought about you. All night. I considered all the different ways I want to kiss you, where I want to touch, how you're going to feel and taste and how awesome it's going to be."

That sounded so good, her toes curled. "So you think it'll be awesome?"

He said with great sincerity, "Given your expectations, I promise to give it my best shot."

Expectations? Oh, wow. She did make it sound like she had great expectations, and of course she did, but she didn't mean to stress him about it. "I'm sorry if I'm making you feel pressured to perform."

He laughed again, and hugged her right off her feet. When he lowered her to the floor again, he said, "I have a healthy ego, honey. I don't feel pressured—I feel challenged." He drew her up and kissed her softly and deeply. Against her mouth, he said, "I offered to help with the fence to give Jesse a leg up."

"A leg up?"

"Yeah." He turned back to the sink and started on the dishes again. "Your landlord is hot."

She deflated, until he said, "But I think you're hotter."

She went still, then stepped up beside him at the sink, trying to see his face. "No, you do not." Oh, God, she sounded desperate for praise, but really, she only wanted the truth.

"Do, too." He hesitated, then with a quick shake of his head he caught her hand, dragged it around in front of him and pressed it...

Right over a straining erection.

"That's for you, Merrily."

Talk about truth! She curled her fingers around him as much as the stiff denim allowed. Wow. "Um...thank you?"

His jaw tensed around a rough laugh. "God, woman, you breathe and I feel it like a stroke."

Speaking of stroking... She brought her fingers up, measuring his length.

Brick braced his hands on the sink counter and dropped his head forward. "Tonya doesn't hold a candle to you."

Merrily knew that was nonsense, but it pleased her to hear him say it all the same.

It pleased her more to explore him. She lowered her hand, cupping him where he was softer, and he caught her wrist.

For a suspended moment, he held her hand

pressed against him, his eyes closed, heat pouring off him.

Finally he eased her hand away. "Let's save that for later, okay? Much more and I really will blow this."

Fascinating. "Blow it how?"

He gave up on the dishes and dried his hands. Teasing again, he said, "I don't want you gossiping with the other waitresses, claiming I'm a lousy lay."

"I would *never* do that." This all felt so special to her, she had no intention of making it fodder for gossip.

"Yeah, you won't. Because I'm not going to be lousy." He tipped up her chin to kiss her. "Back to Tonya."

Talk about a buzzkill.

"I figured Jesse would appreciate an intro. That's all." And then, "How could you even think I'd look at her with you in the room?"

Well, he had looked—enough to say Tonya was hot. But he claimed she was hotter. Merrily shook her head. "Because I'm just…me."

"Before we're through, you're going to know just how insanely sexy you are. I guarantee it."

Before we're through. Because whatever they shared wouldn't last long. He'd been very clear about that. And, oh, God, an awful thought occurred to her.

"What is it now?" Brick asked.

It unsettled her how easily he read her moods. While smoothing a hand over his chest, covered by the soft cotton of his dark T-shirt, she said, "When we're through, given that you think Tonya's hot…"

"Any guy with a pulse would think the same about her—and about *you,* too."

She didn't care what any other guy thought about her—well, except… Merrily looked up at him. "Jesse, too?"

His teeth worked together. "Jesse's not blind, but he's also not stupid."

"Meaning?"

"We're good friends, have been for years." Brick cupped her face, rubbed his thumb over her cheek. "That makes you off-limits."

Well. That seemed rather territorial. To make sure she understood the dynamics of his and Jesse's friendship, she clarified, "So even after you and I are through—"

"Yes." He scowled at her. "For all eternity, in fact."

He looked very put-out, even though she'd only repeated his own words back to him. But what did she know of male friendships and boundaries? Nada.

"I understand. So then, do you think you might… That is, would you…" She couldn't say the words and instead made a lame gesture toward him with her hand. "With Tonya, I mean?"

"If you're asking me if I'll come back here at

some later date and start sniffing after her, the answer is no."

She wasn't so worried about him sniffing as she was touching, kissing or the like. But, yes, sniffing would be bad, too—especially if she had to witness it. "I don't mean to nitpick. It's just that, with me living right next door, it could be…" Awful. Humiliating. Heart-wrenching. "Awkward."

Brick scrubbed both hands over his face and muffled a laugh. "Merrily, listen up, okay? I'd have to be a total dick to do something like that, and while I'm not an angel, I'm not that lost, either. So don't worry about it, okay?"

Not worrying would be tough, given Tonya's draw. She sighed. "I like Tonya a lot, you know. She's been a really good friend and a wonderful landlord. But she's…stunning, and I see how men get around her and turn all goofy."

"You know, that's usually how women are with Jesse." Brick touched her cheek. "But you haven't been falling apart at the sight of him."

"Of course not." She knew Jesse was attractive, but with Brick around, who cared? She thought about it and shook her head. "Actually, Jesse hasn't been goofy, either." Interested, definitely. Attentive, sure. But unlike most men, he came off as confident instead of love-struck. "I've seen contractors, delivery men, servicemen all act pretty outrageous with her. Even guys driving by stare at her. I know she's aware of the attention, but she usually ignores it."

"She's not ignoring Jesse."

No, she wasn't. Interesting. "Hmm."

Brick tipped up her chin. "Can you really be that unaware of the attention you get?"

She didn't get that kind of attention, but she was done talking about Jesse and Tonya. "I don't want to wait, Brick."

"Yeah, I get that," he said with gentle amusement. "You've been pretty clear." He ran his fingers through her hair, rubbing it gently, then lifting it to his nose. With his forehead almost touching hers, he whispered, "You sure you don't want to hold off until tomorrow, love? Maybe slow things down a little so we can both get a grip?"

Love? The affected way he said that made her want to swoon, but she was smart enough to realize a lot of it had to do with Brick being her first real romantic involvement since her bad breakup and her mother's death.

"No, I don't," she said again.

He drew two slow breaths. "I'd probably be in better shape without all this teasing—"

"Brick," she said with an edge of pleading. "Please don't make me wait."

His gaze met hers. His eyes narrowed—and he nodded. "God, I hope I survive this."

Merrily had no idea what he meant by that, and he didn't give her a chance to ask.

Keeping her tucked close to his side, Brick strode with her to the doorway that led into the living room.

Surrounded by both dogs and two of the cats, Tonya sat in a chair. Jesse sat on the edge of the couch, and they were laughing about something.

Brick cleared his throat, and as one, they looked up.

Jesse lifted a brow. "What's up?"

"I'm going to stick around awhile."

Jesse didn't even come close to teasing. "Gotcha." He pushed to his feet. "Then I'll walk Tonya home."

"I live right next door," Tonya said. "I think I can make it on my own."

"But what fun would that be?" He gave Brick a determined look. "I'll be back tomorrow to help with the doggy door and to take some measurements for the fence and to—"

"Yeah, fine, whatever." Brick waved that off. "I wasn't cutting you out."

Confused by that exchange, Merrily looked at Tonya, but her friend didn't appear to find anything amiss.

It took only moments for Tonya to gather her purse and say goodbye to the pets. Given that Brick held Merrily close to his side, Tonya merely waved to her. To Brick, she offered, "I can fire up my grill tomorrow, if you think you'll be here that long."

Jesse answered for him, saying, "I'll bring the steaks."

Moments later, they were alone, and Merrily felt such a smoldering rush of excitement she could barely contain herself.

Brick turned her to face him. "Your fence out back isn't secure enough to leave the dogs out alone."

"I know." She planned to work on that while they put in the doggy door.

"Do they sleep with you?"

"Sometimes."

"I figured." He held her upper arms, his thumbs caressing. "You have a spare room?"

She nodded while staring at his incredible mouth, thinking about his kiss, his taste.

She saw his smile and met his gaze.

"You wanna show me where it is?"

"The spare room?"

The smile widened. "We don't want the dogs joining us, honey."

"Oh." She glanced around and saw that only Eloise ignored them. Stan and Tom, Dundee and Dolly all waited with eager vigilance. "I have treats."

The animals went nuts over that. Rushing back to the kitchen, Merrily dug out doggy biscuits, rawhide bones, catnip balls, kitty kibble…everything she could think of that might keep her menagerie happy for a while.

The animals were so content with the treats, they didn't even notice when she closed a gate to keep them in the kitchen. "That's what I do when I have to clean the floors."

Voice thick, Brick said, "Works for me." He took her hand and tugged her down the hall.

With each step, Merrily's heart beat harder and her breath grew more shallow.

His thumb rubbed over her knuckles. "You're going to have to trust me on this."

Her body felt tight and achy in key places. "On what?"

In her bedroom, Brick flipped on an overhead light, closed her door and looked around at her neatly made bed. "The second time will be better." He caught the top of her comforter and tossed it to the foot of the bed. His hot gaze landed on her. "Because I don't know how long I'll last with the first."

BRICK TOLD HIMSELF to slow down, to ease her into things—but the second he faced her, she was on him. Arms tight around his neck. Her mouth seeking his. Her belly against his erection.

Damn.

A virgin shouldn't be so hot, so sexy.

Turning her, Brick pinned her to the wall and took over, kissing her so thoroughly that she subsided and gave in. By small degrees, she fell into that slow, deep kiss, her hands now clinging to his shoulders, her breathing harsh. He kept his hips angled in to keep her still; if she squirmed against him one more time, he'd lose it.

He held her jaw in one hand, and with the other stroked down her waist to her hip. She gave a ripe moan of encouragement.

He walked his fingers, inching up the skirt of her dress until the material bunched in his hand. She tried to ease her mouth free, but he turned his head and recaptured the kiss again. He wanted her drugged with pleasure, giving without reserve, but not so anxious.

Cupping the back of her neck to keep her steady, he stroked his tongue into her mouth at the same time he slid his hand into the back of her panties.

Soft, sleek, warm skin...

She jolted, but he crowded in closer, gentling her while exploring those incredible curves. Against her mouth, he whispered, "Okay?"

She moaned again.

He kissed her jaw, her throat, down to her shoulder where he nudged aside the insubstantial strap of her sundress. "I love your ass, Merrily." And he did. If he wasn't already strung so tight, he could spend hours on that plump, resilient flesh. "Stand still, okay?"

Putting a few inches between them, he clasped her wrists and brought her hands down to her sides. Her eyes were heavy, and her thick lashes left shadows over her cheeks as she watched him. Lips parted, she drew in shaky breaths and nodded.

In an excruciating tease, Brick caught the straps of her sundress with his pinkies. Slowly he eased both down to her elbows, down, down until the material dragged over her nipples, and exposed her full breasts.

It took him a second to form the words. "Damn, you're beautiful."

With just his fingertips he touched her left nipple, and saw her shimmer in excitement. "I'm rushing things, sorry, but I can't..." He shook his head and bent to draw that tightly budded nipple into his hot mouth.

As he sucked softly, her back arched and she sank her fingers into his hair, holding him close, closer still. On tiptoe, she offered herself up to him, but that wasn't enough. He gripped her bottom and lifted her more, holding her suspended like that while he drew on her.

"Brick..."

Throbbing, rigid with need, he switched to her other breast. Merrily squirmed, her heat against his abdomen, and with every pulse-beat of time her breathing became more ragged.

"Oh, God, *Brick...*"

No way. He released her nipple to look up at her and saw everything she felt in her expressive face. Close to release, eyes closed and head back, she panted through parted lips.

A rush of heat slammed over him. He reached behind her, found a zipper on the dress and, lacking all finesse, wrestled it down. For half a minute he struggled with tangled arms and straps and then, finally, pushed it down and over her lush hips. It fell to the floor, a soft cotton puddle of color that emphasized the creaminess of her bare skin.

"Damn." He soaked in the sight of her wearing no more than a miniscule scrap of white lace. "Nice panties." He pressed a hand to his erection, but there'd be no containing his lust, not now with her standing there almost naked and so incredibly perfect.

Flattening her hands on the wall behind her, Merrily drew one leg close, bent at the knee in an unconsciously seductive pose. She turned her head to the side and her hair fell forward to half cover her face. Her nipples were wet and tight from his mouth, her belly sucked in, her skin flushed.

Standing there like that, shy even while on the edge of release, she was the most stunning woman he'd ever seen.

"Don't move, love. Stay just like that." Brick reached back and grabbed a fistful of his T-shirt to strip it off over his head.

She peeked at him, breathing faster, attention rapt.

He kicked off his shoes, shoved his jeans down and took off his socks at the same time.

Merrily's gaze dropped fast to his dark, tented boxers, but he didn't dare remove those yet or he'd never survive. He fished his wallet from his jeans pocket, quickly located two condoms and put them on her nightstand. He kicked the jeans aside.

Taking his time looking at her, he stepped closer again. "You nervous?"

"No." She met his gaze. "Not with you."

He braced his hands on the wall at either side of her head. "I'm on the ragged edge here, honey." He tried to draw on lost reserves, but he had none. He put his forehead to hers. "I don't want to rush you, but I—"

"Shh." Tentatively, she touched his chest, stroking through his chest hair, up over a shoulder, down his side. "Do you know how you look?"

"Like a really horny guy? Yeah, I know." He put his nose to her temple and breathed in her warmed scent. It wasn't enough, not even close. He kissed her cheek, nipped her earlobe, opened his mouth on her throat.

If he could just hold it together long enough to get her caught up again—

Ah, hell. Her small hand gripped him through his boxers, sending his breath to hiss out in a rush of sensation. "Merrily…"

"I want to take my panties off now."

"Yeah, okay." He panted. "You gotta turn me loose first, love." It took everything he had to lift

her hand away from him, then he forced himself
to step back. "Go on."

She blushed, either with embarrassment or excitement, he couldn't tell.

He tortured himself by watching as she put
her thumbs in the narrow waistband, bent at the
waist—damn, but her breasts looked amazing
when she did that—and straightened again.

Naked.

His heart rapped so hard into his ribs, it almost hurt.

"Your turn," she said.

Without taking his gaze off her body, he shoved
his boxers away and reached for her. "Come here."
Pulling her in close he took her mouth while touching her everywhere, over her breasts, down her
narrow back, over that amazing backside.

Between her thighs.

When she started to reciprocate, Brick tumbled
her into the bed and pinned her hands down. She
tried to complain, but he kept on kissing her even
while locking both her wrists together with one
hand.

With the other, he explored her sweet little body,
over her breasts, her ribs, the slight rise of her
belly.

She twisted her mouth free. "Not fair."

"Tough," he whispered while watching her
face. He pressed his hand between her legs and
instantly stilled her struggles. "Mmm. You like

that?" He touched his fingertips over her, delved down, pressed in and found her creamy, wet, swollen and hot.

"Brick."

Such a thin, sweet voice. "Merrily." Seeing her like this both exacerbated his loss of control and softened his need. "Just relax and let me enjoy you." With his fingertips now damp, he found her clitoris, touched oh-so-gently.

Her back arched and her heels pressed into the mattress. *"I want to enjoy you, too."*

That near desperate demand made him smile. "You will, love. I promise." He licked a nipple, circled with his tongue and said huskily, "But first things first." He suckled at her breast while continuing to finger her so carefully.

Every little move she made, each raw sound from deep in her throat, made him that much more determined to see her climax as a foregone conclusion. He knew once he got inside her, he'd last a minute, maybe less.

"You're so sweet, Merrily," he whispered against her nipple. Carefully, with the very edge of his teeth, he tugged on her. "So soft, and so wet."

She twisted, panted.

He dipped his finger into her, pressed a little more until he heard her breath catch. "So damned tight, too." He paid close attention to what she liked—and what she loved.

When he wedged a second finger into her, she

didn't pull away, even though he knew he stretched her. Using her wetness, he slicked his thumb up over her and saw her teeth clench.

Yeah, she liked that, liked being filled while he stroked her little clit.

His testicles tightened, but he fought off the surge of release. At that moment, he wanted to see her come so bad, he could almost taste it.

That thought made him groan. Yeah, he would taste her, soon, but not just yet. He didn't want to do anything that might interrupt the rise of her pleasure.

He tugged at her nipple again, kept the sweet friction going between her legs, and suddenly she bowed, crying out, her thighs trembling. Her moisture bathed the fingers he had buried inside her, and it almost pushed him over the edge.

As soon as she started to quiet, the second her body slumped back into the bedcovers, Brick sat up and ripped open the condom packet with his teeth. He rolled on the protection, turned to her, moved over her.

"Open those pretty knees for me, Merrily."

Still gasping shakily, eyes closed and body lax, she shifted her thighs. Brick settled on her, used his fingers to part her hot, wet sex, and slowly entered her.

CHAPTER SIX

"Oh." What a wake-up, Merrily thought, as Brick pressed into her. He was so large and solid, and while she felt slight discomfort, it didn't really hurt.

In fact, once she got her eyes open and looked at him, she found it wildly exciting. "Brick."

"Yeah," he growled. "Me—and only me."

Never had she seen a man look as he did, sort of savage, clenched all over and very hot.

Braced above her on his forearms, his teeth locked, his gaze devouring her, he pressed relentlessly forward.

With excitement spiking through her again, Merrily put her hands to his bulging biceps. His skin burned with an inner fever. God, he was... incredible.

"Okay?" he asked through his teeth.

For an answer, Merrily slowly wrapped her legs around him, locking her heels at the small of his back. "I won't break, you know." She stroked his jaw. "You don't have to hold back."

"Don't."

One word, a warning, but she couldn't stop the curious exploration of her fingers over his furred chest—or the automatic flexing of her inner muscles as she tried to accommodate his solid length.

"Ah...*God.*" His big body tensed, strained, and he growled, "Sorry" before filling her in one strong thrust.

She gasped. Okay, now that hurt a little.

Shocked, Merrily held on to him, but she didn't have time to worry before he was rocking slow and deep, his face in her neck, his powerful chest brushing back and forth across her sensitive nipples.

Discomfort faded beneath the sweet, sliding friction.

And deep inside her, with each long stroke, he touched...something. Oh, yes. *There.* She lifted into him more. Dug her fingers into his solid shoulders to better brace herself. "Brick." And then, as sensation spiraled away. *"Brick."*

She'd thought it was amazing before, but now, with him in her, over her, a part of her...

He gave a long, vibrating groan, went still for one taut, suspended moment of time, then thrust more urgently and Merrily knew he was coming, too.

She couldn't imagine anything more perfect.

She couldn't imagine doing this with anyone else.

Big as he was, it felt nice when Brick sank down to rest on her, one of his hands tangled in her hair and cupped around her skull, the other scooped under her bottom. His heartbeat rocked them both, and heat poured off him.

After a minute, he stirred, his mouth touching her shoulder, over to her throat. With great effort he lumbered up to his forearms again.

Saying nothing, he watched her, almost looking into her heart.

Would he know that she'd already fallen in love with him, that she'd fallen hard the first time she saw him sitting in her section of the diner?

Until she'd met him, being a virgin hadn't even factored into her busy life.

After meeting him…would she ever want anyone else? Doubtful. After Brick, all over men would pale in comparison.

All too solemn, he bent down and took her mouth—and…seriously? He kissed her like he planned to start all over again.

Shivers chased over her skin, and she wrapped her arms around him, holding him tight.

When his hand slid down her side to her hip, she accepted that, yes, he planned to do this again.

Oh, boy. She hummed approval, gave him her tongue when he came looking for it, and lost herself in ripe sensation.

With Brick making love to her, she couldn't worry about tomorrow. She could only enjoy right now.

EVEN WITH BOTH dogs in the room, Eloise roaming over the foot of the bed, Brick slept soundly. Not that she minded. He was so beautiful she could have stood there all day looking at him. On his stomach, one muscled arm folded up under his head, one hairy leg exposed from beneath the sheet, he was the most incredible man she'd ever seen.

Even in her imagination, she couldn't drum up a vision more appealing than him.

Her breath shuddered out in a long sigh. Dundee tipped his head, unsure what they were doing, curious and a little worried at the idea of a big male in the bed.

Still. Because he'd stayed the night.

Did that mean anything?

Dolly circled the bed, trying to find a way up, but it was too high for her and Merrily didn't lift her up. Not yet.

Should she wake him? She dragged her gaze away from his magnificent body—and it really was incredibly magnificent—to see the clock. How late did he usually sleep?

He'd made love to her twice last night before leaving her collapsed and numb in the bed while he went to check on the animals. He came back, woke her to say that he'd taken them out to the yard for a bit, given them more treats and they were now content and asleep.

Then he'd started seducing her all over again. She hadn't realized that men were so voracious. Or maybe Brick was more voracious than most. He was certainly more…everything else. Bigger, more muscular, incredibly handsome—he was *more* than any other man she'd known.

Afterward, she'd been too spent to protest when he'd brought a cool washcloth to the bed and tended to her, then tucked her in close to his chest, covered them both and told her to sleep.

Just before dawn, he'd awakened her with small kisses along her arm down to her wrist. The second she got her eyes open she saw the heat in his and knew what he wanted. Or at least, she'd known part of what he wanted. The rest… What a surprise.

He'd sucked at her fingertips with blatant suggestion until she felt the tug of his mouth everywhere on her body.

She learned it wasn't at all the same when he *did* kiss her everywhere, telling her again to "part her pretty knees" and making her insane with the stroke of his tongue, the touch of his teeth and a devastating suckle that had her shivering again just thinking about it.

She closed her legs together tightly to contain

the memory, both of what he'd done and the things he'd said.

More than once, he'd called her "love."

He said such nice things, telling her she was sweet, treating her as if she were somehow special to him… Oh, how she loved it.

Because she loved him. Did she stand a chance of winning him over before he tired of her? Would it be unfair of her to try, when he'd told her upfront what he wanted—and what he didn't?

She wasn't a virgin any longer. But she was still new to sex, so maybe that'd be enough, for now, to keep him—

"What's wrong, love?"

Her gaze shot to his face. "You're awake."

"And you look melancholy." He rolled to his back, stretched those long limbs out with a soft, deep groan and came up to one elbow. Dundee turned circles in excitement, so Brick called him over, gave him a few pats, then reached down and scooped up Dolly to help her into the bed.

Merrily's heart swelled in her chest.

"Come here, you." He reached out a hand to her.

She set the coffee aside and let him draw her to sit near his hip on the bed. He fingered the T-shirt she wore as if he might want to remove it. But with both dogs being so attentive, he contented himself with touching her hair, tucking it back. "Good morning."

"Good morning."

His hand settled on her hip. "Did I disappoint you last night? Did I underwhelm you? Is that why you look so glum now?"

"No!"

The corner of his mouth kicked up, letting her know he only teased. "I expected to find you all smiles, maybe even giggling, especially after that last time when you—"

Merrily smashed her hand over his mouth, then looked nervously at Dundee, who looked back. "Shh."

After kissing her palm, he lowered her hand and muffled a low laugh. "He doesn't understand, honey."

But Dundee continued to stare at her, and it made her uneasy. "You don't know that for sure."

He turned to the dog and said, "She is incredibly hot, Dundee. So hot I still feel singed. She wore me out with her excesses. Sorry, bud, but it's true."

Dundee barked—and it almost sounded like agreement.

"Oh, stop." She noticed how Tom and Stan strolled in and joined him in the bed, too. He now had a highly interested creature audience. "I made coffee."

"Did you? Damn, woman, could you be more perfect?" A glance at the clock, and he groaned. "You should have woken me up. Jesse will be here soon." He went still, then quirked a brow. "Unless he stayed the night next door?"

"I didn't see his truck when I went out for the morning paper."

"Then he struck out." Brick grinned, and in contrast to his expression, he said, "Poor guy."

Merrily took Dolly and moved aside. "You should have time to shower."

"But I don't have time to have you again." With no reserve at all, he threw back the sheet, stretched again and left the bed—gloriously naked and awesomely aroused.

It left her speechless.

"Morning wood," he said by way of an explanation. He lifted her chin to bring her attention to his face. "You wanna shower with me?" But before she could answer, he shook his head. "No, scrap that. I've been excessive and I have to cool it before you think I'm a sex-starved ape."

"I wouldn't—"

He cupped her face, gave her a resounding smooch and headed for her bathroom. "Give me ten minutes, then I'd love a cup of coffee."

At his retreating back—and sexy backside—Merrily said, "Towels are in the cupboard. Help yourself to whatever you need."

He lifted a hand in acceptance and continued on his way.

Wow.

In something of a fog, she pulled on jeans, then turned and headed out of the room. The animals all padded after her.

To keep herself busy and avoid dwelling on Brick in her shower, Merrily started breakfast. She had bacon cooking, eggs on the counter and bread in the toaster when Brick strolled in shirtless, hair damp, face freshly shaved and jeans unsnapped.

"Smells great," he said while she ogled him. He came right up to her and kissed her more thoroughly. "Sorry, love, but I made use of your razor and toothbrush. Hope you don't mind."

Still mute, she shook her head, making him grin.

"Look at you, being all domestic." He clutched his heart. "It's almost too much, I swear." And without missing a beat, "Coffee?"

"Oh." She set aside her spatula and fetched a mug from the cabinet. "Creamer in the fridge and sugar on the counter."

"I take it black." He poured himself a cup, sipped, and hummed his appreciation. "Damn, love, but the whole package is a little much."

"Whole package?"

He saluted her with the coffee cup. "Looking like you look, being as sweet as you are, smokin' hot in the sack, then proficient in the kitchen, too. And to top it off, you love animals. What else is there?"

"Uh…I don't know." He left her so confused she had no idea what to say. "I think you're…the whole package, too."

"Perfect." When Dundee went to the backdoor, Brick automatically opened it to let him out, then stood there to keep watch. "I think I'll use that to segue into tomorrow."

"Tomorrow?"

"I want to come back. Or stay over." He shrugged. "Your choice. I prefer the latter, but if I stay, I'll at least need to head home for supplies."

She was starting to feel like an idiot with her one-word questions. "Supplies?"

"My own toothbrush and razor. Clean boxers." His gaze darkened and he looked her over. "More rubbers."

"Oh." The bacon popped, and she jumped. She quickly removed it from the pan and put it on a plate. Before cracking the eggs, she willed her jumping nervousness to quiet, kept her back to him and asked as casually as she could manage, "You mentioned staying over again?"

Without her hearing his approach, his hands settled on her waist. He nuzzled behind her ear. "Mmm. I need more of you, love. What do you think of that?"

The egg she tried to crack smashed into the pan. She stared at it dumbly.

Brick eased her aside. "Why don't I do the eggs? You can check on Dundee and Dolly."

She watched him scrape her egg mess into the garbage can, then expertly crack four eggs into the skillet. Talk about perfection... No man should look that good in his jeans, be such an incredible lover and know how to cook, too. It just wasn't fair.

She used the excuse of calling in the dogs to get herself together. If she ever hoped to be more than a convenient bed partner, she had to take control of this situation right now. After drying the dogs' paws from the dew-wet grass, she closed the door and returned to Brick.

He had the plates on the table and was buttering the toast. "How many eggs do you want?"

"One."

He put it on her plate and took the other three for himself.

Merrily squared her shoulders. "I'm not a virgin anymore."

For only a second, Brick paused. "Nope, definitely not." He put the toast on the table and pulled out a chair for her.

She hesitated to get that close to him when they had so much to talk about, but if he could be cavalier, she would be, as well. "Thank you."

After she sat, he kissed the top of her head, her temple, and near her ear he whispered, "You're a sexy, barely tried ex-virgin and, again, Merrily, I want more." He moved away and sat across from her. "So what do you say? Wanna play for a while?"

Boy, did she ever.

Pretending great thought, she sipped her coffee. "How long are we talking?"

That took the good humor out of his expression. "Need it spelled out, do you? Should we draw up a contract? Maybe specify an ironclad end date so that I'm not underfoot too long?"

"You're angry?" For some reason, that made her feel better, less confused. "Recall, Brick, you said you wanted me to understand that you wouldn't be getting involved—"

"I know exactly what I said." He stabbed into a fried egg with his fork. "But I figured we'd play it by ear. Let things unfold naturally. Not…" He put his fork back down—with egg still clinging to it. "I don't want to get sent packing too soon."

"How soon is too soon?"

A flush of color slashed his high cheekbones. "Damn it, you are hung up on time frames, aren't you?"

She had to bite back a smile of relief. He wanted her. More of her—however much that might be. Elation filled her heart.

"I'm sorry." Teasing, she asked, "Have I hurt your feelings?"

He looked so dumbfounded by that possibility,

and then bemused as he realized it was true, that Merrily laughed.

Maybe he cared more for her than even he realized. Why else would he get so riled over it?

"Virgins are the devil." While eyeing her, he ate an entire strip of bacon in one bite. "Go ahead," he said at her continued giggling. "Keep me in suspense. I probably have that coming."

Because he sort of did, she took her time eating most of her egg, a few bites of toast, but she couldn't bear the silence or his watchful gaze.

After finishing off a strip of bacon, she reached across the table for his hand. "You were so incredible, Brick."

Grudgingly, he said, "Thank you." His warm fingers curled around hers. "Given how you affect me, I might not have been at my best."

Lord help her. "You were more than I expected. More than I knew was possible."

"I'm listening."

"I would love to continue having sex with you." She thought to add, just in case she spooked him, "For as long as we're both having fun, so please, go get a toothbrush and boxers and whatever else you need. Definitely more condoms. Maybe bring a whole box."

His gaze dropped to her mouth. "Yeah?"

She nodded. "Let's play some more. I want to

have as much fun as I can." And because maybe he needed reassurance, she added, "With you."

Staring at her, Brick breathed hard, shifted, then glanced at the clock. "If only we had enough time…"

A knock sounded on her door, sending the dogs into fits.

Brick groaned. Over the din, he said, "I'll have you know, love, I'm hard. Again. Around you it appears to be a perpetual state but most definitely when you talk about having fun and playing— with me." He shoved the rest of his food into his mouth and put his plate in the sink. He pulled out her chair.

Merrily smoothed her sleep-rumpled hair. "I need my own shower."

"Go on, then, while I get the door and Jesse and I finish off the coffee. Take your time, okay? I'll clean up the kitchen."

That sounded so nice—almost like the partnership she'd always wanted. Brick Carlisle really was the whole package.

How long would she be able to keep him?

BRICK PULLED THE section of wire fencing taut, added new staples to the post, and Jesse hammered them in with a little more force than necessary.

Curious at Jesse's tight-lipped mood, Brick

moved down to the next section. "I take it sexual frustration is adding to your fervor today?"

"None of your business."

"I know you didn't spend the night."

"No, I didn't." Jesse checked that the fencing was still adequately buried under the ground, found one spot that was a little loose and used a looped stake to secure it.

"This is a nice yard." Brick admired their work. "Big enough, with plenty of shade. And now that we have the fence secure, the dogs are going to love the freedom."

"Yeah." Standing, Jesse wiped sweat from his brow with a forearm. "I like that they don't have close neighbors on either side."

"Private but not so secluded they aren't safe."

Jesse looked toward Tonya's porch. They could both see her hot tub, now covered, in the corner of her porch. "She's coming to my shop on Monday to check out the wood."

"Ah, well, then things must be looking up for you."

"Don't be juvenile," Jesse groused, but he grinned.

"What?" All innocence, Brick shrugged. "I meant that you've still got some opportunities with her. It had nothing to do with her seeing your wood."

"Yeah, right." Jesse nodded at where the women worked the grill. "So how's it going for you?"

"Okay."

"Just okay? Because I know that you *did* spend the night."

Brick rubbed the back of his neck, scowled, then blurted, "She had me damn near begging this morning."

That got Jesse refocused real fast. "Begging for *what?*"

"Now who's being juvenile?" He peeled leather work gloves off his hands. "More time with her."

"She doesn't want more time?"

"I think she does, but I gave her my damned spiel going in about no commitments and now she's...well, she's holding me to it."

"What a dunce." Quickly, Jesse clarified, "You, not her." And then, "Why the hell would you go into all that with her?"

"Seemed like a good idea at the time."

"Because you always lay it out there with women?"

"Yeah." Frustration bubbled over. "Thing is, she's not like any of the others."

"Duh. I could have told you that." He clapped Brick on the shoulder. "You knew her a month and didn't ask her out, but every time you look at her, it's clear to anyone with eyes that you've got it bad. That alone sets her apart from other women."

"Yeah." Brick thought back on his hesitation, all the lame reasons he'd given himself for steering clear. "I've been an ass and now I have to figure it out."

"Fuck me sideways. You actually admit it? Just like that?"

"Yeah. Just like that." After having Merrily last night, he'd known deep down that he didn't want to let her go. Not now. Not anytime soon. Probably not ever.

That thought was so uncomfortable, he glanced at Jesse. "She thought I'd want Tonya."

"No."

Jesse's predicament was far more amusing than his own. "Pay attention, man. I'm head over ass, so there's no reason to mean-mug me. Tonya doesn't interest me. Take a breath and get a grip."

Jesse bent to pick up tools. "She spelled it out last night. Friendship is the only thing on the agenda."

Huh. Usually Jesse scored with ease. Outright rejection had to burn his ass a little. "Better luck with the next one."

Jesse didn't seem to hear that sentiment. "It's not just me, though. She said all guys are off-limits."

Brick remembered the hot tub comment and scowled. "She's into women?"

"Nope." He narrowed his eyes. "I asked."

Wow. That had to have been an interesting conversation. "Probably too many bozos hitting on her, then, her looking the way she does and all."

"Maybe, but I get a feeling it's more than that." Uneasy, Jesse chewed on his thoughts a bit before saying, "There's something about her, something sort of... Hell, I don't know. Maybe wounded."

And that would change everything. Brick started them toward the house. "So what are you going to do?" No way in hell would he let Jesse muck this up for him. He wanted Merrily for the long haul. A disgruntled friend of his pushing her neighbor could wear out the welcome for them both.

Jesse rolled one shoulder. "She has a lot of stuff that needs to be done around the house, and I don't mind doing it, so I'm going to be her friend. For a little while, anyway." He stared at Tonya as they neared the porch. "After that...I dunno. Guess we'll have to wait and see."

CHAPTER SEVEN

A LITTLE WHILE turned into a month.

Brick was having the time of his life. He came in from work greeted by berserk enthusiasm from the dogs and purring acceptance from the cats. Merrily showed more subtlety; she'd smile, wrap her arms around him and kiss him senseless.

He loved it. Hell, he loved her.

He hadn't exactly told her yet, not with her holding that invisible timer. Instead he showed her in every way he knew how and hoped she ended up caring enough to want to get all legal with him.

They took turns cooking and cleaning and caring for the animals. Brick helped to free up her time so she could dedicate more attention to her class work. She got along great with Jesse, and it hadn't taken her more than two minutes after her introduction for her to win over his brother, Evan, and his sister-in-law, Cinder. Of course they loved her—who wouldn't?

Whenever possible, be it morning, afternoon, or evening, they burned up the sheets. And every time got better. He hadn't officially moved in, but he spent far more time at her duplex than he did at his own place. For him, life was pretty damned sweet, almost as sweet as Merrily herself.

But poor Jesse hadn't gained any headway at all.

He was still hanging around, and both sides of the house had been rehabbed in numerous ways. Tonya now had a nice fence surrounding her hot tub and a new patio for it to sit on. She'd insisted on paying something, so they'd let her buy materials—at cost—and donated the labor.

On Merrily's side, they'd built a deck that now held an assortment of outdoor furniture and a nice propane grill.

Jesse, using every excuse he could to continue hanging around, currently put the finishing touches on a small house for the dogs and connecting perches for the cats. The pet "condo," as Merrily called it, was elaborate and decorative and looked great in the yard.

But so far, it freaked out the animals. They walked a wide path around both structures.

Poor Merrily worried that her animals would hurt Jesse's feelings, and that left Brick cracking up.

"You're so tenderhearted." It was one of the things he loved most about her.

While Jesse nailed in the last shingle on the roof of the "condo," Dundee snarled.

"Oh, no." Hand to her mouth, Merrily fretted. "I feel terrible. It's so awesome. I mean, look at it. It's like their own little home. Not just a doghouse, but something really special."

Yeah, special enough that it had taken Jesse two weeks to build. Sure, Jesse enjoyed the work, and he even seemed to enjoy Tonya's platonic friendship.

But Brick wasn't fooled.

"Put a few treats in there," Brick suggested. "The dogs will like it more then."

"Great idea!" Merrily rushed inside to get some dog chews.

Brick strolled out to Jesse. "You can only put so many nails in there, bud."

He gave one more whack of the hammer and relented. "Yeah, it's done." Standing back, he admired it. "Looks good, huh?"

Dolly got close—ran past—and slowed again. Dundee walked over and lifted his leg on the side.

"Great." Jesse laughed. "If he's marking his territory, then he must be willing to claim it as his own, right?"

Brick ignored that. "Tonya's usually home by now."

"Yeah, I know."

"Should be here any minute."

Jesse looked up at the setting sun, then off to

the side. "I have to take off soon anyway." He bent to gather his tools. "I have a date."

Why that shocked Brick, he couldn't say. Hell, Jesse had shown more patience than any healthy guy could be expected. "Damn."

He glanced up at Brick. "What?"

Brick dropped to sit on his ass, his wrists draped over his knees. "Something just occurred to me."

"Yeah, what's that?"

"Merrily's ex."

"What about him?"

"He waited for Merrily. For a long time, in fact."

Jesse pulled his shirt back on. "Not as easy as it looks, ya know?"

"I can only imagine."

"Lucky you." Jesse shook his head. "Try living it."

"Her ex did. Try to live with it, I mean."

"It's not the same, Brick." Jesse sat in the thick grass, too, with the tree shading him. "She had reasons, right? She was younger and she had her hands full with some really heavy responsibilities."

True, all of it. But it didn't make him feel any better. Would he have been any better? Would he have waited for Merrily?

Could he have waited? He just didn't know.

"I don't suppose Tonya's given you any reason for...?" What could Brick call it? Not lack of interest. He gestured. "For the hands-off policy."

"Not a clue."

They both heard a car door and knew Tonya was home.

Brick eyed him. "You sure you don't want to stick around and have dinner with us?"

"Nope." He pushed to his feet.

Brick did the same. He wasn't a busybody old lady, and he sure as hell wasn't a matchmaker. But damn it, now that he was so happy, he wanted the same for Jesse. "Talk to her one more time, okay?"

"Let it go, Brick."

"Spell it out to her. Ask her to confide in you." He gave Jesse a shrug. "What d'ya have to lose?"

ARMS LADEN WITH doggy treats and toys, Merrily started out but hesitated when Tonya tapped at the front door.

She rolled her eyes, knowing Tonya had seen Jesse's truck and knowing her friend wanted to see him. But instead of going around back to where the men waited, she came to the front.

"Come on in."

Tonya stuck her head in the door, saw Merrily standing there alone, and smiled as she walked in.

She wore another fashionable suit, this one beige with a coffee-colored blouse beneath. It looked amazing with her pale hair, but then, Tonya could wear a tent and make it look good.

Leaving the front door open, she walked in to

admire the repaired baseboard in the living room.
"I like it when you have a boyfriend. Things get
done."

"Wait until you see the house Jesse built for the
animals. It's incredible." She shook her head on
a grin. "I've taken shameful advantage of them
both."

"Nonsense." Tonya relieved her of half the dog
toys. "Men in love are happy to help out."

"Jesse is in love with you?" Wow. And here
she thought they hadn't gotten past the talking
stage yet.

Tonya laughed at her. "Of course not. Jesse and
I are just…friends."

"Uh-huh." Merrily set aside her load and folded
her arms. "You want to be more than friends.
Admit it."

Her smile dimmed. "I can't." She, too, set aside
the toys. "But I was talking about Brick anyway.
It's clear he's madly in love with you."

Hearing that shot Merrily's heart into her throat.
She shook her head in denial, even while hope
filled her. "He's not."

"Oh, hon, of course he is." Tonya took her
hands. "You can't tell?"

"I…" She didn't know what to say. "He's wonderful."

"Yes, he is. But wonderful men aren't necessar-

ily in love. There's a difference. Brick *is* in love—
with a capital *L*. Just ask him."

"No!"

Tonya smiled. "Afraid?"

She pressed a hand to her churning stomach. "I
don't want to rock the boat."

"Oh, please. I know men, and Brick will be
thrilled to hear it from you. He's probably doing
his own share of fretting, unsure how you feel
about things."

That distracted Merrily. "If you know men so
well, then why don't you realize how invested Jesse
is? He's done everything he can to win you over."

Tonya bit her lip—and another knock sounded
on the door. Both women turned, and Merrily fell
back a step. "Kyle."

"Who?" Tonya asked.

Her stomach dropped again, this time for a very
different reason. "He's my ex."

"No way." Tonya looked up, saw Kyle smiling as he stepped in uninvited, and quickly sidled
around Merrily to head for the kitchen. "I think
I'll just go get Brick."

Merrily barely heard her. Kyle was back, but
seeing him didn't have the effect she'd expected.
It didn't hurt to see him. It wasn't a relief.

Honestly, other than regretting the interruption,
she felt absolutely nothing at all.

What about that?

BRICK PACED IN the kitchen. Damn it, he did not want to leave Merrily alone in the living room. Not with Kyle.

Especially not now that he'd stopped thinking of her ex as a villain.

Seated at the kitchen table, Tonya and Jesse watched him with something close to sympathy. It irked.

"He's a big guy," Jesse noted.

"So?" Brick didn't care if he was a linebacker. He wanted to kick him to the curb. Right now. Before he had a chance to schmooze his way back into Merrily's good graces.

Over and over in his mind, he kept hearing her say she'd loved the guy, that she'd been hurt when he broke the engagement.

"From what I knew of him," Jesse said, "I expected…I dunno…a dweeb, maybe."

"He's handsome," Tonya stated, then caught herself. "I mean…well, like Jesse, I expected something different."

"I don't know why." Both dogs followed Brick as he continued pacing the kitchen floor. "Merrily could have her pick of men." And damn it, she'd picked him.

He hoped like hell she remembered that.

"He said he heard that her mother had passed," Tonya whispered. "That's why he's here now."

"He's hoping to worm his way back in," Jesse added. "Why are you in here?"

Brick shook his head. "She asked for a moment with him." But even now, she looked a little distant, a little confused and he didn't like it. "Gotta respect her wishes on that." Even if it killed him.

When their voices rose, everyone froze to listen, even the dogs.

"You moved in with someone else, Kyle."

"Only because you kept me at an emotional distance."

"It was the physical distance you objected to."

"Any man would, Merrily. Look at you." Oozing sincerity, Kyle murmured, "It was torturous not having you."

Merrily snorted.

But damn it, Brick had to agree—that would be torturous.

And because Jesse suffered it firsthand, he shifted easily. Tonya got up from the table to get a drink from the refrigerator.

"Merrily, honey, we were both different people then."

"I haven't changed," she said.

"But you have," Kyle argued. "Your situation has."

Face going red and eyes narrowing, she whispered, "You mean because my mother is gone now?"

Kyle had the good sense to hesitate, but then he forged on. "You're…free now."

"Actually…I'm not." She looked over her shoulder at Brick.

Taking that as a cue, Brick surged in. "No, she isn't." He put an arm around her and hauled her to his side in a possessive show. "Sorry, bud. Snooze, you lose."

Kyle looked between them. He worked his jaw. "That didn't take long."

"Long enough for you to be a distant memory, pal."

Merrily elbowed him for that brutal bit of truth—at least, it better be true.

She gave a sweet smile to her ex. "Really, Kyle, it's past history. I've moved on. I don't hold any ill feelings, and I hope you don't, either."

"I have only wonderful memories of you, Merrily."

"Course you do," Brick said. "Because she's wonderful." He crowded her in closer to his side. "And now she's mine."

"You don't own her," Kyle insisted.

"Nope, but I'm hoping to get her legally tied all right and tight, so don't hold your breath waiting for me to screw up like you did." He felt Merrily stiffen beside him, but so what? She had to find out his long-term intentions sooner or later. Now seemed like a really good time to him. "Then again, go ahead." Brick smiled at her flummoxed ex. "Hold your breath, why don't you?"

Merrily turned to stare up at him. "What are you talking about?"

"Send him away, and I'll go to one knee to expound on things."

With high color in her face, she rounded on her ex. "Sorry, Kyle, but I need you to go now." She put a hand to his shoulder and half urged, half shoved him toward the door. "Thanks for stopping by, but you probably shouldn't do that again."

When Kyle suddenly planted his feet, Brick said, "She'd like you to go." And just because he did pity the idiot, he said, "Sorry. Tough break and all that."

Kyle gathered steam, bunching his shoulders, fisting his hands. He opened his mouth—and Brick stepped in front of Merrily.

Very quietly, he said, "Don't do it, dude. Take my word for it—any insult from you won't end well. Keep your dignity intact. Close your mouth, turn around and mosey on away."

Luckily for all concerned, Kyle did just that, slamming the door on his way out.

"Huh." Brick looked down at Merrily. "You like 'em big, huh?"

Tears welling in her eyes, she touched his chest, then his shoulders and nodded. "Obviously."

He frowned at the tires squealing out of her

driveway, but Merrily still had hands on him, still waited, so he forgot all about Kyle.

"Am I big enough to keep?" Gently, he cupped her face. "Because I want you to keep me, Merrily." He kissed her trembling lips. "C'mon, honey. Tell me I can stay. I mean, stay with you. Not necessarily stay here."

"Hey," Tonya complained.

"Not that I don't like the house. I do." He shrugged. "I just meant—"

"You love me?"

The smile pulled at him and happiness expanded. "How could I not?" Dundee jumped up against his leg, and the happiness escaped as a laugh. Dolly circled them both, trying to find a way to worm in. "The dogs love me." He glanced toward Eloise, Tom and Stan, lazing on various pieces of furniture. "I think even the cats are fond of me."

"They all adore you, and you know it."

"Sounds like you're outnumbered then, huh? You may as well give up and adore me, too."

She threw her arms around his neck and squeezed him tight. He felt her soft breath on his throat when she said, "I love you so much."

"Thank God." When he pretended weak knees, the dogs scattered, then surged back with excited barks. "Way to drag out the suspense, woman."

"Good work, Brick." Jesse leaned on the wall,

a big smile on his face. "That was incredibly smooth."

"I try."

Tonya stood a few feet from Jesse, her hands together and her gaze soft. "You succeed."

"So…" He nodded at them both. "If you two will excuse us for a bit—"

Another knock sounded on the door. Thinking her ex had returned, Brick turned, then stiffened at the sight of the police officer standing there.

What now?

IT WAS LATE at night, and moonlight filtered in through the open window. At the foot of the bed, two cats snored. On the floor, Dundee and Dolly curled up together. Eloise sat in the window, watching the night sky.

Brick knew Merrily wasn't asleep yet. After the busy evening, they'd only been in bed a short time.

He kissed the top of her head. "You okay?"

She nodded, snuggled a little closer. "Poor Tonya."

"Yeah." The cop had come for her. Really bad news, news that made him crush Merrily closer. "She'll be okay. Jesse is still with her." They'd been with her, too, and they'd done what they could.

"She knew her sister had problems. She said she'd lived with constant worry for a few years now, always waiting for this day."

"That's rough." It seemed Tonya's sister had taken a bad path. Too much drinking, too much partying. "Doesn't sound like she'd been much of a mom to her kid."

Merrily's hand wandered over his chest. "Tonya tried to help out where she could, but she and her sister were estranged. And now…"

"Now she'll be the one raising her nephew. At least he's not a baby."

"He's twelve, Brick. That might be even harder."

Remembering himself at that age, Brick nodded. "Yeah, probably." He had a brother, and he knew he'd die for him. He couldn't imagine what Tonya must be feeling.

Merrily levered up over him, her arms folded over his chest. "Thank you."

He smoothed his hands down her back to her plump behind. "For what, exactly?"

"Being you. And being here with me."

"There's nowhere I'd rather be. I love you."

She bent to kiss him. "You know, I pretty much fell in love with you the first day I saw you."

"Same here."

Disbelief beetled her brows. "Baloney. I had to practically throw myself at you."

Silly woman. "I knew you were different. How you made me feel was different. I knew if I ever once had you, there'd be no going back." He lifted to take her mouth, then said against her lips, "And I was right."

She settled against him, her cheek to his heart-beat, her fingers toying with his chest hair. "Tonya said now, she wishes she'd taken advantage of Jesse's attention when she had the opportunity."

"Who says she can't still?"

She lifted up again to blink at him. "She's going to have a twelve-year-old boy to care for."

Brick nodded. "She'll have her hands full, that's for sure."

"Well..." Merrily considered everything. "Tonya said no man would want a part of that."

"So you both expect Jesse to bail, huh?" Brick snorted over that. He was starting to think Tonya knew even less about men than Merrily did. "He won't. If anything, he'll be more determined to hang around."

Stunned, Merrily stared at him. "You're serious?"

"Jesse isn't a dummy. And after a month of celibacy, it's obvious he cares for her. Otherwise he'd have moved on long ago." Brick touched her cheek. "I'm not saying he won't date. Or...find relief somewhere. But he'll want to help Tonya if he can. Count on it."

She bit her lip. The tears glistening in her eyes caught and held the moonlight. "You think Tonya is doing the right thing?"

"Absolutely. Family is there for family, always."

"You'd have felt the same about my mother? About the time I had to give to her?"

Catching her shoulders, Brick rolled her beneath him. The cats scattered with a meowing complaint, but otherwise the room remained quiet. "You did the right thing, honey—the only thing you could do. For my family, I'd do the same." He didn't know if he'd have been able to wait, but he did know one thing—he was glad Kyle hadn't. "Tonya and her nephew will have a rough road ahead of them. But we'll be here for her and for him, too. And no matter what happens, you will never again be alone."

"Because I have you." She wrapped her arms around him. "I'm so glad you were my first."

"And your last." Brick kissed her. "And best of all, your one and only. Forever."

* * * * *

BEACH HOUSE BEGINNINGS

Christie Ridgway

Dear Reader,

I want to take you away! I have a special place for you to visit, with sun and sand and magic. Not the hocus-pocus kind of magic, but the kind of alchemy that occurs when two strangers meet and know instantly the moment is a game changer. Their hearts beat faster and there's an exuberant lift in their bellies and even if they don't want to feel like this, they just...do.

Beach House Beginnings is also connected to three full-length works available now: *Beach House No. 9, Bungalow Nights* and *The Love Shack.* I hope you'll enjoy this first look at Crescent Cove as the sunshine breaks through the coastal fog to reveal a gem of a setting and a man and a woman who are about to uncover treasure...in each other. Both Caleb McCall and Meg Alexander have fractures of the heart that only the act of committing to each other can fully mend. I hope you'll root for them and return for more Beach House No. 9 books.

And look for the first book in my new Cabin Fever series, *Take My Breath Away,* coming soon!

Christie Ridgway

www.ChristieRidgway.com

CHAPTER ONE

TWO MILES OF magic.

Trudging through soft sand, Meg Alexander remembered that's how she'd thought of her childhood Neverland, Southern California's Crescent Cove. Even after ten years away, she recalled how lucky she'd felt growing up here.

Meg's great-great-grandfather had purchased the land as a location to make silent movies such as *The Courageous Castaways* and *Sweet Safari,* and the tropical vegetation he'd trucked in for authenticity in 1919 continued to thrive at the cove today. The buff-colored bluffs rising up from the beach were made more colorful by the bright green fronds of date palm trees and the salmon-and-scarlet flowers of bougainvillea that nestled beside the native sagebrush. Closer to shore, floppy-leaved banana plants, chunky Mexican fan palms and colorful hibiscus shrubs surrounded the fifty eclectic cottages, most of which had been built during the 1920s through 1950s.

Each of the beach houses at Crescent Cove was

different, their form-following whims now long forgotten. Their paint schemes were as varied as their shapes and sizes, though the colors selected blended well with the landscape of sand, earth and vivid flora. The single similarity was that in every one, windows peered oceanward.

Meg didn't dare look in that direction, herself.

Growing up, her mother had told Meg and her little sister, Skye, that merfolk lived in those waters offshore, protecting the cove with their supernatural powers. Growing up, Meg had believed in that, just as she'd believed that sand dollars were the merpeople's currency and sea glass the discarded pieces from some mysterious merchildren's board game.

But Meg didn't believe in magic or mystery anymore.

"Good morning," an elderly male voice said.

Startled, Meg looked up. "Hey, Rex. Good morning, yourself." Rex Monroe, ninety-some years young, was the only full-time resident at the cove other than Skye, who had managed the property since their parents' move to Provence, France. Yesterday, for the first time in a decade, Meg had met up with the nonagenarian as he walked along the sand. Like now, the clouds had been low and damp, the typical gloomy "May Gray" weather conditions. "Getting in your daily constitutional?" she asked.

Rex patted his belly, covered in a flannel shirt tucked into soft chinos. "It's not just you ladies who have to watch your figures. Are you settling in okay?"

"Oh, sure," Meg said, waving a hand. It was actually weird being back in her childhood bedroom, ten years after leaving the cove at nineteen, but her sister had been invited to the out-of-town wedding of a former college roommate. How could Meg have refused to step in? Memorial Day weekend was the kick-off of the Crescent Cove summer season. Someone had to be on hand to pass out keys to the bungalows and handle minor crises.

Even if it was a major crisis, in Meg's mind, to be back here.

"I see you have a satchel of tools," Rex said, pointing to the canvas bag she carried. "Something need fixing already?"

"Not really. Just trying to keep busy." Anything to prevent her from thinking of the last summer she'd spent at the cove. "I'm going to scrape the deck railing at Beach House Number 9. I understand that Griffin Lowell has been staying there the past couple of months, but since he's away for a few days, Skye hired a contractor to take care of the blistering paint while he's gone."

Rex gave Meg a piercing look that reminded her he was a former war correspondent, one who'd won a Pulitzer during World War II. "What? The man Skye hired doesn't have some sort of electric paint-removing machine?"

"Uh, well…" Meg glanced at the simple metal scraper at the bottom of her bag, sitting beside a few other basic tools and her bottle of water. "You know what they say about idle hands. I thought I'd do the work myself." An idle mind was even more dangerous, Meg had decided. She had to stay busy to avoid thoughts of that last summer. Of Peter.

Rex nodded as if he understood all she didn't say aloud. "You come visit me if you'd like some company, all right?"

"Thanks, I will," Meg said with a bright smile, though she knew she wouldn't. She didn't want company. Company might bring up Peter. Company might ask her why she'd run away from her childhood home and never returned. Company might make her admit how much she'd lost, including the happy-go-lucky girl she'd once been.

Meg was too smart to allow that to happen.

"Enjoy your walk, Rex," she said, and then continued down the beach.

The south end of Crescent Cove was bounded by a sea cliff that pushed into the Pacific. Though the top of it was wide and flat, there were steep trails snaking up its side that led to various outcroppings from which, she remembered, daredevils used to launch ocean jumps. Skye had posted warning signs against the practice, but from the look of those clearly defined routes, it remained an enticement. The last cottage in the cove snuggled next to the bluff, a two-story, brown-shingled building with blue-green trim and a large deck extending over the sand.

A driftwood sign was tacked to the outer railing, words painted in the same color as the trim. *Beach House No. 9.*

Meg mounted the steps that led from the sand to the surface of the deck. She dropped her bag on the umbrella-topped table and took in the rest of the patio accessories: single chaises, a double lounger, a stack of extra chairs and a barbecue.

Everything looked in order. Though the current resident was gone for a few days, he'd return for the month of June. After that, No. 9 would have different occupants in July and August. Skye had said almost all the cottages were booked up for summer. That was good, because those months were when Crescent Cove paid its way. It would quiet in the fall and the rentals would be mostly vacant throughout the winter and spring.

Meg frowned at the peeling rails. Her sister was right to be annoyed that the paint hadn't stayed tight to the wood. Maintenance was accomplished in the off-season and a company had been out in February to refurbish, but their efforts hadn't lasted.

On the plus side, it gave Meg something to do, besides think of—

No one. No one was on her mind.

Yanking a hair tie from her front pocket, she gave another frown at the blistered railing as she bound her mass of caramel-colored hair. Then she consciously relaxed her facial muscles. "Watch it," she murmured to herself. "You don't want to groove permanently grumpy lines."

Then again, she *was* a twenty-nine-year-old accountant. Grumpy might already be permanent.

Ignoring that unpleasant thought, Meg tackled the task she'd assigned herself, starting at one end of the railing. Paint chips flew until they covered her feet in their rubber thongs and were scattered over her hands and forearms. They drifted onto her jeans and T-shirt, too, almost obscuring the word blazoned across her chest: Meh.

Which kind of summed up how Meg had been feeling about herself and her life.

Meh. Meg. Just one letter off.

Contemplating that made her thirsty again. She'd nearly drained the puny little bottle of water she'd brought. The May Gray was locked in battle with the sun, and though right now gray was winning, it had definitely warmed up. With the last drop in her still-parched throat, Meg decided to dig through her bag for the cove's master keys, and dash inside No. 9 to refill her water at the kitchen sink.

Since No. 9's occupant, Griffin Lowell, had summered in this very bungalow as a kid and they'd been friends back in the day, she didn't think he'd object. Although according to Skye, Griffin barely resembled the devil-may-care boy who had vacationed with his family at the cove. Now a journalist, he'd spent a year embedded with the troops in Afghanistan and had come back to the beach a loner who wanted nothing more than to be left to himself. Meg hoped he'd find what he was looking for here, though her own return to Crescent Cove had yet to bring her peace.

The sliding door leading from the deck to the living room was heavy, so she left it open as she hustled inside, leaving her paint-chipped footwear behind. It only took a moment or two to replenish her bottle and twist on the cap. As she hurried back out, her bare soles slid on the hardwood floor. She felt herself going down and dropped the container to catch her balance on a floor-to-ceiling bookshelf. Steady again, she saw the plastic cylinder of water rolling toward the sliding glass door. Rolling toward shoes.

Shoes?

As she looked up, the sun won the war, breaking from behind the clouds. The light dazzled, and made the figure in the doorway a dark silhouette.

A male silhouette, with a big shaggy-haired dog at his side.

Meg's heart shot high, fueled by pure exhilaration as she recognized the masculine outline. Her fingers tightened on the bookshelf. Peter. *Peter!*

In one single moment she experienced all the blazing joy of that summer ten years before when she'd met a twenty-two-year-old recent college graduate. She'd fallen for him, fallen so deep that there'd been barely a splash, and he'd been equally smitten. The feeling had held all the thrills and enchantment her mother had promised about that thing called love, as happy-ever-after-ish as Meg had fantasized since she was a little girl swooning over the Disney version of *The Little Mermaid*. Peter Fleming had been her prince.

That summer, she'd thought she'd met her future, and they could have fed the entire world's energy grid from the unending pool of their mutual bliss.

And here he was! Again! Her heart raced, thrumming against her ribs. Peter...

Did she say it out loud? Because the dark figure shook his head, then stepped into the room. The dog followed, his nails clicking smartly against the floor. "I'm Caleb," the man said. "Caleb McCall."

She stared at him blankly, her racing heart braking to a screeching halt, her brief joy subsumed by the grief she'd experienced that summer, too. Her body began to tremble, an aftereffect of shock.

As she watched, the man swooped down for the bottle, then paced toward her, holding it out. "It looks as if you could use this," he said.

She released the bookshelf to take it from him, her senses still working at recovery. Of course this man wasn't Peter. Peter had been gone for ten years, drowned by a rogue wave, it was presumed, when he'd gone out kayaking one afternoon at the end of August.

The stranger might look a little like Peter had he lived, though. Same golden tan, same sandy brown hair—though cut short when Peter's had been long. The man—Caleb, he'd said—was gazing at her with narrowed brown eyes, concern written across his handsome features.

Now that she was breathing again, she felt a little visceral tug in her midsection. Handsome? He was more than that. The way he held himself radiated a confident sexiness, as if he understood his place in the world and liked it as well as he liked himself.

"Are you going to be okay?" he asked. His voice was low, a deep sound that suited him.

"Sure. You just…startled me. I—" Tensing, Meg broke off, suddenly aware she was alone, at the nearly deserted cove, with a man—albeit a good-looking one—whom she'd never before met.

Her sister had admonished her to take precautions with her personal safety. The water bottle was a crappy weapon, but she did have her cell phone in her pocket.

"Rex told me where I could find you," Caleb said.

The tension in her shoulders eased. "You know Rex?"

The handsome stranger shook his head. "I just met him on the beach. But when I told him I wanted to check into the cottage I rented, he said you'd be here."

"Oh. Sure. Right." Though Meg had thought no one was expected today.

The dog chose that moment to whine. Meg glanced down, noting Caleb soothing him with long, masculine fingers, but when her gaze shifted from the man's hand to the canine's bicolored eyes, her heart took another jolt.

She knew those eyes.

She knew this dog.

Her fingers tightened on the water bottle, causing the plastic to make a snapping sound. "Who... who are you?"

"I said. Caleb McCall." His eyes were serious and trained on her face. "I'm Peter's cousin. Do you remember me, Starr?"

Starr.

The name pierced her chest, triggering a sharp ache in its empty cavern. Starr was listed on her birth certificate; Starr was what she'd been called from infancy until nineteen, but nobody had used it in years. She'd made sure of that.

Once she could breathe past the pain, she hastened to correct the man still staring at her with a steadfast gaze. "Call me Meg," she said. "I'm Meg now."

The second thing she did was drop to her knees to pet the dog. Her palms stroked over his rough-soft fur. "Bitzer." She glanced up, Caleb's quick nod confirming it *was* Peter's dog. He'd been a one-year-old when his master had gone missing, and now had a muzzle that was nearly gray.

She pressed her cheek against it. "Bitzer," she repeated. It was Aussie slang for a mixed-breed dog—"bits of this and bits of that"—and since he looked to be some bit Australian shepherd, Peter had thought the name fit. The animal wiggled his hindquarters and seemed a pleased recipient of her affection, though she didn't expect he actually remembered her.

With a last fond pat, she stood. Clearing her throat, she glanced at Caleb again. "If you'll follow me back to the property management office, I'll check you in."

The walk up the beach was quiet. Meg was grateful the man didn't try to chat, because she needed the silent minutes and the cool breeze to pull herself together. Those milliseconds when she'd mistaken him for Peter had shaken her, taking her back to that time when she'd been a naive nineteen-year-old who never anticipated gathering clouds on the horizon. Caleb's use of that old name, Starr, had been yet another painful reminder of the girl she'd been.

But she was all grown up now. More important, she was *Meg,* a completely different person. A practical, common-sensical, reality-grounded woman who had moved on from that ten-year-old tragedy. A little sadder, yes, but a lot wiser, too.

Completely free of romantic fancies.

She powered up the computer on the desk in the office and checked the reservation log. "You were due to check in two days ago." It was why she hadn't expected him—he should have arrived before Skye left.

"I had a last-minute appointment," he explained as she handed over the keys.

"Too bad you missed part of your getaway." The computer screen said he was checking out Monday and it was already Wednesday.

"I hope to still get what I'm looking for." His gaze met hers, and she felt another tug, a feminine quiver accompanied by a distinct inner whisper. *You woman, he man.*

She dropped her lashes, surreptitiously checking out the rest of him. Dressed in a T-shirt and battered jeans, he had heavy shoulders, lean-muscled arms, a broad chest. You woman, he man? *Thanks, but I could figure that out for myself.*

Her appreciation of his male form didn't diminish when, after a brief goodbye, he turned around and left the office, dog at his side, keys in hand. The hem of his shirt brushed the rear pockets of his jeans, drawing her attention to the curve of his very male backside. Nice.

He man, you woman.

Be that as it may, Meg had no expectation of seeing him again, not until he checked out, anyway. So she proceeded with her day, making more progress on the railing, then returning home in the late afternoon to shower. The fog rolled in again, and she dressed in jeans, a sweatshirt and a pair of warm sheepskin boots.

By five, she was in the kitchen and opening a bottle of wine. Dinner hovered at the back of her mind, but she hadn't decided on anything in particular. If she got lazy, she could take the one-mile walk up the beach to Captain Crow's, a restaurant/ bar situated at the north end of the cove. It had an expansive parking lot on the Pacific Coast Highway and was a popular spot year-round, thanks to an open-air deck that sat right on the sand. During inclement weather, plastic screens were unrolled to protect diners from the elements without obscuring the sights or sounds of the pounding surf.

Meg was holding up her glass, appreciating

the glow of the garnet-colored merlot, when she heard a rap on the front door. A little surprised, she set down the drink and headed for the entry. With her hand on the knob, she paused, remembering her younger sister's anxious expression when she'd warned Meg about locking up and staying safe. It niggled her now, just as it had then. Skye hadn't seemed her usual buoyant self. She'd been dressed in what appeared to be their father's cast-offs, her hair bound in a tight braid, her face devoid of makeup. Yes, she'd been preparing for a six-hour drive, but still…

Another rap sounded against wood.

"Who's there?" Meg asked.

She heard the jingle of a dog collar first, then Caleb McCall's deep voice, identifying himself. Without anyone to witness, she didn't bother suppressing the little shiver of awareness that wiggled down her spine. How had he found her? she wondered. Rex again, she supposed, pulling open the door.

Caleb was still in a T-shirt and jeans. Still exuding that masculine confidence. "Sorry to bother you," he said.

"What's the problem?" She reached out to Bitzer, smiling when he licked her fingers.

"You should do that more often," Bitzer's owner said abruptly.

Meg blinked. "Do…?"

"Smile. You have a great smile."

The compliment made her girlishly flustered. Which was ridiculous. She was twenty-nine and though she'd lost a lover long ago, there'd been men in her life since. Compliments. Even sex on occasion. But something about *this* man made her feel flushed and breathless and fidgety. "Uh, thanks," she said, hoping her voice didn't squeak. "Did you need something?"

"Sorry, yes. The oven doesn't seem to work...or I'm not skilled enough to figure out how it should."

"Hmm, I don't think lack of skill is a problem you often encounter," she murmured, then felt her face go hotter. Good God, that sounded like flirting!

He grinned at her. "All the same."

The cottage he'd rented was just a hundred yards from her childhood home. When he unlocked the door, she smelled a touch of the citrus-scented cleaning products they used. And something else. Already there was a masculine spiciness in the air. Another clutch of awareness fisted in her belly. She pretended it wasn't there.

In the kitchen, more good scents. Tomato sauce. Garlic. She saw a casserole on the stove and evidence of prep work on the cutting board, including a knife and strips of glossy, plum-colored skin. "You cook?"

He grimaced. "Learning. I think I make a decent eggplant parmesan, though," he added, nodding at the dish.

"Smells like it," Meg said, then turned the dials of the stove. No preheat light came on. She pulled open the door and there wasn't a hint of warmth. With a little sigh, she played with the dials again, trying different combinations: Bake, Broil, Roast. Nothing woke up the uncooperative oven.

Frowning, she glanced at him over her shoulder. "Can you fridge that food? I'm sure I can get this fixed tomorrow. For tonight, we'll pick up your dinner tab at Captain Crow's, or anywhere else you'd like to eat. Just bring me the receipt tomorrow and I'll reimburse you."

"What were you planning for dinner?"

"Me?"

His smile was charming. "I could bring the casserole to your kitchen. Use your oven. Feed us both."

Bitzer pushed his nose into her hand as if he thought it a good idea, as well. "I don't…uh…" More girlish flutters in her midsection embarrassed her.

"I could use a critique of my recipe," Caleb said. "You'd be my first."

Her eyebrows rose.

"To eat my home cooking," he clarified, a laugh sparking glints in his dark eyes.

It was the laughter that got to her. Meh Meg

needed a little more of that in her life, especially now. Especially at Crescent Cove. Caleb could be the distraction she needed.

So that's how she found herself pouring a second glass of merlot as the delicious scent of herbs, onion and tomato sauce filled the air at the house where she'd grown up. They took the wine to the front porch and the pair of generous-size chairs that sat side by side. Bitzer collapsed at their feet with a happy sigh.

Meg slid a look at Caleb. His expression gave nothing away beyond a simple contentment with the moment, not unlike the dog's. "So...what exactly brings you to the cove?" she asked, working herself up to what she knew needed to be addressed, now that they were sharing a meal. It likely wasn't mere serendipity that brought Peter's cousin to this particular stretch of beach.

Caleb's long legs stretched out, then crossed at the ankle. "Needed a break. The thought of here, it sort of...came to me."

"So you're familiar with Crescent Cove?"

He turned his head, a rueful smile curving his lips. "I didn't think you noticed me then."

Then? Suddenly she recalled earlier that afternoon, when they were at No. 9 and he'd asked if she remembered him. The question hadn't processed, rocked as she was by that moment of mistaking him for his cousin and by the sound of her former first name on his lips. "You…you were here before?"

"I was the skinny kid who came to visit my aunt, uncle and cousin a couple of weekends that summer."

She had the vague memory of a flop of hair and baggy board shorts. "That was you?"

"I'll take your surprise as a compliment." He smiled again. "I grew a lot in my early twenties."

"And now you're…?"

"Thirty."

Just a few months older than Meg.

They exchanged more life details then. He had spent the past four years with a cell phone app start-up, working insane hours but enjoying himself immensely. Meg realized he didn't live far from her in the San Francisco Bay Area, where she worked for a large accounting firm that sent her out to smaller companies for independent audits.

"So you left Southern California?" Caleb asked.

"First time I've been back in a decade," she said lightly, and explained about her parents relocating to Provence and her sister attending a wedding in Arizona.

Caleb slowly straightened in his chair, then shot her a considering look. "What happened here a decade ago—losing Peter—that was a tremendous blow."

A fatal blow to Meg's heart. Still, even now,

something inside her chest gave a painful, ghostly squeeze. Resisting the urge to rub the spot, she turned her thoughts to Peter's family. They'd lost someone vital to them, as well. "Your aunt and uncle were devastated, I know."

"They were," Caleb agreed. "Me, too. Peter was the big brother I never had. I missed him so much that his parents gave me Bitzer."

At the sound of his name, the dog raised his head. Caleb fondled a soft ear, his gaze on his pet. "We've been good company for each other, haven't we, boy?"

Then his eyes shifted to Meg's face. "How did you get through your grief?"

By running from that summer and from this place. But no one wanted to hear those kinds of truths. "One day at a time," she said instead. Noting the sober look in Caleb's eyes, she hastened to add more, not wanting him to think she was mired in the past. "It was ten years ago. Of course I'll always feel sad about it, but I'm not pining away."

"Good," he said softly. "Good to know."

"I'm not even that same person anymore."

"Hence the Meg."

She nodded. "Starr still had stars in her eyes. When I left the cove, I felt like I was different, more of a down-to-earth woman than that sentimental, romantic girl."

"Why does 'down-to-earth' sound like a synonym for pessimistic?"

Meg swiveled on her cushion to face him. "I'm not. I just don't believe in fairy tales anymore."

Before he could reply, the oven timer dinged. They got to their feet and trooped to the kitchen. Bitzer padded behind, exuding enthusiasm. "Still likes to eat, huh?" Meg asked.

"Likes to be part of the crowd. I even take him to the office."

As they dished up the eggplant parmesan, Meg discovered that the start-up Caleb worked for was actually *his* start-up, and the apps his company developed were software products used by the triathlete crowd, from route analyzers to workout logs. As they sat at the kitchen table, plates accompanied by a bowl of tossed salad, the wine and a pitcher of water with a second set of glasses, she again sized up his broad shoulders and lean-muscled torso…for informational purposes only, naturally.

Ignoring the little heated pulse of reaction she experienced just looking at him, she picked up her fork. "Triathlons, huh? I take it that's your competition of choice."

He glanced up from his serving of casserole. "I've cut back, actually," he said. "I'm trying for a…tamer lifestyle, I'd guess you'd say."

Tamer? A man like this, self-made, self-possessed,

flat-out sexy, didn't have a tame bone in his body. Not even his pinkie was domesticated. Not even his little toe.

He laughed. "You look like you don't believe me."

"I don't believe you."

He laughed again, and at that moment, they both reached for the pitcher of water. Their fingers tangled somewhere above the handle. And for a woman who no longer believed in magic, there had to be something else to account for the hot thrill that rushed like pinpricks up the tender inner flesh of her arm. Biology? Chemistry? A reason both logical and objective, likely involving pheromones as well as adrenaline, because two conflicting compulsions were at war inside her: to get closer to Caleb, and to run very far away from him.

Really, she should have paid more attention in her science classes, she decided, because she'd feel better with a solid explanation for why her skin felt hot, why her blood ran itchy through her veins, why her nerves were speed-dialing messages to random parts of her body.

Her belly tensed.

Her toes curled.

Her fingers clutched at his.

"Meg." His quiet voice made her shift her gaze from their joined hands to his eyes. There was heat in them, and a curious kind of humor, too. "Are you seeing someone?" he asked.

The question gave her the impetus to slide her fingers from his. "No." She watched him fill her water glass, then his, without spilling a drop. If the pitcher had been in her hand, it would have wavered all over the place. "I had a man in my life a while back, but he wanted marriage and that's not for me."

"Really?" Caleb asked, one brow rising.

"Really," she said, finding his skeptical tone irritating. All women—even those approaching the supposedly dreaded 3-0—weren't focused on white lace and promises. So she tossed her hair over her shoulder and said the first flippant thing that came into her head. "I'm more into short-term, for-the-physical-release-only affairs."

Then she thought of how that sounded. Tackiness aside, some might construe it as an invitation. Her fingers tightened on her fork. "I mean, I…"

She had the distinct impression he was laughing again, though his mouth was closed as he chewed a bite of the eggplant dish. He swallowed, wiped his lips with his napkin, then gave her an encouraging smile. "You mean…?"

"I don't know what I mean," she mumbled, once again feeling out of her depth. It was infuriating, really, this nervous, edgy feeling. Meg never felt nervous in that way. Men didn't put her on edge.

"It's okay," Caleb said, his gaze shifting to his plate. "I'm a little unsteady myself."

She didn't press for clarification of that, though she didn't believe for a second that he was anything less than rock-solid. He appeared cucumber-cool as he continued calmly with his meal, eliciting more information from her—that she belonged to a book group that read nonfiction only; her favorite recent film was an award-winning documentary about the Great Depression—and offering up some additional details about himself—he had two nieces that he took to Disneyland by himself every year; his favorite movie was the latest blockbuster adaptation of a best-selling fantasy series.

Even as he laughed when she admitted she'd once sabotaged the book group's secret ballot process so they didn't pick as their next read the best-selling, but looked-long-and-boring biography of an obscure former president, and she laughed at the recounting of his determined quest to hunt down the Magic Kingdom's Cinderella to obtain for his nieces a coveted photo—"I began to think the princess was like the fabled but elusive unicorn"—that edgy, breathless feeling did not abate.

It was sexual awareness, of course. Sexual tension.

An exhausting state of being, truth be told. By the time she stretched foil across the cooled, left-over casserole so he could return with it to his cottage, she felt as if she'd spent the past couple of hours on the narrow ledge of a high building. During heavy winds.

Yes, he was a charming companion in many respects, but she was glad the evening was coming to an end as she walked him to the door. Bitzer pressed against Meg's knees as she stood in the entryway with his master. She patted his warm head in goodbye, then gave in to impulse and knelt down beside him to place a kiss on his soft doggy cheek.

Rising, she met Caleb's smiling eyes. He held the casserole dish in one hand and gestured toward Bitzer with the other. "Do I get one of those, too?" he asked.

"Uh…" *Oh, why not?* that voice inside her asked. It was impulse again, or perhaps curiosity that brought Meg up on her toes. What woman wouldn't want to get a little closer to such a perfect specimen of male-in-his-prime?

She leaned in, prepared to buss his lean cheek.

His large hand speared through the mass of hair at the back of her head, bringing her mouth to his. He didn't go for a simple peck, or a gentle lips-to-lips brush, either. This was a full-on, fiery kiss, his mouth firm on hers, his tongue sliding inside without hesitation.

A sound came from low in her throat—surprise, appreciation, wonder—and she clutched at his shoulders. Her body flushed hot and she moved closer to his as if pressure could assuage the sudden ache between her legs and the tender heaviness of her breasts.

Caleb's kiss continued until her head dropped back. Murmuring something, he slid his mouth along her cheek and down her neck. Goose bumps broke out on that thin skin and then shivered down her spine. The sensation jolted her back to reality and she took a hasty step away, staring at him as she inhaled great gulps of air.

Caleb stared back, then he shook his head, a rueful smile curving his lips. "Wow. I didn't expect it to be quite all that."

Meg, part embarrassed, part pleased, felt her face heat. Now there was a distinct throbbing between her thighs and her nipples were so tight they almost stung. "I don't know what to say."

"Say we can try that again," Caleb answered, then wrapped his free hand around her upper arm to pull her close again.

She went willingly, her mouth already parted, eager for his tongue, his taste. *Why not this?* she thought, her mind going woozy as he licked her bottom lip. Maybe one of those quick, physical releases she'd claimed were her thing was in order. A reward for doing her sister a good turn.

Caleb's tongue slid against hers and she moaned.

Yes, *yes*. A casual fling. Nothing worrisome, because didn't he look just like a casual kind of man?

Moving nearer, she accidentally jostled the hand that held the casserole and felt him stiffen. "Oh, no," she cried, shifting back. "Did it burn you?" She could see the splash of tomato sauce on his shirt, where he'd held the dish against his side.

"No, it just surprised me," he said, looking down at himself, his expression sheepish. "I completely forgot about the eggplant parmesan."

She took it out of his hand and hurried toward the kitchen. "Take off the shirt and I'll run it under cold water. Maybe it won't stain."

"It's an old shirt," he protested, trailing her.

"Take it off, anyway," she said, letting her smile bloom, because she knew he couldn't see it. Her blood was still thrumming in her veins and with his chest bare, she'd be one step closer to the possibility of a doesn't-have-to-mean-anything hookup with a beautiful, casual man.

Lucky Meg, she told herself. Though she wasn't usually so impetuous, being with Caleb just felt right. And, after all, didn't she deserve some good fortune?

Setting the dish on the counter, she whirled around. *Oh, yes.* Caleb had his T-shirt in hand, leaving for her appreciation a wealth of tanned skin and muscled chest.

In the middle of which was a clearly new, very serious-looking, four-inch scar.

CHAPTER TWO

CALEB MCCALL DIDN'T waste time anymore. Actually, he'd never been much of a time-waster, but now he was a definite time-*appreciater*. As he walked southward along the beach of Crescent Cove, that's what he did—appreciate. The fresh, fog-laden air was almost intoxicating. Not that he needed a buzz; he'd had one since kissing Starr—*Meg*—the night before.

Yeah, a buzz and a hard-on, he thought, grimacing. It wasn't his most comfortable night, but he'd had worse, and he held hope that last night's frustration was a temporary circumstance. Though he figured she'd need some persuading to explore this…this situation between them.

He couldn't blame her for being gun-shy. Losing Peter had affected them all in ways big and small. His cousin had been open-minded and big-hearted, the kind of person who had friends of all kinds, from tech geeks to varsity jocks. It was Peter who had given confidence to his scrawny younger cousin, encouraging Caleb's interests in both sports and computers that had come together in the successful business he'd now built. But upon hearing the news of Peter's death, for a long time Caleb had felt as if nothing could go right with the world again.

Meg must have experienced something similar. After all, she'd actually left this beautiful place. No wonder seeing his scar—that four-inch symbol of man's mortality—had shut her down. Oh, she'd gone through the motions of rinsing out his shirt, but she'd used the activity to avoid looking him in the eye. Short minutes later, he, Bitzer and the casserole dish had found themselves on the other side of her front door.

But Caleb wasn't acceding defeat, not yet.

Because even before that explosive kiss, he'd been drawn to Crescent Cove—drawn to *her*—and he was a very determined man. To that end he'd developed a plan in the long, sleepless hours of the night. He was going to get past her newly erected guard, get her into bed and then figure out if what seemed more certain all the time was really destined to be.

Yeah. Destiny.

Looking death in the face had a way of making a man believe in such a thing.

The property management office was a one-room clapboard building with a white picket fence surrounding it and a small plot of grass. The gate was cocked open, as was the front door, and Caleb assumed the occupant couldn't hear him approach over the crash-and-sizzle sound of the waves hitting the sand.

He halted in the doorway and, just like yesterday when he'd seen her in Beach House No. 9, was struck dumb by her beauty. Ten years ago, Caleb had liked the view, too. Despite the fact that she'd been his cousin's girlfriend, despite the fact that he could tell his skinny teen self didn't make a blip on her consciousness, he'd looked. A blonde girl, a skimpy bikini—what guy wouldn't?

But now…now the sight of her struck him in the solar plexus, a fateful blow over newly healed skin. She looked just as he remembered from that odd dream he'd had while in the hospital. Not like the girl she'd been a decade before, but like this woman, with a Rapunzel-ish fall of wavy golden-brown hair and eyes that were an otherworldly green. Dressed in knee-length shorts and a T-shirt that read Tax Season Rocks, she scrutinized a piece of paper on the desk. Then she half turned, revealing the slenderness of her back and the sweet curve of her ass.

He studied her profile then, too, noting her high brow, the curl of dark brown lashes, a straight nose and the full pink curves of her lips. He'd kissed them—*God!*—and the lush softness had nearly blown off the top of his head. His heart had pounded so hard against his ribs that if he hadn't already known he was completely well, the fact that he'd survived his tongue in her mouth would have convinced him.

He wanted to taste her again.

Crossing the threshold, his determined footstep sounded loud on the hardwood. Meg startled, her hand catching a box on the desk, toppling it. Keys spilled like doubloons from a treasure chest, clattering against the floor.

"Sorry," he said, hurrying over to kneel beside her. "I didn't mean to scare you."

She scooped up some of the metal pieces and tossed them back into the box. "I'm not afraid," she scoffed. "I just didn't expect to see you again."

Sending her a quizzical glance, Caleb let a stream of keys trickle out of his palm and into the container. "Meg." He waited until she glanced his way. "You thought I'd just go away and leave you alone after that?"

Pink color suffused her cheeks, a contrast to her deep green eyes. "I don't know what you mean."

"After last night." He knew she didn't need further illumination, because her gaze slid away from his. Still… "After those incredible, incendiary kisses." Let her try and deny just how incendiary.

"You…you asked for one," she said, clambering to her feet and plunking the key-laden box back onto the desk. Then she stomped around to the chair behind it, putting distance and a solid piece of furniture between herself and Caleb. "It was just a friendly 'thanks for dinner.'"

He crossed his arms over his chest, watching as she fiddled with a pad of paper, centering it with precise movements. Denial, not just a river in Africa.

She darted a quick glance at him, then returned her focus to the desktop. "Can I help you with something?"

My aching hard-on, he almost said, just to provoke her. Her discomfort in the aftermath of their passionate embrace didn't bode well for his plans. Seeking inspiration, he took a moment to glance around the room. There was a large, impressionistic painting on one wall that was quite well-done, in his very uninformed opinion, and clearly depicted the cove. On a set of shelves sat photographs—the Alexander family, he presumed—as well as jars of beach glass and seashells. None of them gave a clue as to how he could pierce Meg's armor.

He swallowed a sigh. "I thought you'd like to know the repairman came and went. Oven works fine now."

Her shoulders relaxed and she lifted her gaze to his, this time letting it linger. "Yes, he stopped by afterward to deliver his invoice. I hope it wasn't an inconvenience."

"Not at all."

"Good. Well." Her gaze dropped when he continued to stand there. "If there isn't anything else…" She swept her hands over the desk as if to point out the multitude of tasks facing her. Too bad it was nearly empty.

He ignored the hint and took the chair on the other side of the desk. All his instincts told him now was not the time to back off. She peeped at him again, her mouth pursing in a way that made him think more of kissing than of disapproval.

"You didn't ask about my scar," he said in a conversational tone.

A moment of charged silence passed. "Well… you know, it's none of my business."

"I'm not sure about that. It's what brought me here, after all." *It's what brought me to you.*

Her eyebrows rose and she gave him her full attention for the first time. "How is that?"

So cautious was Meg, so different than the Starr of ten years before, who had seemed to welcome life and love as if they were her due. He remembered her racing into the surf, dolphin-diving into the face of an oncoming wave. Would she even let the water wet her feet now? *No,* Caleb thought, and it took everything he had not to reach out for her, to grab her hand and tug her into his lap where he could whisper in her ear, assuring her he would always be her safe harbor.

But he knew she wasn't ready for that. Hell, he wasn't even sure he was ready, though it didn't seem he had much choice in the matter. Those kisses last night had proved that ready didn't mean squat. When something so bright, so sure, came your way, you just grabbed for it with all you had and held on.

Looking death in the face made that Lesson Number One.

"Caleb?"

Right. He was supposed to be explaining his impetus for renting a beach cottage, though he'd better keep the exact details to himself for the moment. "I was in the hospital when Crescent Cove… uh, the idea of it just popped into my head. I knew I had to visit as soon as I was well."

When he didn't continue, she threw him a disgruntled look. "Fine, I'll ask. Why were you in the hospital?"

"How much do you know about hearts?"

"Are we talking physical or metaphorical?"

Both were important when it came to the two of them, but Caleb would address that later. "Physical."

"Size of a fist," she said, placing hers against her breastbone. "Four chambers. Blood pumps in, and it sends the de-oxygenated stuff through the lungs to pick up O_2 before being sent back out to the body."

"Right. The blood returning from the lungs goes into the left atrium—one of the chambers of the heart. From there, a valve, the mitral valve, opens to let that blood flow into the main pumping chamber, the left ventricle. I had a wonky valve, causing mitral stenosis."

Her fisted hand dropped to the desktop. "Sounds serious."

"It made some of my blood flow backward to my lungs, meaning my heart had to pump harder to get the necessary volume through my veins. Provided the leak is slow and only gets worse progressively, your body can compensate for years."

She covered her fist with her other hand, as if to comfort it. "And when it can no longer compensate?"

"Then you experience shortness of breath and extreme fatigue."

"You knew this when you were a competing triathlete?" she asked, frowning at him.

You say that as if you cared. "*Because* I was a competing triathlete I caught on to something being not quite right. Turns out the bad case of strep throat I had as a kid likely developed into undiagnosed rheumatic fever that caused the damage. So I had surgery to fix me up, all right and tight."

She tilted her head, that glorious hair falling over one shoulder. "What kind of surgery makes you 'all right and tight'?"

"Open-heart," he said. "I have a mechanical valve now, and take a blood thinner every day, but that's it. My long-term prognosis is the same as for any other thirty-year-old."

A moment passed, then she slapped her palms on the desktop. "Well. Congratulations." She rose to her feet. "I'm glad to hear you're in good shape."

"Excellent shape," Caleb said, standing, as well. She was in that hurry-him-out mode, just as she'd been last night. "Meg—"

"Sorry, but I don't have any more time to chat right now." She snatched up her purse and looked ready to push him out the door.

He rooted his feet to the ground. "Let me take you out to dinner tonight."

"I don't see why you'd want to."

His eyebrows rose. Stubborn woman! "Let's start with that we both need to eat."

"We don't need to eat together. We already did that."

Caleb rocked back on his heels. "I really do scare you."

She frowned. "Of course not. But you recall what happened last night."

He damn sure would remember it for the rest of his life. "Didn't you enjoy yourself?"

Her cheeks turned pink again and her green eyes narrowed. "Can't you take no for an answer?"

"I haven't actually heard you say that word,"

Caleb pointed out, rubbing his knuckles along his jaw. "Not last night. Not now."

Meg looked down at her feet, then inhaled a long breath. "All right. Here's the deal. Last night…last night was nice. You're fun. You're funny. I'm sure I'm not the first woman to let you know you're attractive. After those kisses, I even considered sleeping with you."

Now, why didn't that sound like a victory?

Her gaze lifted to his, and a hint of a smile curved her lips. "Now *I'm* scaring *you*."

"Hardly. Setting the sheets on fire does not inspire fear in me." He thought of his hands fisted in her hair, of his mouth on hers, his tongue stroking deep. "When can we make that happen?"

"We won't. I considered it, but decided it's not in my best interest."

"Why don't you give me a chance to change your mind?" he asked, taking a step toward her.

Meg held him off with a hand. "No. Really."

Caleb could see the tension in her body. She was worried about him getting close, and he thought he could understand why. "I realize that after what happened to Peter you might not want to take a chance—"

"Don't bring Peter into this."

"But he's here," Caleb said. "Because he was your first love." Though if destiny played out the way he hoped, the way he thought it should, he planned on being her last one.

"Love." Meg shook her head. "It wasn't that. What we had was a potent mix of young adult hormones and summer sun. I was more than ready to drink the pre-sweetened Kool-Aid after a childhood overstocked with Disney princess movies and long hours of pretend."

Caleb stilled. "You don't think you fell in love with him."

"I don't believe in falling in love," Meg said. "I don't ever want to."

It was only later, after she'd once again put him on the other side of her door and he was taking a long walk on the beach, that Caleb absorbed her last words. Then grasped their inherent contradiction. If you truly didn't believe in the phenomenon of falling in love, there was no reason not to want that to happen.

Looking toward the water, he grinned. "I'm not giving up on her, cousin," he promised.

AT ABOUT 4:00 p.m., behind the closed and locked door of the property management office, Meg decided she needed a nap. Sure, it was classic avoidance of issues she'd prefer not to face, but it was also…a nap. Rarely did she allow herself one of those and she thought a prize was in order. She'd checked in everyone expected to arrive at the cove that day. More important, she'd held out against Caleb's still-smokin' sex appeal.

He'd strolled in, wearing that confidence of his like a second shirt. When she'd clearly been trying to get rid of him, he'd made himself at home in her visitor's chair. What perversity inside of her thrilled to that obstinate quality of his? It was almost as if he was bone-certain she enjoyed being with him. That she was supposed to *be* with him.

Someone as sensible as Meg shouldn't be swayed by such persistence. Didn't she know there was nothing to be gained by a roll in the sack with him? Yes, scratching an itch could provide temporary pleasure, but good sense warned her that being with Caleb would come with a price.

And she'd already paid once, hadn't she? Ten years ago she'd lost her head and then effectively lost her family home.

In the corner of the office was the shabby leather recliner that had been her father's favorite. Approaching it, she had to smile, imagining her mother insisting to Dad as they prepared to move to Provence that the recliner belonged at the cove. Mom had detested that chair the moment her father had brought it home from an estate sale, but since he'd been so delighted with the find, she'd never said a word against it.

Her parents had been married for thirty-plus years. Any mature person knew it couldn't have been a happy-fest 24/7 for all that time, but they were still together. He brought her flowers every Friday. She never grimaced when he practiced the saxophone each afternoon. Starr—the girl she'd been—had considered both proof of connubial bliss and lasting love.

Meg didn't have an opinion of or an explanation for their continued devotion. Her brain couldn't conjure one. There was an empty place in her chest where her heart—which might have weighed in— had once resided. If forced to guess why her parents' togetherness worked, she'd say blind faith. But the scales had fallen from Meg's eyes long ago.

Just something else to dodge mulling over. Settling into Dad's old chair, she closed her eyes and willed herself to sleep.

The cracked leather creaked as she wiggled against it. Breathing deep, she listened to the surf, hoping its ceaseless ebb and flow would sweep her consciousness away.

It didn't work.

Long minutes passed.

Then she heard a strange scratching against the front door. Nothing human. Something…canine. She popped out of her chair, certainty making another smile break across her face. No surprise, it was Bitzer on the other side of the entrance. That summer ten years ago he'd shown up at her door just like this, signaling his arrival in the very same way.

She went to her knees, her arms wrapping around his neck. "Bitz! Do you remember me, you adorable dog?" Burying her face in his ruff, she reveled in his furry warmth. He accepted her embrace, body writhing in delight.

His doggy grin was wide as he trotted into the office. Then he wandered about the room, nose peeking into the attached bathroom, then nudging the items on the bookshelf opposite the desk.

Meg watched him, a little buzz of joy rolling through her. Something had survived of that summer. Bitzer was his outgoing, all-accepting self. Sliding onto the leather seat, she rested her head against its back and closed her eyes again, hearing the clack-clack-clack of his nails against the floor. With the dog as company, sleep seemed possible now.

Then something sharp prodded her arm. Meg's eyes popped open. "Bitzer?"

He had a plastic DVD case in his mouth, which he then dropped in her lap.

"Where did you find this, boy?"

While he didn't answer, she figured he'd discovered it during his explorations. On the bookshelves, perhaps, or in the oversize reed basket beside it that held a collection of magazines and DVDs that guests were welcome to borrow.

Turning it over in her hands, she determined it wasn't labeled. Her father was an avid amateur "filmmaker"—translation, he loved his video cam almost as much as his sax—so it could be a Crescent Cove sunset or perhaps several minutes of cavorting seals.

On a whim, she popped out of the chair and crossed to the computer on the desk. A moment later, an image bloomed on the screen. "Bitzer," she breathed, casting a glance toward him. It was the dog, racing along the sand and then plunging into the surf after a Frisbee. Not a gray hair in sight.

Then the image changed. Meg tensed, her hand jerking away from the keyboard as if it burned. The monitor showed a girl and boy walking on the beach, coming toward the camera, but oblivious to it. Peter, lean and smiling, his long hair ruffled by the breeze. The girl that was once Meg—Starr— her arm hugging his waist, her face turned up to his. Smiling, too.

Bitzer raced toward them, and Peter took the Frisbee from his mouth, flung it again. The dog leaped into the water, splashing Starr with cool drops, and she squealed a little, following that up with a laugh.

Peter turned her to him for a kiss.

They looked so young, Meg thought. So young and carefree.

Without thinking, she reached toward the screen, tracing the teenager's bright hair, following the young man's grin with her fingertip. She was smiling, too, she realized, appreciating their happiness. Then the couple continued strolling. The camera followed them and Meg noted the golden stretch of sand, the waves rolling in, the bright-colored beach cottages that had been her childhood playground.

How beautiful it all was, she thought, from those delighted lovers to that cloudless sky.

For the first time in a decade, gratitude rose like a warm tide in her chest, displacing the cool bitterness of disillusionment and grief. She'd grown up in this wonderful place. Starr and Peter had enjoyed a spectacular summer. Nothing, not even his death, could take the reality of that away.

She still ached that Peter was gone, but the rush of good memories of her life here, and of that golden summer, was unstoppable. She saw bonfires in her mind's eye, smelled the delicious blend of coconut oil and roasting corn on the cob, could almost taste the salty flavor of the ocean on her lips.

Meg didn't try warding off the recollections as was her usual practice. Instead, she let them roll through as she continued watching the home movie—an assortment of moments from that last summer—taking in each scene of the visual playlist. Her dad trying to catch a fish in the ocean, her mother at her easel on the bluff, Skye still turning cartwheels at seventeen. And always Peter and Starr, smiling into each other's eyes like the rest of the world and the future didn't matter.

Maybe they didn't. Maybe the fact that their present had existed once upon a time was enough.

Nobody got forever. That couple, Peter and Starr—they seemed like old friends to Meg's fond gaze now—had lived large for three glorious months. *Let them go now,* a voice inside her said. *Let them continue on their walk down that sunny beach.*

Meg, let go.

When the screen finally faded out, she rose from the chair, her legs almost weightless. Everything about her felt lighter, and she drifted out of the office, then drifted up the sand, Bitzer at her side. Fog lingered over the beach, and strains of music carried toward her on the breeze, the sound of Happy Hour cranking up at Captain Crow's.

She could use a drink.

Her timing couldn't be better, she realized. A tradition went back to the 1950s when the same group of families summered at the cove year after year. They celebrated the arrival of 5:00 p.m., cocktail hour, with a special ceremony that was still carried on at Captain Crow's today.

As she approached the restaurant's deck, many of those crowded at the tables cleared out, gathering around a flagpole at the base of the steps that led to the sand. Meg stood at the periphery of the ragged circle, watching as a man in low-slung shorts and a faded sweatshirt lifted a conch shell to his lips. A loud blast from it caused the people around him to cheer, then they saluted as a blue flag was run up to flutter in the breeze.

"The martini symbol," an amused voice said near her ear.

She didn't need to look behind her to know it was Caleb's warm breath that stirred the hair at her temple. "All hail revelry."

"The cove's a place for good times," he said, as the others tromped back up the steps to their seats.

"I'm starting to remember that," Meg admitted.

Caleb's fingers curled around her upper arm and he turned her, his gaze searching her face. "You look…relaxed."

She shrugged, trying not to show how something as simple as his sure touch made her belly quiver. His thumb caressed the vulnerable flesh of her inner arm and she had to put some starch in her knees to keep from leaning into him. "Thanks to Bitzer."

"Yeah?" He slanted a glance at his dog. "I've been looking for you, buddy—but you're forgiven for running off if you've been doing good works."

The dog responded with waving tail and toothy grin.

Then Caleb's palm slid lower to take Meg's hand. "I can do good things, too," he told her, the corners of his mouth curving up. "You should give me a chance."

She considered it, trying to drum up all the reasons it was wrong. But they were hardly a match against that weightless feeling she still enjoyed and Caleb's potent physical presence. He was so damn good-looking, with his hair falling over his brow and the intriguing dichotomy of his serious eyes and smiling lips.

His warm hand clasping hers—when had a man last held her hand?—was irresistible. "I'll give you a chance to buy me a drink," Meg said.

The sun broke from behind the clouds.

Really. Not that it was uncommon for it to finally shine after being held back for most of the day, but the warm, yellow blast of it against her face felt like a benediction. Caleb grinned, correctly interpreting her wonder. "The universe is on my side."

Oh, arrogant man. But it was hard to disagree as they were given the best table on the deck, in a corner close to the railing. It was an intimate two-top, and she angled her chair so that the ocean wasn't in her line of sight. The move brought her closer to Caleb, who didn't seem to mind the quick, innocent bump of her knee against his. Instead, he moved his leg so the denim of his jeans was pressed lightly against her bare calf.

Bad man. Because he left it there, a reminder of his male heat, and even played with her fingers as they waited for his beer and her margarita. In her veins, her blood started chugging hot and heavy, and her skin turned ultrasensitive, the breeze blowing against it feeling like a caress. On her other side, Bitzer leaned against her knee, caging her against his owner—though she no longer felt inclined to move away. As her icy glass was set in front of her, she sighed a little.

Picking up his beer, Caleb cocked a brow. "Problem?"

She lifted her drink and tapped the rim to the lip of his bottle. "I'm just thinking about the futility of delaying the inevitable."

"Yeah?"

"I should have gone to bed with you last night." She smiled when she saw him freeze, relishing the surprise crossing his face. But really, hadn't the conclusion felt foregone? It seemed the only answer to this helpless, girlish flutter she felt just looking upon his face. The only way to manage it. "What have we wasted? Twenty-four hours?"

With a deliberate movement, he set down his beer. "Believe me, sweetheart. We're not going to waste another second."

CHAPTER THREE

As MUCH AS Caleb would have liked to throw down some bills and drag Meg to his bed, the time-appreciater in him wasn't going to act so rashly. Especially as he was aware that she'd pulled out a metaphorical stun gun by announcing her sudden willingness for sex. She thought to get the upper hand on what was going on between them by taking it down to its basest level.

Hell yeah, he wanted to kiss her, touch her, taste her, take her, but he was in this for a much longer game. That weird dream during surgery had intrigued him enough that he'd made the trip here, but it was Meg herself who held him now. Her beautiful face, her rare smile, that empty place inside her that made him want to pull her close, to fill her up, to treasure her forever.

Tearing off her clothes and driving himself inside her was not the way to make that happen. So he sat back in his chair, picked up his beer again to take a swallow, then caught the server's eye and asked for a couple of menus.

Meg shot him a suspicious glance.

He hid his smile behind his bottle. "Got to fuel us up, you know," he explained. "Want to have plenty of energy to deplete."

She twitched. "Maybe I'm not hungry."

Oh, yeah, now that she'd made a decision, she was desperate to race forward. Caleb caught her hand in his and brought it to his mouth. He kissed the back of it, then tickled her knuckles with his tongue.

With a low noise, she snatched it away.

He gave her a lazy grin as the menus were laid in front of them. Taking his time, he reviewed the food offerings. She didn't give them a look. "Shall I order for you?" he asked politely.

"God, no," she said, and opened the folder.

Caleb bit back another smile, knowing he was on the right track with her. No doubt she wanted to maintain control of the situation and of herself. But he thought he needed to force her to release the reins. Only that way could she reclaim the missing stars in her eyes. Meg would never be Starr again and that was fine with him, because he was after the woman she was now, not the girl she'd been— but first she needed to trust that a man could care for her without leaving her unhappy.

She had to let go in order to love again.

That's what he wanted…her love.

He ordered a full meal, from appetizer to salad

to entree and he even said he might leave room for dessert. Meg stared at him, then tossed back the rest of her margarita and fidgeted while waiting for the second she ordered.

"Relax," he said.

Her green eyes glared at him. "Let me tell you something. 'Relax' is the worst word a man can say to a woman. It can put her right out of the mood."

Her second margarita was delivered and he pushed it closer to her. "You'll be in the mood."

The shrimp cocktail he'd requested came on a bed of crushed ice. He dipped one piece of seafood in sauce, then held it to Meg's mouth. Pressing her lips together, she snatched it from his hand, then bit into it with furious relish. "Yikes," he said, his voice mild. "I hope you'll be more gentle with me."

A reluctant smile dug a dimple in her left cheek and he saw a little of her tenseness fade. "You're trying to make me crazy, aren't you?"

"I want to," he admitted. "Because I'm crazy for you back."

She didn't fight so hard after that. When he pushed the appetizer to the center of the table, she dug in alongside him. When their salads came, she shared a taste of her field greens and heirloom to-matoes. He offered a forkful of spinach and red onion and she took it with good grace.

They were almost mellow companions as they slowly worked their way through a steak—him—

and a serving of grilled swordfish—her. At the end, as the plates were removed, she flopped back against her seat. "Maybe," she said, sliding him a look from beneath her long, curly lashes, "I'm too full for sex."

"We'll have to work off some of the food, then," he answered, and tugged her up by the hand. Bitzer tried to follow, but a soft command settled him back onto the deck. Then Caleb drew Meg away from the railing and toward a parquet dance floor where a few couples were swaying to something slow and sultry.

She tried hanging back. "I don't dance."

"What? Why?"

The fingers of her free hand wiggled. "It's too…"

Yeah, he knew. Personal. Private. Intimate.

To her mind, dangerous.

His chest aching, he pulled her close and pressed his forehead to hers. "I've got to learn how your body moves, honey, if I'm going to do my best work."

"You can learn that in bed."

But he didn't want her just in bed.

"C'mon," she whispered in a seductive tone, her palms traveling up his chest to circle his neck. She laid a kiss on his chin, and then she gave it a little nip. "I'm ready. I'm…wet."

Caleb's pulse rate and his dick both shot up.

He'd already been semihard, and now the lower half of him was screaming for relief. But he gritted his teeth and slid his arms around her waist, then started to sway back and forth. "Look," he said, twirling her in a small circle, "it's just this easy."

But it wasn't easy to ignore how right she felt against him. He pressed a palm to that sweet curve of her lower spine, bringing her against his hips. She glanced up, a glint in her eyes. "Why Grandma, what a big—"

His kiss took the last word from her mouth. It seemed to settle her a little, and when it was over, she pressed her cheek against his shoulder. The song changed, Steve Goodman crooning the heartbreaker "California Promises," and they kept dancing.

God, this was good, Caleb thought, stroking her wealth of hair. All those hours he'd spent on his business had meant not enough time for dancing with a woman in his arms.

Though it wouldn't have been *this* woman.

Steve's final guitar note rang out. Meg lifted her head from Caleb's shoulder to look into his face. "Have you made your point?"

Probably not, but his patience was gone.

He paid the bill. Maybe. The act of it didn't sink into his consciousness, which was preoccupied with her scent, the feel of her curves under his hands, the absolute carnality of what came next. *I'm wet,* she'd said.

He should have hauled her off then!

Their arms around each other's waists, they walked toward his rental. Bitzer ran ahead and ran back, then circled them, clearly happy they were all moving in the same direction.

It was full dark when Caleb unlocked the front door, the porch light casting shadows on Meg's face. Her eyes were pools of darkness as she hesitated to cross the threshold. "It will be all right," he whispered to her.

"Of course it will," she snapped back, then marched briskly into the cottage. Stifling a grin, he followed behind her, noting the smart sway of her hips as she moved toward the bedroom.

The only light came from the half-open door to the attached bath. Meg approached the bed, then, glancing over her shoulder, began to undress with her back to him. Fascinated by her quick movements, he leaned against the doorjamb. "In a hurry?"

Her perfume scented the air as she whipped the T-shirt over her head, displaying the supple line of her spine and the delicate angles of her shoulder blades. Next, her bra fell to the floor with a soft plop. Anxious for her to turn and face him, Caleb felt his breath catch in his chest. Just then, Bitzer's nose nudged his knee, making him jump a little, and he turned to direct the dog back down the hall. "Sleep," he told his furry best friend, pointing toward the living room where one doggy mattress waited. There was another in the corner of the bedroom, but now wasn't the time for canine company.

Bitzer, bless his brilliant heart, took the hint and trotted away. When Caleb turned back, there was a naked woman a foot from him.

Lust burned through his bloodstream like a gasoline fire. He reached for her, fascinated by the sleek expanse of creamy skin. She went into his arms, her body fragrant, her flesh warm, the feel of her breasts against his chest making his balls tighten and his dick go even steelier.

He took her mouth, his hands sliding around her narrow back, then down to her hips, tilting them into his aching stiffness. She moaned, her lips opening so his tongue slid inside. His palm cupped one rounded ass cheek, his fingers kneading the sweet flesh of it.

Crazy for her. Yes. There was no other term for it.

Her hands slid beneath the hem of his shirt, her fingers moving over his belly and his chest. He lifted one arm and gripped the back of his shirt at the neck, breaking the kiss so he could lift it over his head. Then he returned to kissing her, grinding their mouths together, helpless not to, because she was rubbing her breasts against him, going on tiptoe so that her taut nipples brushed his.

He groaned, then held her away so he could look at her breasts, cupping the round weight of one before bending his head to the crest. His tongue licked it first, then he gave in to desire and sucked, sucked it strongly, reveling in the way her fingers bit into his scalp to hold him there.

Yeah, he thought, this was what he wanted. Meg needing him, holding him closer, realizing he had what it took to please her. He moved his mouth to the other nipple, tasting her sweet flesh while his hand toyed with the one he'd already dampened. Her moan was louder as he squeezed the little nub, then released it, torturing her with a tiny bite of pain even as he worked the other with a hot yet easy suction.

He took his free hand from her ass, working it around her hip toward heaven. Her belly twitched as his fingertips brushed across the velvet skin there, and she whimpered, a needy, ego-boosting noise. "Shh," he said against her breast, then ran his tongue around the areola. "I've got you. I'll take care of you."

He should have known it was too soon for sentiments like that. Instead of cooperating with the next step in her seduction, she stepped back, giving herself room to work on the fly of his jeans. "Meg, no," he protested, groaning, but she pushed his hands away when they tried to manacle her wrists.

"I want to see you," she said, then dropped to her knees to work his pants and boxers toward his knees.

"Oh, hell," Caleb said, his head falling back. He knew he should be intent on unraveling her, but with her pretty face at the level of his cock, she had him at her mercy.

The wet slide of her tongue tasting him from crown to balls made him groan again. Her hands cupped his hips and then her tongue was on the move once more, sliding up before she took the head into the hot cavern of her mouth. The top of his skull took off for parts unknown.

She played with him, sucking, sliding, tasting, teasing. One of his hands was curled in a fist, the other found its way into her Rapunzel hair. His fingers were deep in the soft wavy stuff as she continued ratcheting his need until he was gritting his teeth and writing pieces of Java programming code in his head to keep control.

It was no use. Pulling away, he looked into her face, her lips swollen and wet. "Get on the bed," he said, his voice guttural. "Get on the bed now."

Instead of being alarmed by his harsh command, instead of damn doing what he said, she licked her lips and then took him once more into her mouth. Her big eyes stayed trained on his face as she went back to her sensual torment. His breath was stuck in his lungs and he felt the climax rolling up from his heels.

At the very last second, though, he remembered his mission.

This was about her. This was about Caleb making Meg let go.

Gritting his teeth, he wrenched from her and bent down to pull her up by the arms. Half-hobbled by his clothes, he had to toss her onto the mattress, then step out of them. She was rising up as he reached the bed, but he pushed her back with one hand on her shoulder.

Triumph rose in him as she settled on the mattress. He took advantage of her acquiescence, catching her mouth in an aggressive kiss as he lay down beside her, slinging his thigh over hers. She wiggled a little, testing the bond, and he continued restricting her movement as he slid his tongue deep between her lips.

Her hands came up and he shackled both wrists with the fingers of one of his. "Keep still," he murmured.

Her hips rose, however, tilting up in blatant request. He tore his mouth from hers and looked down into slumberous eyes.

"Yeah," he whispered. "You watch what I can do to you." *What nobody else can. What nobody else will ever give you but me.*

Then, still clasping her wrists, he slid down her body. Her thighs parted for him, and she made a helpless sound as he used the span of his shoulders to open them wide. His free hand pushed them even farther apart. "Put your heels on the bed, baby," Caleb coaxed. "You gotta let me in."

She made a little sound of embarrassed distress, but he ignored it, licking at the seam of flesh in front of him, pushing his tongue into her until the softness bloomed open to reveal all the delicious wetness awaiting him. He lapped at it, studiously avoiding the knot of nerves at the top of her sex, feeling his own desire burn as he felt her skin heat and heard her panting breaths. His mouth moved lower and he licked into her. On either side of his shoulders, her thighs went rigid. So he did it again, sinking his tongue deeper into her slick, smooth channel.

"Oh, God," Meg said, and then again as he withdrew and flattened his tongue to bathe all the sensitive, aroused flesh.

He continued exploring her, his pulse loud in his ears as he stoked her fire. She was whimpering nonstop now, wordless, sexy pleas that he could live on like food. Glancing up, he saw her watching him, her bottom lip caught between her front teeth. Her gaze snared by his, he lifted his head to slide his first two fingers in his mouth, wetting them with his saliva.

She stilled, tension in every muscle. "Caleb," she breathed.

Then he brought them to the entrance of her body, speared deep. Her hips bowed. He withdrew, pushed inside her again.

"Caleb."

Desperate now to assuage the neediness in the one word, he dropped his head, finding the knot of her clitoris. He gave it a glancing lick, then another, then he held it between his teeth and flicked it with the tip of his tongue. Her knees pressed against his shoulders, then she started to shake, and Caleb plunged his fingers deeper yet and sucked her into his mouth with a tender yet insistent rhythm, coaxing out every tremulous pulse.

When she finally quieted, he moved up her body again, pressing kisses to her closed eyelids, her forehead, her mouth. She remained lax and sated for several minutes, one of her hands sifting idly through his hair until he bent his head and gave one soft, pouting nipple a tiny bite.

She jumped, opened an eye.

He smiled. "Shall we sleep a little?"

Even in the dim light he could see a flush rise up her face. "No," she said, her gaze flicking to her breast. The tip had hardened again, responding to the edge of his teeth. He bent to the other, gave it the same treatment.

"Oh, God." Meg urged him over her with eager hands. "Come here. Come here, I need this."

He wanted her to need him, he thought, as he reached into the bedside drawer for a condom, one of those he'd packed in his toiletry kit and then stashed here, just in case. Like a Boy Scout, always prepared. She tried to help him roll it on, but her touch was no aid at all. Wrenching to the side in breathless laughter, he told her to leave this part to him. "You just concentrate on opening for me, baby." Protection donned, he moved back to her.

Let me have you, Meg.

Let me in.

Holding tight to his control, he carefully watched as he breached her tight heat. She drew in a breath, held it, and he went still, talking her through the first inches of penetration.

"That's right," he murmured. "It's okay. I won't hurt you. I'll never hurt you." He pressed deeper, felt her flinch. Again, he halted his progress.

"Caleb…"

"Take your time. Your body will adjust to me, sweetheart. Go soft, honey. You're so wet, your body's ready for me. Let your mind catch up to that." Her muscles were clamped on him like a velvet vice, and he knew she was caught between coiling desire and feminine defense. How could he blame her, when he wanted it all?

He gave a gentle kiss to her mouth, then drew in

her bottom lip, sucking it sweetly. "Let down your guard," he whispered to her, and slid his palms beneath her bottom.

"Please." There was frustration and desperation in her tone. "I want it, Caleb."

"Shh, shh, shh. I know," he said, tilting her up for a better angle. "Just loosen up and let me in."

Then she lifted her head, taking his mouth in a torrid kiss. The minute her tongue skimmed his, her inner muscles eased, and he slid straight to the hilt. They both groaned.

His body took over then, enticed by her sleek heat. He surged into her over and over, aware that their breaths were in sync, that he was holding her down to the mattress so that all she could do was writhe against him, pinned by his lunging cock.

It was the hottest sex he'd ever had, until he opened his eyes and looked at Meg's beautiful face and it hit him again, another heart smite, and he stopped breathing altogether at the wonder of it all. Could it really be…? But of course it could, because nothing had been like this before, no woman made him feel so much tenderness and lust and crazy certainty that they had to make this happen.

That they had to be together.

"Meg," he said, but his voice was too gruff for such declarations.

She moaned, wiggling some more, and her inner muscles clenched again, this time in demand. His lust spiked at the feel of her squeezing him and he knew the crisis was at hand. He put his mouth to her neck, compelled to mark her with a tiny bite. She cried out, lifting herself upward and he slid one hand between their bodies, a nudge all that was needed for her to detonate again.

His was a slower explosion. The orgasm shuddered through him, rattling his bones, quivering his muscles, making him spasm in absolute, astonishing pleasure.

When it finally faded, he withdrew from Meg, then dropped to the mattress beside her. Rolling his head to look at her, he pushed her hair from her face, then used his thumb to caress the love bite he'd left on her neck.

"You'll have a bruise," he told her. At that sign of his possession he felt very primal—and not the least bit politically correct. "Should I say I'm sorry?" Though he wasn't. Not at all.

She was his, damn it. Forever.

"No worries." Her smile was sleepy and sweet. "It's temporary, just like us."

MEG REALIZED TOO late that she should have slipped out after the spectacular sex. By the time she opened her eyes, it was past daybreak, and there was a man sitting on the mattress with a mug of coffee in his hand, watching her.

"Good morning," she said, meeting his gaze

square-on. The sex had been a mutual choice, and she wasn't going to start feeling shy about her part in it now. Still, she worried about striking just the right note. It had been a one-night stand and she didn't want to give him the impression she expected anything more than that.

"I think it is a very good morning," he said, and held out the mug.

With the sheet clutched to her bare chest, she struggled to a sitting position and then claimed the coffee. It smelled delicious and a little like… "Cinnamon?" she asked, sniffing.

"A trick I learned from my sister. You sprinkle it over the grounds before brewing."

"You really are trying to become domesticated."

"After my heart surgery I decided I needed a few more dimensions to my life," Caleb said.

Meg didn't like thinking of him in a hospital, his chest being opened. She'd kissed him there the night before, right over the scar, just before drifting off to sleep. It was covered now by a simple T-shirt, the pale green color a contrast to the golden tan of his skin. Taking another sip, she noted the newly shaved skin of his face and the shininess of his damp hair. Really, he was ridiculously handsome, she thought, as warmth started pooling in her belly.

Not a good idea. Remember—one-night stand!

"What time is it?" she asked, glancing around

for a clock. The overcast sky she could see through the window made it impossible to guess.

"About nine."

"Nine?" She squeaked and shoved the mug in his direction, preparing to leap from the bed. "I never sleep late. I have things to do—"

"Like what?" he asked, pushing the coffee back into her hands.

"I… Well, something. People will be checking in today."

"What time? How many?"

"Several families. But not until three this afternoon," she admitted.

"So there's plenty of time for coffee, breakfast, followed later by the picnic I've planned," Caleb said.

Meg scowled. She should have told him an army was expected by ten! "Caleb…" Thinking back, she replayed the moment on Captain Crow's deck when she'd offered to sleep with him. Hadn't she made clear it was a single session she was after, a way to address and then eliminate the almost adolescent fascination she felt for him?

Damn, she realized she'd not been clear after all.

A flush crawled up her neck to her face. "I should have said… It's not that last night wasn't nice—"

"From my side of the blankets, it was damn fabulous."

It was hard not to be pleased about that. "Well, yes, for me, too."

"Good." He leaned in and pressed a kiss to her mouth, the touch gentle and unassuming.

Beneath the sheets, her toes curled. "Still," she said, rallying her good sense. "I wasn't supposing, you know..." God, how to say this?

"When I came to the cove I wasn't supposing anything, either, Meg," he replied. "So how about we stop concerning ourselves with expectations and just enjoy the day? I've become quite good at that."

Since the surgery, he meant, and the second reference to it quelled her objections. She could have a picnic with him, she supposed. It didn't mean anything would go further than that.

Another night in his bed wasn't a foregone conclusion.

But enjoyment—that did seem to be foregone. Caleb had already proved himself a charming companion and that didn't change as he coaxed her into exploring the cove with him, Bitzer at their heels. They wandered along the hiking paths winding around the hillside behind the cottages, finding evidence of the small creeks that kept the tropical vegetation lush.

She found herself telling him about her great-

great-grandparents, Max Sunstrum and Edith Essex. The moviemaker and the ingénue. Their love affair and subsequent marriage were the stuff of legends. "Some accounts say he was so obsessed with her he made her quit acting. He didn't want her to have any other leading man but him."

"Isn't there something about a missing piece of jewelry?" Caleb asked. "Given to Edith by her final costar?"

They stopped in the shade of a palm tree, and the breeze made a silvery sound through the fronds. "An old Hollywood rumor," Meg said. "Our family has never really bought into it. It's purported to be a magnificent choker nicknamed 'The Collar,' inspired by the last movie made here, *The Egyptian*."

"There's Cleopatra's barge and everything in that one, isn't there?"

Meg glanced over. "You've seen it?" At his nod, she smiled. "When we were kids, we wished the barge had survived way more than some dumb necklace."

"I can't imagine growing up here," Caleb said. "It must have felt like being shipwrecked on your own private island."

"Sometimes," she admitted. "Especially in the off-season when my sister, my parents and I were often the only ones here." That's when their mother would tell her stories about the merpeople and every day had felt enchanted.

After eating the lunch he'd provided—Caleb admitted to stocking up on deli stuff before moving in to his cottage—they continued their walk on the beach, starting at the tide pools on the northern end and strolling along the sand to the southernmost point, right in front of Beach House No. 9.

They paused there, staring up at it. "The numbers on the houses refer not to their geographical location, but to the order in which they were built. My mom always claims this one holds a special charm for lovers, though, just like in the song 'Love Potion No. 9.'" Meg slanted a look at Caleb. "Sentimental stuff, huh?"

He opened his mouth as if to speak, then shrugged, and bent to pluck something from the firm sand. A clam shell, bone-white with gray rings toward the outer edge. His thumb stroked over the surface. "I bet you collected a thousand of these in your lifetime."

"Maybe a million," Meg said. "My sister, Skye, and I pored over our beach treasures like other kids did trading cards."

He glanced up. "I remember one particular treasure you had.... A piece of abalone shell, I think it was, that you'd strung on a leather thong for Peter. He wore it everywhere."

"Yes." Her fingers found Bitzer, and she rubbed

his thick coat. That fragment had been part of her collection forever, and one of her prized possessions because it was shaped like a heart. She'd given it to Peter that summer ten years ago, and told him it was just that. Her heart. "He wore it all the time except when he went into the ocean."

Caleb petted the dog as well, his lean hand caressing Bitzer's flank. "So you have it, then."

"No. We don't know what became of it. Maybe that day, that time, he kept it on when he went out…though it was never recovered." Even when Peter's body and his kayak had shown up a day later, on a beach five miles south of the cove.

A beat of silence went by, the quiet only filled by the rush of the waves. "I'm sorry if my mentioning that made you unhappy," Caleb said. He stepped around the dog to pull her close.

Although she knew she shouldn't, Meg leaned against him. "It's all right," she said. "There are those sad memories, but so many happy ones at the cove, too."

"Tell me," he urged, taking her hand and turning to direct their walk back up the beach.

And the next thing she knew she was doing just that, mixing up her mother's merfolk stories with the real-life escapades of the cove kids who had run wild every summer. She laughed out loud, remembering the games they'd invented, the sand abodes they'd built, the miniature popsicle-stick boats they'd launched or the real-life rafts they'd attempted to construct out of driftwood lashed together with rope.

Before she knew it, it was nearing three o'clock and she had to rush to the property management office to meet the newcomers. When her duties were over, she locked up, only to find Caleb and Bitzer on the sand right outside.

The dog sat beside his master. Caleb was staring out to sea, the wind ruffling his hair. Again she couldn't help but admire the width of his shoulders, the strong muscles of his back that she could see through the thin cotton of his shirt. But it was that calm stillness that attracted her most, she thought, as if the mere act of breathing in air was something to which he gave his utmost attention.

Apparently sensing her presence, he turned his head. "Business done?" he asked, holding out his hand to her.

She went toward him, drawn like a magnet. Once her bottom touched the sand, he drew her close. It was the most natural thing in the world to drop her head to his shoulder.

"What should we do now?" he asked idly.

She should tell him what they should do now was head to their separate lives. But it didn't seem right to upset the affable mood. So she shrugged.

"We could go for a swim," Caleb said.

"I don't go into the water anymore." She didn't

even gaze upon it. Right now her eyes were focused on the beach. In her peripheral vision she could just glimpse the white foam stretching toward their feet, but that was the closest look she allowed herself.

Caleb drew her more snugly to his side, then sighed. "I guess it's sex, then."

The words took a moment to sink in. Caught between amusement and exasperation, she turned her head to look at him. "What? Isn't that a trifle presumptuous?"

"My mother always said that about me."

Meg laughed, then pushed at him. "You stop."

He fell to the ground, then pulled her on top of him. "Not gonna." With a roll, he had her flat on the sand and his weight was on top of her, the effect more thrilling than she cared to admit. "Haven't you ever heard of afternoon delight?"

"No," she lied. "And even if I had, I remind you we're on a public beach."

His mouth touched her eyebrow, her cheek, her nose. "There's nobody around."

"You didn't even check!" she protested, giggling when his mouth tickled the rim of her ear.

Giggling. The realization stunned her for a moment. When was the last time she'd made such a sound? A little alarmed by it, she twisted from beneath him, squirming away so she could jump to her feet. Then she started sprinting for home.

"Don't think you'll get away from me!" he called out.

Her legs churned faster. Bitzer started barking, a joyous sound, and Meg took that to mean Caleb was in hot pursuit. More laughter bubbled up in her throat as she put on the afterburners.

He pounced twelve feet from her front door. When his hands gripped either side of her waist, she shrieked, then felt herself going down. Caleb saved her, though, landing first and then rolling them both to their sides. He grinned at her, and she could feel an answering smile stretch across her face.

"I win," he crowed.

"And I suppose you've already picked out a prize," she said, trying to look stern and stand-offish, even though her pulse was a flurry in her throat and at her wrists. She tried pulling in her smile, pursing her lips in a prudish gesture.

He made a noise—a sort of groan—then swooped close for a kiss. "That mouth of yours is going to do me in," he said upon coming up for air. "You've ruined me for any other lady's lips."

Absurdly pleased, she allowed herself to touch him as she wanted, pushing those boyish locks of hair off his forehead. "You're funny."

"I'm serious." His smile died then, as his gaze searched her face. "Meg, where do you see your-self in five years?"

She considered the question, then gave him an honest answer, she who hadn't wanted to give him anything beyond a one-night stand. "I see myself visiting here. I haven't been back, you know, not ever, and now I think I'd like to return every once in a while. Maybe more often than that."

"You don't want to stay?"

"No. I like where I live. I like my job."

"Me, too," Caleb answered. "Though I'm mending the worst of my workaholic ways. Coming here has been very good for cementing in me the notion that there's more to life than my business. I don't plan to forget that."

Meg nodded. "Being at the cove has been good for me, too. I was feeling a little 'meh' lately, but I think I have the bounce back in my step."

Mischief sparked again in his eyes. "Is that what we're calling it now?" She felt his hand creep under her T-shirt at the small of her back. His forefinger moved in circles and curlicues, some kind of pattern, she thought.

"What are you doing?"

"A game from my childhood," he answered. "I'm spelling out a word." His finger moved again. "This is what I want to do to you."

She sat up in faux outrage. "I know that word!"

He yanked her back down. "You're going to get it before I'm through."

They did make it to his house while they were

fully clothed. But the garments came flying off once the door was shut behind them. Then they tussled on the bed, laughing and kissing and writing words on each other's skin with fingers and tongues until there was no teasing left in them and the desire had to be sated through a more serious touch.

They lay on their sides again, and he drew her thigh on top of his as he opened her with his fingers. Then his erection was there, the thick knob of it rubbing against her clitoris, making her gasp, before he began to push inside. One of his hands was curled over her hip, his fingers steadying her as he penetrated.

Hot chills flashed across her flesh as he entered her, the possession so achingly sweet that she moaned. Her breasts were tender, heavy, and the nipples, still wet from his mouth, tightened impossibly more.

"Caleb..." she breathed.

His gaze was on her face as he continued moving into her. "You feel so good. So wet and hot, sticky and sweet, like honey."

She slid her knee farther up his flank, allowing him further entry. He kept coming inside, heavy and so thick it stung just a little, and the shuddering pleasure of it made an ache of tears start behind her eyes.

When he was seated inside he did the same

maddening, wonderful thing he'd done the night before.... He didn't move for long, long moments. She felt full and possessed and needy and desperate and her fingers clutched at his shoulders. She wanted to urge him to move, to insist he start rocking inside her, but this was so good, too, as if they were two interlocking pieces of one whole.

"So right," she whispered.

And then Caleb smiled, as if she'd uttered the words he'd been waiting to hear. His hips began to move in time with the pulse of the ocean. Meg gasped, the ebb and release a rhythm that she'd been born hearing, that she'd absorbed to her marrow during the first two-thirds of her life. Now she moved, too, the counterpoint second nature to her, as they stared into each other's eyes and rode each wave toward final bliss.

When it was over, they lay together, still tangled. Caleb stroked her hair, then her cheek. "You said it feels so right."

Meg felt tension infuse her lax muscles. "I—"

"No." He put his fingers over her mouth. "It feels right to me, too. *You* feel right."

"Caleb, I can't—"

"I know. Just don't run on me again, okay?"

"You don't understand. I thought something was right before." Panic robbed her lungs of air. "'Right' doesn't always lead to a good place."

"I understand why you'd think that." He brushed

another soothing hand over her hair. "It's because you lost something. You lost what belongs right here." His fingertips touched the center of her chest.

She couldn't say he was wrong.

"Give me a chance to get it back for you," he said. "I have two more full days at the cove. Let me spend them with you."

And Meg, who had woken up that morning with a one-night stand behind her, couldn't make any promises...but she didn't refuse Caleb, either.

CHAPTER FOUR

MEG TOLD HERSELF it wasn't because she was superstitious. After all, she'd learned a decade before not to believe in irrational ideas like fated mates and forever-afters. Still, that didn't stop her from hedging her bets and steering clear of Beach House No. 9 while Caleb continued as a cove visitor—just in case there was a kernel of truth to the idea it was some sort of architectural love potion.

No sense in risking infection.

It was bad enough, she realized, just spending time with him at his rental or at her family home, or anywhere for that matter...even in the car on the twenty-minute ride to the nearest grocery store— by SoCal standards, a near-epic distance—because everywhere they went he slipped in mentions of the future. "I've got to take you to this great fish market I found in Tiburon," he said, as they perused the butcher section and the packaged selections offered there.

When they peeked into the small gallery at the cove, he insisted on buying her a pair of earrings, tiers of tiny shells strung on multicolored silk thread, that she adored so much she swallowed her third round of protests. "Have you ever poked around the jewelry stalls along Fisherman's Wharf in San Francisco?" he asked as he watched her don his gift. Without even waiting for a response, he tacked on a "We'll have to do that this summer."

Meg found it exasperating and bewildering at the same time. He seemed like an intelligent human being, and one with adequate hearing, too, but each time she demurred or even flat-out ignored his comments, it didn't give him pause.

Maybe, she thought with a stab of guilt as they cleaned up the dinner dishes on his last night at the cove, that was because she also didn't hesitate to let him kiss her, touch her, hug her whenever he wanted. And she kissed, touched and hugged him whenever she wanted, too. They were in the small kitchen of his rental, and their hips kept bumping and their shoulders kept rubbing as they moved about, putting everything to rights.

His warm palms circled either side of her waist as she dried her hands on a towel. Drawing her back against his chest, he whispered in her ear, "Are you too sore for sex? I've been giving you quite the workout."

Heat flared over her face and then spread down her body. Between her thighs, she *was* tender, but the minute he talked to her in that rough-soft voice, she felt herself going soft there, and wet. Turning her head, she pressed her lips to his. "I wouldn't want to deny either one of us on our last night together."

He stilled a moment, then smiled and swept her along to the bedroom. There, he undressed her with a staggering gentleness that would make a more emotional woman weep. Next, he slid her under the cool sheets and before they'd even warmed up, he was beside her, his body a furnace, his mouth scalding the side of her neck, the fragile skin inside her hipbone, the drenched tissues between her legs. Except there was no pain in the burn, only the deepest, farthest-reaching pleasure.

When they'd both climaxed, he held her against him, her head in the hollow of his shoulder. *This is it,* she thought, closing her eyes against the stinging ache behind them. *Tonight is our last.*

"What's a good evening for you next week?" Caleb asked, his fingers sifting through her hair. "I leave the office at five o'clock these days, which means I could make it to you by… What? Five forty-five? Six?"

Instead of being alarmed by the question, Meg realized she was…was…tempted.

Oh, God.

How he tempted her.

The realization was enough to goad her into sitting up. Clutching the sheet to her throat, she glared at him. "Caleb, I told you. Really, I was clear. I've been very clear. There's no future—"

"Of course there is," he said, in that calm, certain manner of his.

"There's no reason—"

"There's no reason why not."

"I don't do this," Meg protested. "A…a relationship is not what I want."

Caleb reached over and turned on the bedside light. "Because you're afraid."

She blinked against the sudden brightness. "Because I don't believe in happy endings…only endings."

Sitting up, too, Caleb took her free hand in his. "Sweetheart. Believe me—"

"Why should I?" Meg said, tugging even as his hold tightened. "Why should I believe this thing we have would turn out any better than what I had with Peter?"

Caleb stared into her eyes for a long minute. "For the simple—or maybe not so simple—reason that I already died, Meg. Three months ago, on the operating table, they lost me."

Her skin went cold. "No."

"Yes." He brought their joined hands together and kissed the back of hers. "And when that happened, I had what I've been calling a dream, though perhaps 'out-of-body experience' is a better description."

Meg wanted to move, but her muscles wouldn't obey her commands. "Caleb…"

"And while I had this whatever-we-want-to-call-it, several scenes played out before my eyes. I saw you here, Meg. This you, not the younger you, and I knew I needed to come here to the cove and be by your side. I saw us in the future as well, happy, together, a couple. In love."

"No." She yanked her hand and then slid away from him, toward the edge of the mattress. "You're not with me just because of some odd dream."

"No, not just because of some dream," he agreed. "The fact is, I've thought of you over the years. You might not have noticed me that summer, but I definitely noticed you, the way you sparkled, the way you seemed to embrace life with wide-open arms. And I only admired Peter more for winning you. After he was gone, you would come to mind from time to time and I'd wonder…"

"Wonder what?"

"If I should try to contact you." He shrugged. "I talked myself out of it, though, until that day I woke up from surgery and was told that I'd survived the crisis and would have a complete recovery. Remembering my dream, I knew I had to follow it. I had to at least come to the cove and see what might happen between us."

"I might not have been here!" she said. "I haven't been back since that summer."

He shrugged again. "Fate at work?"

Meg swallowed. "It's ridiculous to think something like fate or a dream had a hand in…in our meeting or anything that came after."

"It didn't have a hand in what came after. When I arrived and met you, not the dream you, but the real woman, that's when I fell in love. That's *who* I'm in love with. You, Meg. You still sparkle, you know. And I think that hand in hand, the two of us could do a damn good job of embracing everything life has to offer."

She was already in her clothes. Without even being aware of it, during that speech she'd found them and quickly pulled them on, like armor. Caleb didn't seem interested in stopping her; he just gazed on her with a steady, self-possessed regard.

It made her want to throw things.

It made her want to throw up.

It made her want to fall down on her knees and cry.

Instead, she ran away, returning to her childhood bed where she crawled under the blankets and pulled them over her head, though she knew such an action never kept the monsters away.

THE NEXT DAY, aware she'd have to face Caleb sometime, she couldn't stand hanging around the property management office. Instead, at about eleven, she left a note on the door, saying she'd be back after a thirty-minute walk.

Then she took off down the beach, the wind fluttering the hem of her sleeveless cotton dress. The sun was out early, the morning was as warm and beautiful as high summer, and the smell of sunscreen was in the air as she traipsed past small groups on the sand, their camps delineated by bright beach towels and low fortress walls made up of coolers and beach chairs. Meg waved when people called out her name, but didn't stop to chat. She'd have to pass Caleb's rental and she wanted to be moving at full steam when she did so.

Yet her feet came to a sudden, panicked halt when she caught sight of him at the water's edge, bare-chested and wearing a low-slung bathing suit. With a kayak.

Her mind flashed back ten years before. Peter, giving her a jaunty wave as he started off that late afternoon.

Never to return.

Her rubbery legs still managed to break into a run and she raced toward Caleb. "What are you doing?" she screeched.

"Going out," he said calmly. He was already in the water up to his knees and was stepping into the molded plastic watercraft.

Without even thinking, Meg waded toward him,

barely registering the cold water on her toes, her ankles, her shins. "You shouldn't do this!"

But he was already moving off, stroking with the aluminum-and-plastic paddle. A small wave tilted the kayak's nose higher, and she saw a lei nestled in the bow.

"Why do you have flowers?"

He glanced at her over one bronze shoulder and raised his voice as he moved farther from her. "A tribute for Peter. Would you like to go out with me? This is a two-seater."

"No." Anxiety was churning in her gut, swirling like the sea water around her legs. "Please, Caleb. Please come back."

He looked at her again, the kayak still cutting through the water. "Of course I will, sweetheart. Keep the faith."

I don't have faith. I don't have anything like that. But her throat was too tight to say the words and he was now too far from her to hear. Her eyes still on him, she walked backward to shore. Once on dry ground, she continued to watch him, noting as he stroked off toward the cliff at the south end of the cove.

That's what Peter had done that day, she remembered, panic rising again. Peter had paddled in that direction, then gone outside the cove, and neither her feelings for him nor the merpeople magic had been strong enough to keep him safe.

Something wet touched the back of her knee. She looked down. "Bitzer," she whispered, dropping low to take him into her arms. His fur was warm against her face. "Bitzer, I don't know what to do."

The dog seemed to have a plan. After allowing her a long hug, he started trotting down the sand, his gaze on his master, who was skimming through the water about fifty yards offshore. Then Caleb angled, clearly intending to head around the bluff.

Throat tight, Meg followed in the paw-steps of the dog, the both of them keeping pace with the man in the kayak. But as she and Bitzer ran out of cove, Caleb edged around the waves crashing against the rocks at the base of the cliff and disappeared.

At that, a short, harsh sob caught in Meg's chest. Still looking out to sea, Bitzer whined, and she dug her fingers into his fur, hoping to bring him comfort. "It will be all right, boy," she croaked out. "It will be all right."

Please, Caleb. Please come back.

Of course I will, sweetheart. Keep the faith.

With some vague notion of climbing the bluff for a view from the top, Meg headed toward one of the paths that led up the rocky side. But then her gaze caught on Beach House No. 9, and she felt compelled to go toward it instead. Griffin Lowell was still absent, so she and Bitzer wouldn't be disturbing anyone. Calling the dog to her side, she trotted toward the steps leading onto the deck. There, with the furry canine leaning against her leg, she kept watch, waiting for the first glimpse of Caleb.

Waiting for her love to return to her.

More panic churned in her belly at the thought. *Love?*

"I love him," she told Bitzer, caught somewhere between dread and awe. Caleb, with his confidence, his laughter, his pure enjoyment in every breath he took, had found his way beneath her long-held defenses. He knew exactly who he was and what he wanted, and she…she… "I've fallen in love with him."

The dog shot her a craggy grin, then redirected his attention to the ocean. Meg did the same, all the while feeling as if No. 9's deck was that of a rocking ship in the midst of a storm, and she was struggling to get her sea legs.

I've fallen in love with Caleb.

How had this happened? Despite her past, despite her fears, the man had found an ember of hope inside of her and with his very breath nurtured it into a full and steady flame. He'd brought her to life, too, by making her love again. By making her love him.

Time passed. Minutes? Hours?

Bitzer's vision was better than hers because he

let out a burst of a bark before she could detect any sign of Caleb or kayak. Then she saw them both, and as the dog took off down the steps, so did she, racing through the soft sand, damp sand, wet sand, until the water rushed over her toes. Even then she didn't stop. Instead, she kept on going, until the skirt of her sundress was drenched and plastered against her thighs. Caleb was calling to her, saying something, but she couldn't make out the words because she was laughing and crying and now she was actually swimming toward him.

Her hands clutched the side of the kayak and he was smiling down at her—the man she loved was alive and smiling at her!—all the while shaking his head. "What are you doing, sweetheart?"

The explanation stuck in her throat. So she attempted clambering into the watercraft. It took two tries, the second one aided by Caleb and also— she decided to just go with the wild thought—the supportive hands of the merpeople she fancied just might be watching out for her after all.

She fell against the sun-warmed man, winding cold arms around his neck and pressing wet kisses to his handsome face. His own arms closed tightly about her. "I told you I'd be back," he said, soothing her with his big hands. "I told you."

"I didn't believe," she said. "I didn't believe in anything."

They were floating on the water, the cove's bay

cradling them with a gentle rhythm. "I know," Caleb said, holding her away a little so he could look into her eyes. "Because you'd lost this."

Then he held up the necklace she'd given Peter. The heart-shaped shard of abalone shell gleamed in the sunlight, its dark, pearlized rainbow both beautiful and mysterious. Like life. Like love.

Meg gasped. "Where did you get it?" she asked, staring as it swung gently from Caleb's hand.

"It was another part of that dream. Peter showed it to me, Meg. He showed me where he'd stashed it that day, and told me it was way past time for you to have it back."

She gave her head a little shake. "No—" But then she remembered that she believed in love now, and was that any less a strange and wondrous miracle than a dream filled with portents or a man surviving critical surgery and near-death? Her hand reached out, her fingers closed over the abalone shell.

Caleb released the thong it was strung upon.

Letting her lashes fall, Meg cradled the shell in her palm as if it were something precious. In her mind's eye she saw Peter standing on the beach, saw his brilliant grin, saw him take his young lover by the hand. The girl clasped his fingers, then threw a happy smile over her shoulder at Meg as the two turned to stroll along the sand stretching endlessly in front of them.

And this time, finally, forever, Meg really let them go—both Peter and her younger self. *Goodbye,* she thought, squeezing the shell to cement that last, sweet vision of the pair. *Farewell.*

Then she lifted her lashes and turned her gaze to Caleb. "This was Starr's heart."

He nodded. "Yours again."

"No," Meg said. "Though I've kept it deep under wraps, I actually have—had—my own."

Caleb's brows came together. "'Had'?"

"So I think I'll return this one to the merfolk whose it was in the first place." With that, Meg held her arm over the side of the kayak and let the necklace fall. It drifted atop the water for a few moments, and then it started to sink beneath the ocean. Maybe it was her long-suppressed imagination coming alive again, her old belief in magic, but she could swear she saw the slim, pale fingers of a mermaid reach up to close around the shell and then disappear.

Warm hands cupped her shoulders. Caleb turned Meg to face him. "'Had'?" he demanded again, his expression serious.

"It's yours now," she confessed, her voice a little hoarse with emotion. "I'm in love with you, Caleb, and when you get me, my heart is part of the package."

His eyes searched hers. Then he smiled, and it was the sun breaking through the fog. "You love me," he said, the smile turning even brighter. "You really do."

"Don't let it go to your head," she teased.

"It already has," he murmured against her mouth, the kiss at first a promise that quickly turned to passionate intent. Then the kayak's rocking rhythm was no longer so gentle. Almost unseated, they were forced to come up for air.

The merfolk urging them to dry land? A joyful bark turned their attention to the beach. Bitzer was there, pacing impatiently, as if he was eager to be part of their happiness.

Caleb slanted a look at Meg as he fished for the paddle that had dropped to the bottom of the craft. "Well, my love? What next?"

"Forward," she directed with a grin. "We have a dog on shore. And a forever just waiting to get started."

* * * * *

STRONG ENOUGH TO LOVE

Victoria Dahl

Dear Reader,

I first met Eve while I was writing *Close Enough to Touch*, the first book in the Jackson Hole series. Another character noticed the sadness in Eve's eyes, and in that moment, I had to know the cause of her pain. I had to know her story. As you might expect, her story is bittersweet, but I promise there's a happy ending! In fact, I wanted to write this ending for everyone who's yearned for that one person you can't have. The person who's off-limits. The person who makes your heart ache.

Eve and Brian have a very special place in my heart. I hope you'll feel the same!

Happy reading, and if you'd like to read more in the Jackson Hole series, check out *Close Enough to Touch*, *Too Hot to Handle*, and *So Tough to Tame!*

Victoria

www.VictoriaDahl.com

CHAPTER ONE

EVE HILL STARED at the man poised above her, his blue-and-black flannel shirt open at the front, exposing a smooth chest and an abdomen ridged with muscle. She watched as his chest rose with a breath, watched the fabric part a tiny bit farther, revealing more of his tanned skin. A breeze ruffled his hair, drawing her eye to the way the sun haloed the blond curls around his head.

"Take off the shirt," she said softly.

He shrugged it off willingly, eagerly even, revealing wide shoulders curved by tight muscles. His skin glinted with a delicious gleam, so dark against the snowy mountain peaks behind him. Pine boughs shushed in the wind and Eve watched his nipples draw tight with the cold.

Her camera shutter snapped in the silence. Eye to the viewfinder, Eve kept her face indifferent and cool. He wasn't a warm smooth body that would cover hers. He was a job. Nothing more. He wasn't an answer to her darkest fantasies. He wasn't company for her long nights. Whatever beauty he offered was superficial, and she'd already tried at that kind of satisfaction and failed.

Eve took the pictures the client wanted, and she didn't need anything more than that.

"I think we've got it," she said. She had no idea what a naked male chest in front of the Teton range had to do with selling five-thousand-dollar watches, but her eye had been drawn to his skin, after all, and all marketing ever wanted was that few seconds of attention. *Look. Look at this. You might not have this chest, but you can have this watch.*

"Thanks, Joseph," she said to the model, signaling that he could put his robe on. "Take a minute while I see if we're done here."

The client, a ferret-faced ad man from New York, waited at the table she'd set up just a few feet away. Eve loaded the pictures from her camera to the laptop and opened a few shots. "What do you think? Between these and the ones we shot this morning with both models, I think we've got more than enough to work with."

"Yeah. Yeah, that's good. Perfect. You really hit it out of the park. And you were right. The clouds cleared just in time."

"They were moving fast. Nothing to worry

about." She tried to hang on to the brief moment of pride she felt at his praise, but it slipped through her fingers as quickly as he'd said them. Something was wrong lately. That high she'd always felt behind the camera was starting to fail her. The excitement of doing something she was so good at. The pleasure of a job well-done. It felt brittle these days. Fleeting.

"Let's pack it up," she called cheerfully, because she refused to subject anyone else to her increasingly restless moods. "Joseph, you're free to go. You were wonderful, as usual."

"Thanks, Eve."

He was gorgeous enough that he could probably make it in New York or Europe, but his husband ran a very expensive ski clinic here in Jackson Hole, so here was where they stayed. But Joseph was one of a few models she was able to promote to clients from the coasts, who were relieved not to have to pay big-city modeling prices and transportation costs. It worked out well for everyone, and Joseph got to go home to a cozy cabin every night with his true love.

Eve told herself she was happy with her cat and her occasional chance to ogle beautiful men. She was, damn it. Even if she did have to fake a smile just now.

"Have fun in Curaçao!" she called out as Joseph left. They were off for a well-earned vacation. Joseph's husband had put in months of nonstop work at the ski clinic over the winter.

Joseph ran back to give her a kiss on the cheek, still buttoning his shirt. He looked like a lover grabbing a quick goodbye before rushing off to work.

God, she missed sex. She missed *good* sex.

She didn't need a husband and a little cabin. She didn't need someone to take care of her and whisk her away on luxurious vacations. But she'd give a lot for an occasional weekend in bed with a man intent on wearing out every muscle in her body. Someone she could laugh with between orgasms. Someone who understood her passions and humor and—

She shoved those thoughts away, shaking her head in panicked denial. No. She wasn't going there. She'd given him up for good. Even thoughts of him. He no longer existed. Hell, he never had, not for her.

"Where do you want these cords, boss man?"

Eve looked up to see Grace standing there, her eyebrows raised in sarcastic question, the wild blue strands in her dark hair vivid in the sunlight.

"Oh, all right," Eve sighed. "I'll help break down, if that's what you're hinting at."

Grace snorted and started for Eve's brand-new black SUV. "You know I can't reach the lights when you put them up that high. But they're turned off and cooling."

"Thanks. I'll get them." They'd used only two lights to add a little ambient warmth to the natural daylight, and she had them broken down and the whole shoot packed up within thirty minutes. Grace carried the last bags up the trail to Eve's truck. Eve was alone for a moment, surrounded by nothing but pine trees and wild grass matted down by the melting snow.

She took a deep breath and turned in a slow circle, taking in the quiet for a moment. It was spring. The mountain peaks would stay white for months, but the first wildflowers would start to bloom in a few weeks. She loved the spring. The scent of the first faint hints of green grass curved around her and filled her lungs, but the wind whipped it away within moments.

She had dreams sometimes that she could capture scent in a photo, that she could hold on to so much more than a picture.

Then again, being able to experience a remembered scent at will was likely a terrible idea. Her heart hurt at the very thought.

Eve clenched her teeth together and started up the trail. She'd go home and work for a few hours, then take that hot bath in the hopes of soaking away this new melancholy.

But her plans for escape were foiled when she found Grace leaning against the tailgate of the truck, a mischievous smile in place. "Hey! You're coming to Jenny's birthday party tonight, right?"

Shit. She'd forgotten about that. And now she had her heart set on a pitiful evening of feeling sorry for herself. "Grace—"

"Nope. I knew you'd try to wiggle out of it, but you're going. Good God, Eve, you're only, what? Thirty-five?"

"Thirty-six," she said, hating that Grace's guess had been so close.

"So you haven't earned your right to a quiet night at home with a microwaved dinner. You've got to put in a few more years of hard partying. Come on."

"I've already put in years' worth of awkwardness, thanks to you and Jenny always foisting men on me."

"We aren't foisting. We're just forcing you to

dip your toe into the water. A few dates here and there never hurt anyone."

"They've been painful enough," Eve grumbled.

"Oh, please. Don't be a wuss. Anyway, I'm not trying to fix you up tonight. Though there will be lots of cowboys there. And cowgirls. Maybe that's your thing."

No, it wasn't Eve's thing, but maybe it would be easier if it were. She'd never been good with men. It hadn't bothered her until a few years ago.

"Come to the party," Grace said. "If you don't, I'll come drag you out of your house in your nightgown. Because I bet you wear a nightgown."

Eve gave her the finger. She didn't wear a nightgown. She wore a men's XXL T-shirt in a very attractive shade of camouflage-green, and a pair of running shorts that had gotten too tattered to wear while running.

"You are a bitch," she said very clearly.

"Employee abuse!"

"You wish."

Grace smiled. "So you'll come?"

"Fine," Eve huffed.

"Good."

She waved Grace into the truck, vaguely remembering the invitation now. She'd been forgetful lately. Somehow she'd been shrinking further and further into herself, seeing everything through a camera filter, pretending that was life.

But it wasn't life. Not yet anyway. Maybe she'd better give it the old college try before she gave up completely. Maybe she should flirt with a few cowboys and see what happened. Then again, the last time she'd had sex it had been so resoundingly mediocre it had turned her off for months. Thank God Mitch hadn't been friends with any of her friends. She'd ignored his calls and never seen him again.

But it had been almost a year now. Eve grimaced and squeezed her eyes shut for a moment. She couldn't just be celibate forever. Could she?

Not yet. Grace was right. Eve hadn't put in the time yet. So she'd go to the party and maybe she'd even talk to a few men. For an hour, tops. Just to say she had. Then she'd hurry home to feel sorry for herself in a hot bath.

A few more years of that kind of effort and she could respectfully retire into spinsterhood and never date again.

OR SHE COULD give up on dating starting tonight.

She couldn't imagine where Mitch had come from or why he was at Jenny's party, but there was no avoiding him, because he'd cornered her near the doorway of the tiny apartment and he was making a concerted effort to reconnect.

This town was too damn small. She'd have to be more careful. If she wanted to scratch an itch, she should do it with men who'd come to town just to ski. They moved on in the spring like migrating wildebeests.

"Oh, there's Jenny!" she said, latching on to the perfect excuse to escape. "I need to say happy birthday!"

"Wait." Mitch reached out as if he'd grab her arm, but pulled back before he touched her. He looked down at his own hand before he let it drop. "I had a really good time when we went out, Eve. I thought you did, too."

"I did," she said in a rush. "Of course I did."

"Right. So I think maybe the…after…was maybe slightly awkward?"

Oh, God. Eve felt her face heating. No. This wasn't happening. She shook her head.

"You didn't call me later, and… Well, I think I mentioned I'd just gotten out of a relationship, and it had been a while since I'd dated."

She shook her head again, more frantically this time, and held up her hands in desperation. "Mitch, it's okay. It was fine. It just wasn't the right connection." She wished she could melt through the floor and be outside and free.

"But what if it was? When we got to your place, I was nervous. I admit it. We both were. But before that, I had a great time. You're funny and smart. It felt natural."

She nodded, trying to give in just enough to give herself room to escape.

"I'd really like to see you again," he pressed. "We could get to know each other a little better this time. Not rush things."

She wanted to say no. She wanted to dodge to the side and dart past him to break free of this awful awkwardness. Surely he could feel it. But he wanted to go on a *date?* How could he even ask?

Then again...as much as she wanted to say no, she had to admit that the guy was brave. And upfront. And honest. That alone stopped her mouth from forming the word *no*.

He was also right. Everything else had been nice, which was how they'd ended up in bed together after their second date. A terrible mistake. She'd remembered the problem as him being awkward, but she couldn't deny his claim that they'd both been nervous. He'd managed to power through and finish the job. Eve most decidedly had not.

She tried to relax her face when she realized she

was cringing at the memory of that uncomfortable goodbye. She'd regretted that night so much, but mostly for reasons that had nothing to do with him.

He watched her patiently, one eyebrow tipped up in slightly sardonic awareness of how strange this was. "Maybe?"

"Maybe. Yes. Okay," she stammered. "Call me. Maybe we can meet for lunch this time instead of dinner?"

His face broke into a slow, wide smile, and Eve remembered why she'd agreed to go out with him in the first place.

"Great," he said simply. "That sounds great."

She wished she could say that she felt the same, but at least she wasn't hoping for the ground to open up and swallow her anymore. In fact, when he excused himself a few minutes later, he left her laughing with a self-effacing joke. Maybe another date wouldn't be so bad. Maybe she'd been too quick to dismiss him.

Grace, who was making a beeline for her from across the room, would definitely say Eve was being too picky. They'd had plenty of discussions on the subject. Grace was of the decided opinion that Eve was single and successful and should be reaping the rewards of that the way a single and successful man would. Eve agreed in principle. In reality, the idea left her sadly cold.

"Hey, boss man," Grace said. "Are you chatting up the hotties?"

Eve couldn't help her smile. What the hell. She may as well embrace the situation. "Maybe."

Grace's eyebrows rose in surprise. "Really?"

"I'm not completely hopeless, you know. I can pick up men and…do the hookups, or whatever you call it."

Grace threw back her head and laughed. "Oh, my God. You're such a dweeb."

"I know."

"But you look hot."

"Yeah, I took my hair out of its ponytail. Pretty sexy."

"I'm serious," Grace insisted. She ran her hand down Eve's hair. "I'm glad you finally gave in to my coloring skills. You look brighter. Not just your hair, though. I'm glad you're starting to relax a little."

Yes, she was finally letting go. She'd fought her life for the past couple of years, white-knuckling it through a sorrow she hadn't even earned. It wasn't so hard anymore. It wasn't so damn lonely. "I need to find Jenny."

Grace pointed her in the right direction, and

Eve set off to give Jenny a hug. She'd been here for thirty minutes. She'd agreed to a date. So she gave herself permission to escape as soon as she'd spoken to the birthday girl. She even gave Mitch a friendly wave as she left.

Maybe the chemistry wasn't there, but when was it ever? She was thirty-six. She'd had two careers and lived in four states. And in all that time, there'd been only one man, one out of the hundreds she'd met as an adult, who'd wrenched her heart and set every nerve in her body vibrating.

Eve walked slowly down the dark street, shoving her hands into her pockets to pull her jacket closer against the cold.

She couldn't keep looking for that, wanting that. Hell, maybe even that hadn't been real. They'd never acted on it. Despite the countless nights she'd spent imagining his hands on her, nothing had ever happened, because he'd been too honorable, or they both had. So maybe all that chemistry would've evaporated the same way her mild attraction to Mitch had.

She nodded, lying to herself. It might've been awful with Brian. Sure. So why did tears spring to her eyes at the loss?

"Stop it, you idiot," she muttered, blinking back the stupid emotions. "You gave that up." She had.

On New Year's Eve, she'd vowed not to spend one more night crying for him. Not one more tear. She didn't have a right to them.

Brian had been her boss. Her mentor. And her best friend. But what he'd been more than anything else was someone else's husband.

And while she hated him for having the strength to walk away, she was so thankful for it that it made her stomach hurt. She'd never touched him, and that was her greatest regret and her best truth, all rolled into one.

"Fuck chemistry," she whispered as she turned off the dark residential street and walked toward the cheerfully lit square that was the center of Jackson. Her studio was one street off the square, but still part of the lively tourist district, and she adored the little apartment overhead. If she hadn't had that, she'd have holed up in some secluded cabin long ago and lost track of the outside world completely.

But here, even on this cool night in the middle of the off-season, people still walked along the western boardwalks of the town, fading in and out of the light cast by old-fashioned lamps.

Even on her street, a man stood in front of the bright windows of her studio, absorbed in a wall-size photo of the Tetons that she'd taken last year.

She loved that picture, even though it wasn't as vivid as the others behind it. She'd taken it in late fall, when all the color had already fallen from the trees. The whole expanse of land looked dead, but the mountains still rose up, solid and unmoving and dominating the world. She didn't mind the browns and blacks and grays. She didn't need the more flagrant shades of autumn to capture the beauty of the place. It stood on its own.

Apparently the man at the window liked it, too.

She was trying to decide if she should speak to him or just sneak past to the narrow staircase beyond when something about the line of his jaw caught her eye. The pace of her boots hitting hollow against the wood slowed. In that moment, she wished she'd worn quieter shoes, because she didn't want him aware of her. She wanted to sneak past. She wanted time to get a good look at him and see—

"Everything is so different," he said, then turned slowly, inevitably toward her. And just like that, after two years, Brian was back.

CHAPTER TWO

EVERYTHING IS SO *different.* But he looked the same.
Nothing about him had changed. The same face,
which had been handsome to her, but could only
truly be called rugged. The same brown hair he
kept cut short so it didn't curl. Even the same
traces of gray at his temples and the sun-worn
creases at the corners of his green eyes.

The same.

And the same awful blow of awareness she always felt near him, though it hit her in a sore spot
now, a place that had only just started to heal.

Eve stared, lips parted, the sudden shock to her
nerves beginning to turn cold beneath her skin.
"Brian?" she whispered, as if every part of her
didn't ache with the knowledge that he was only
five feet away.

"I tried to call," he said. His eyes shifted toward
the sky and he shook his head. "I mean, I tried and
couldn't seem to do it. I didn't know what to say."

"What are you doing here?" she managed to

ask. "Are you…?" But how to finish that sentence? He had a cousin here, but if Brian had come to visit before, she'd never heard. Thank God, because that might have broken her, knowing he was so close and completely unreachable.

But he was close now. And she hadn't broken. Yet.

She forced her shock away and stood a little straighter, tipping her chin to a haughty angle the way she'd fantasized of doing so many times. For months after he'd gone she'd acted out this meeting in her head, of being cool. Of not showing him her pain and rage. But now…now most of that anger was gone and she didn't know what to grab on to for support. So she pretended.

"Are you visiting your cousin?" she finally got out.

"I'm not sure." He shoved his hands in the pockets of his jeans and tipped his head back to blow out a long breath. When he looked at her again, his mouth was serious, his eyes as dark as she'd ever seen. He was a quiet man in public, and his harsh features could lend him a dangerous look, but he'd always been laughing when they were alone, or making her laugh.

"Can we go inside, Eve?"

She inhaled quietly at the way his voice wrapped

around her name. One deep syllable that had always made her wish she was called something longer and more complicated. Genevieve or Isabella. Something that would take him full seconds to say so she could feel it rumble over her skin.

"If you'd rather not, we could grab a coffee or a drink."

He watched her, waiting for an answer, the silence enveloping them. But it felt nothing like her earlier encounter with Mitch. Uncomfortable, yes. And awkward, the awkwardness pushing out from inside her until it hurt to breathe. But this time she didn't wish for the ground to swallow her. She felt as though she could stay here forever as long as he was watching her. As long as he was *here*.

"We can talk inside," she murmured, mortified that she even had to say that. After all their easy hours together, all those months of friendship, he had to ask if she'd feel comfortable seeing him in private. How the hell had they come to this?

She walked toward the staircase, so aware of him behind her. She'd always been aware. That he was right there. Nearby. She'd always been able to feel him. Even when she'd been renting the apartment from him, she'd been able to feel him working in the gallery below. The guilt of it had eaten at her, but not enough to overtake that awareness.

Her back tingled, telling her he was about to touch her, that he was reaching for her right *now*. But she'd learned to ignore that feeling, because it had never happened. And it wouldn't happen now. It was a lie.

Hands numb and heart pounding, she opened the door, fumbling with the keys and then the doorknob, as if there were something complicated about turning it to the right. But she finally made it in and he followed her inside. He still looked grim, his wide mouth flat and his gaze moving away from her.

Why the hell was he here? She felt suddenly panicked by the thought and wanted to scream at him, demand an answer. But more than anything, she wanted him to think it didn't matter. That she was cool and calm and *strong*. That she hadn't lost everything when he'd walked away.

Jesus, how sad was that? There hadn't been anything to lose in the first place.

He took a moment to look around; his eyes seemed to touch on a hundred things. The apartment wasn't neat and orderly, but it never had been, so she let him take in the cameras and lenses and photo books scattered between the magazines and occasional abandoned coffee cup.

"Can I take your coat?" Her voice sounded weak.

He nodded, still not meeting her gaze as he slipped off his jacket and handed it to her. The warm leather swallowed her hands, and the scent of him rose over her so unexpectedly that she had to close her eyes. Oh, God, she'd forgotten that. The smell of his skin. Pain bloomed deep inside her belly and nearly made her knees buckle.

She'd finally gotten over him, and now he'd returned, and for a moment she hated everything about him. Every kindness he'd shown, every wry smile that had forced laughter from her.

He'd made her remember the scent of his skin. Was there anything crueler than that? She hated him and loved him.

Her eyes burned with tears, so she blinked rapidly and hurried toward the closet to hang up both of their coats.

"Would you like a drink?"

"Yes," he said before she could even finish the sentence, as if he were just as stressed as she was.

She rushed to the kitchen and poured two glasses of red wine, stealing a gulp from hers before she even recorked the bottle.

"I remember this one," he said, gesturing toward a photo mounted on the wall.

"The ghost town," Eve said, trying to steady

herself before she joined him in the living room. "It's being restored now."

"Really? I'm not sure how I feel about that. It was perfect the way it was. Eye of the beholder, I guess."

They'd spent the whole day at that ghost town as he'd taught her old-school photography techniques she'd been using digital tricks to achieve. She'd taken hundreds of photos. This one was her favorite. She'd shot a few of Brian when he wasn't looking, and those were locked away on a thumb drive somewhere. She'd nearly deleted the pictures permanently after the night she'd accidentally run across them while going through files.

She didn't tell him that she was happy the ghost town would never be the same again. But she was.

When she handed him a glass and directed him to the couch, he waited for her to sit. She took the chair.

"You look good, Eve. Amazing, actually."

She sipped her wine and said a silent thank-you to Grace for forcing her to go to that party. If she hadn't, Brian would've dropped by to find her in yoga pants and a sweatshirt, her hair still damp from the bath. And not a speck of makeup to cover the fact that she was older and more tired than she'd been the last time they'd seen each other.

She needed to give Grace another raise.

"You look good," she said. "I hope things are going well for you."

He sipped his wine before he set the glass down and met her eyes. "Julia and I finally worked out our differences. We finalized the divorce two months ago."

"But..." Those two sentences didn't go together. She didn't know how to react. She wouldn't know how to react even if she was sure what he'd meant.

His mouth tipped up in the faintest of smiles. "At long last, we're getting along. We had drinks a week ago. It was nice."

"So...you came to tell me that you two are divorced and *dating?*"

"No! No. We're divorced and *friends*. She bought out my share of the gallery in Raleigh. I've spent the past six months showing her the ropes with the finances and paperwork."

"Well, congratulations, I guess."

He frowned. She frowned back. She'd never known how she'd feel about Brian finally getting divorced, but she hadn't expected to feel so numb. "Thanks for letting me know," she said into the silence.

"Eve."

"What?" she bit out.

"I don't know what I'm doing back here in Jackson. I only know that I had no choice. I had to come back. I had to find out."

Her heart beat harder, faster, but she still felt nothing. Nothing except that pulsing beat in her chest. "It's been two years."

"I had to try with Julia."

"I know that," she snapped, but deep down inside, she didn't know. She didn't understand why there'd had to be one more shot at it. He'd been on his third separation from Julia when Eve had come to work at his photography gallery. Julia had lived two thousand miles away in Raleigh. She'd come to Jackson only once that year, and meeting her had been a blow to Eve's conscience. And her confidence.

Julia was a true artist who saw beauty and conflict and emotion in everything. She was wild and spontaneous and confident. Eve, on the other hand, looked at her own best work and saw a need for improvement. She wondered if she could call it art at all. She was steady and analytical and good with numbers. She knew she had passion and life, but it was a quiet sort of wildness that no one ever seemed to notice. Even her photography was quiet. Pictures of the corners of life that no one else saw.

That was Eve.

Julia, on the other hand... Eve had never wondered why Brian had loved Julia. The woman was a flame. Eve just couldn't understand why he hadn't gotten tired of being burned, even when he'd had the option of something safer. Especially then.

"I had to try," he said again.

"Of course." She said it quietly, but she wanted to scream it. Of course he'd had to try again. Because the smallest chance with a woman like Julia was worth more than a sure thing with someone like Eve, any day.

The thought was so ugly and honest that she had to swallow back tears. Regret at her own selfish hurt filled her up. "She was your wife," she rushed to say. "Your first love. I understand."

He nodded. "I had to know it had ended honestly, Eve. Without any distraction or interference."

"Yes. That's what you said in your letter. I remember."

"You never wrote back."

"What was I supposed to say?"

He shook his head, the harsh planes of his face angry in the shadows of the dim lamp next to him. "Jesus, Eve. Anything. You were supposed to say anything."

"There was nothing to say," she bit out. "You

told me you had feelings for me. *For the first time
you admitted you felt something more than friendship, and you were already gone. What was I supposed to do with that?*"

"Eve—"

"You were already gone! You should never have
told me any of that."

"I had to. You were my best friend. I had to
tell you."

"Your best friend?" she snapped. "You walked
away from me. That letter made everything worse.
It made me want things we couldn't have. You just
left me here and went on with your life."

"I had to try to fix my marriage."

"I know that!" she yelled, jumping up from the
couch to rush to the kitchen for more wine.

"Eve." He moved toward her as she uncorked
the bottle. She stared down at the empty glass in
one hand and the bottle in the other. Her hands
shook too hard to pour it.

"It's over now. Julia and I both gave it the best
we had. Maybe we tried too hard. Maybe not hard
enough. I don't know. But it's over now. She's dating again, and I…"

Eve finally managed to pour the wine. She let
his words hover there and took a long drink. She
hated the hope that snuck deep into her veins. She

hated it and she wouldn't indulge it. Closing her eyes, she shook her head, but Brian still spoke.

"I'd like a chance, Eve. If you're not seeing someone else. Hell, even if you are. I'd like a chance to find out if this is something."

She shook her head again, harder this time.

He cleared his throat. "Actually, that's not right. I know it's something, at least for me. I'd like to see if it's something for you, too."

"No," she finally said, the word bursting from her on a wave of panic.

"I know it's not right. How it started. The way we felt. We should have stopped being friends. I should've been strong enough to walk away from you before I did, but you were so… God, I felt at peace with you, Eve. Content. But fucking tortured, too. Please, Eve, just…"

He touched her then. He *touched* her. His warm fingers closed over her wrist with no force at all, just a question. Just a hope.

Oh, God. God, it felt like atoms colliding. Like energy being created in some heretofore undiscovered way. The force of it surged into her veins and heat suffused her whole body. It was all she'd ever wanted. His hands on her. His warmth tangling with hers.

Her lips parted so she could draw more air as

she watched his thumb slide over her racing pulse. Could he feel that? Did he know?

"I can't," she said.

"Yes, you can." His voice had gone dark and rough. "You want it, too. For a long time, I wasn't sure how you felt. I told myself we were just friends, that friendship was all you wanted, and my fantasies were just that. Fantasies. But once I was sure... Jesus, it was all I could think about, Eve. Wondering how you'd react if I kissed you. Wondering how it would be for us."

She pulled her arm away. "I can't."

"If you need time—"

"I can't. You should go. I can't do this. Just..." She hurried toward the bathroom, cradling her warm wrist, trying to hold on to feelings she didn't even want. She shut the door and locked it, needing to shut him out.

He was so wrong. Wrong that she'd only wanted to be friends. Wrong that he was the only one fantasizing. And wrong that she could do this now.

She'd buried all those feelings. She couldn't resurrect them now. He'd left her alone in this damn place with all these memories. He'd had a life and a companion and a new place where he could think without seeing her in every corner. He'd gotten that space he'd needed. The space that men always seemed to take as their right. She'd been left with his ghost and the cruelest of goodbyes. *I think I'm falling in love with you. I have to leave.*

Everything she'd wanted, laid out just beyond her reach. What the hell had he wanted her to say? *Please leave your wife? Please choose me?*

Eve put her hands to the sink and leaned close to the mirror. "Fuck him," she said to her own pale reflection. He couldn't just leave and then step back into her life because *he* was finally ready. *Hey, baby. Thanks for staying on that shelf I left you on. I'm ready now.* "Fuck him," she growled again, glaring into her own eyes. But her eyes failed to convey the hurt and rage she felt. They looked as plain as ever. Brown and a little weary and sad.

Because she hated herself more than him. Hated how much she wanted to sob with relief and fall into his arms. God, that would feel so good. To finally be held by him. To smell the scent of his skin, not because she was holding his jacket, but because he was holding her. She wanted to give in and cry, "Thank you for coming back!"

She was disgusting. And he was an arrogant asshole. And it was too late for them, even if it had never been the right time before.

He knocked on the bathroom door and anxiety exploded through her.

"Eve, are you okay?"

"You h-have to go," she stammered.

"Eve—"

"Please! I can't do this, Brian. I swear, I can't. It's been too long and I don't feel that way anymore. It was a mistake. It wasn't real."

"It was real."

She backed away from the door, afraid he'd get past the lock and push through. If he did, if he held out his arms, she'd… "No. Please just go."

"Come out. Please. Let's talk."

She shook her head, unable to force even the smallest word past her tight throat.

He was silent for a long time, then she heard a quiet vibration of sound, as if he'd put his hand to the door. Or his forehead. "Eve, I'm begging you. I'm begging you for a chance."

He didn't sound as if he was begging. He'd likely never done it before and didn't know how it should be approached. He wasn't a man who begged. But she'd begged before. She'd gotten on her knees and begged God to let things work out for them. To let her have what she wanted. And then…to let her forget she'd ever wanted it.

She knew what begging sounded like. Weak and broken and so desperate you wished you were dead. Brian sounded only determined.

"No," she said, and it felt good for that one brief moment.

He drew a deep breath. She heard the shush of something against the wood, his forehead or fingertips or sleeve. Then he walked away. At first, his footsteps were a relief, but as they moved farther away, her relief gave way to fear. He was leaving. She heard him open the closet for his coat, then move back to the kitchen, where he paused for a moment.

He was about to leave, and what if he never came back? She didn't want to love him, but the idea that she would never touch him was brand-new again in that moment. New and awful and taking over everything inside her.

She wanted him so badly it was a solid weight in her body. She wanted to touch him, taste him, let him inside her. She wanted to feel his mouth and hands and cock.

"Oh, God," she whispered, pressing a hand to her mouth to hold back a groan of pain.

She wanted him that way. Needed it. It would never, ever leave her, as long as she lived. It hadn't faded at all.

The front door opened. She lunged forward. She jerked the bathroom door wide, but he was gone, her door already shut and Brian out in the night.

Taking a deep breath, she rushed for the front door. When she opened it, she found him standing there, head down, his wide back filling her vision before he turned.

"One night," she said.

"What?" Snowflakes drifted through the black behind him, glinting when they caught the light from her apartment.

She swallowed hard and made herself say it again. "One night. But that's it. Nothing else. No love or promises or hope. Just one night to get this out of our systems."

"That's not going to work, Eve."

"It has to. I'm not going to give you anything else. Just sex."

She thought he'd be pleased with that, at least, but he looked furious. "It won't be *just sex.*"

"It has to be. Take it or leave it."

"Are you involved with someone? Is that what this is about?"

"Just give me an answer. Yes or no."

For a long, terrifying moment, she thought he'd say no. The hard edge of his jaw jumped with rage. He didn't like being backed into a corner, and she was remembering now that his wife had been fond of ultimatums. Well, that was too damn bad. But if he wasn't going to budge on this, then what would

Eve do? Now that she'd had the idea, she couldn't give it up. She needed this. She couldn't just go on with her life, never knowing what it was to have him.

She waited.

"Fine," he finally bit out. He started to step forward and she held up a hand.

"Not here. Not in my bed."

"Jesus Christ. Are you kidding me?"

"No. I'll come to your hotel. I can't have any more memories of you here."

He closed his eyes for a moment and his lips pressed hard together. A heartbeat passed, then two. "Fine," he said again.

"Tonight?"

A huff of humorless laughter parted his lips. "Sure," he said drily. "Tonight."

"I'll meet you there in thirty minutes."

"This is ridiculous. After everything we've had together, you want to try to force it all into a one-night stand? You really think that's going to do anything but make it worse?"

"It can't get worse," she said. "Not for me."

His anger broke for a moment then. His features softened into regret. His shoulders lost their rigid tension. "I'm sorry, Eve. I didn't have a choice."

"Maybe not. But that doesn't mean I have to

tell you it was okay. It wasn't okay, Brian, so we can't just pick up like you never left. I'm sorry if that's what you came here looking for. All I can give you is tonight."

He watched her for a long moment, studying her eyes, then her mouth, before he finally nodded. "I'll take tonight."

He gave her his hotel name and room number, and then he left, moving down the stairs to the street below. Eve closed the door, leaned against it and slid slowly to the floor.

This wasn't happening.

BRIAN LOOKED UP at the stars for a moment, at the crisp white flickering against that deep blackness. He hadn't seen a Wyoming night sky in two years. There was no filter here. No haze of humid atmosphere to dull the light. But looking up at these stars felt like a memory, and so did hesitating outside Eve's apartment before walking away.

How many times had he done that? How many times had he stopped and wondered if he should go back, knock again, pretend he'd forgotten something and then…

He turned to look back at her door and felt that horrible tug of need, but he walked away like he always had. Only, this time it wasn't the end of the night.

Jesus. This couldn't be happening.

As he walked toward his hotel, he was so deep in confusion that he knew he was scowling at the people he passed, but he didn't give a damn.

He hadn't known how she'd react to his return. She had a right to be pissed. Of course she was hurt and angry. But he'd hoped that she might still greet him as a friend. He'd even hoped her initial shock would melt into something much warmer. But she'd been so cool to him when he'd turned to see her. Her eyes had swept over his face as if she were trying to place him.

And he... Jesus, his heart was still pounding so hard he could barely hear the clop of horse hooves as the tourist stagecoach rolled past him and made its slow way around the square.

Brian ignored it and slipped into the side door of his hotel.

Seeing her had been like seeing cool running water on a torturously hot day. Relief. That was what she'd looked like. Relief, if he could get close enough. If he could touch her and end the gnawing ache that had lived inside him for two years. More than two years, actually. Since the moment their friendship had pulled him too deep. He hadn't meant for it to happen, but by the time he'd realized the danger, she'd felt like the only real thing in his life. His marriage had been a phantom.

Shit. He'd had to try one last time. He'd been with Julia almost twenty years.

They'd been opposites. At first, he'd believed the old adage that opposites attract. She'd made his world exciting. And he'd made hers safe. She could count on him, lean on him, and at first, that had been what she'd needed. But she'd loved drama and passion, and after ten years of steadiness, she'd left.

They'd tried again. And again. When she'd left him in Jackson and gone back to Raleigh, he'd thought it was the end. Hell, he'd wanted it to be the end, even before he'd met Eve. But he'd tried one more time, because Julia had asked. For the first time, she'd volunteered to try therapy. She'd wanted one more shot. After twenty years of love and history, he'd owed her that.

Leaving Jackson had been the hardest thing he'd ever done, but it had been right. He and Julia had finally learned to speak to each other as adults, even about the stuff that hurt. Even about the most painful truth of all…that their marriage had been over for years. In the end, they'd walked away as friends.

Which was more than he could say for himself and Eve.

He'd hurt her badly. But he'd make it up to her. She'd forgive him. She had to, because what would he do if she didn't?

Brian let himself into his room. He tossed his jacket over the chair and walked immediately to the window to stare out toward her studio.

She'd walk that same path soon. She'd skirt around the square and come up to his room and she'd be here.

This couldn't be happening, because it was a mistake. He didn't want to touch her like this, with anger and finality between them. He wanted this to start the way it should have, with all the love and yearning he'd felt for her two years ago.

He should've said no to her ridiculous idea. But his *no* wouldn't have mattered, because his body didn't care about the hows and whys. His body was tight and energized with the knowledge that she'd be here in minutes, and his cock swelled with the anticipation of touching her. Finally.

Brian couldn't count the number of times he'd fantasized about it. In prurient ways, certainly, but in smaller moments, too. In quiet moments, when she'd sneak past his distraction with some quiet joke that would catch him by surprise. He'd laugh then, at the unexpected humor, but also at the happiness she brought him, and he'd almost lean toward her. So many times. It had seemed the most natural thing in the world to lean in and kiss her.

But he'd never let himself. He'd had to pay his dues. He hadn't had a choice. And he didn't have a choice now.

He couldn't walk away. It wasn't possible.

His hands shook. His heart pounded. This wasn't happening. It wasn't what he wanted. But he needed it more than life.

CHAPTER THREE

SHE'D SHOWERED AND dressed for the party earlier, but Eve still stripped down and tried on ten different pairs of panties, hoping to find something that would make her feel sexy. It didn't work. She didn't own anything scandalous, and she wasn't twenty anymore, so after a few long minutes of staring hopelessly at her not-quite-taut body, she pulled on a pair of black panties and a matching bra and left it at that. He could close his eyes and imagine something sexier, if that was what he wanted.

She put on the only little black dress she owned, added the matching heels, then left before she could worry that she looked as if she was trying too hard. This was the one memory she'd have of him, and she'd write it the way she wanted, with his hands sliding soft black fabric off her shoulders.

And that image was all it took. Her anger fell away and her pulse quickened. She was on her way to Brian's hotel room. To his bed. To his arms.

As soon as her heels touched the walk, she turned without hesitation and moved quickly toward the next street. He was only two blocks away. The cold hadn't even started to sink in when she reached the hotel and stepped into the warmth created by the lobby's fireplace.

Eyes averted, she walked straight past the reception desk to the elevator, a little afraid she'd see someone she knew. If she did, what could she say? That she was on her way up to a party? A reunion? Wearing nothing but a little black dress and heels? Eve kept her head down, and nearly jumped into the elevator for the ride to the third floor.

Would Brian try to talk her out of this? Would he hesitate? If he did, she'd just take off her dress.

Her mouth went dry at even the thought of being so brazen, but when the elevator doors opened, she stepped determinedly off. She was done with being denied. Done with doing the right thing. Done being careful. Tonight she'd take what she wanted and she'd deal with the consequences tomorrow. But she had to keep moving. If she stopped, if she really thought this through... No. She wouldn't give this up out of fear.

She was determined to remember every second of this, but even walking down the hallway felt a little hazy and far away. When she found his door and raised a hand to knock, it was someone else's hand in someone else's dream. But when the door opened, there was no doubt whose fantasy this was, because Brian stood there, still angry, but softer somehow. His sleeves rolled up to reveal his strong forearms. His hair mussed as if he'd scrubbed his hand through it. He looked as he had so many times with her when he'd been working for hours and was losing the light he wanted.

Eve's mouth watered.

She knew how to get rid of his tension. She'd always been good at that, but this time, it wouldn't be about making him laugh. This time she'd distract him with something different.

His eyes slid down her body as he stepped aside to let her in. She set down her purse and watched him as he edged past her. She had no idea what to do now. She'd instigated this, but all those years of forcing herself never to touch him had trained her muscles. She couldn't just reach out and press her hand to his chest. She couldn't step into his arms. So she watched him.

"You look beautiful," he said.

She whispered, "Thank you," clutching her hands together as her thoughts dissolved into nervous chatter. She was filled with the truth of how much she wanted him and how much this scared her.

The room was dim, but the single lamp he'd left on let her see him clearly enough. Despite her heels, he was still inches taller than her, and his wide shoulders made him seem even larger. She wanted to stroke her hands along those muscles. She wanted to clutch them.

But she surprised herself. When he took a step toward her, she stepped back. That didn't dissuade him, thank God. "Eve," he whispered, moving closer, and suddenly the wall was at her back and his body was only a few inches away.

Instead of touching her, his hands pressed to the wall on either side of her arms. His head ducked, but he didn't kiss her. Instead, his mouth hovered near her temple. "This is a mistake," he breathed.

"I don't care," she answered, trembling with the awareness that he was right there. So close. But he didn't move closer.

"Eve," he said again, that one syllable fraught with pain and doubt and helplessness. "Not like this."

She tipped her head up, forcing his mouth to brush over her cheek as she turned toward him. "Does it feel like a mistake?" she breathed against his parted lips.

Brian groaned, and then he kissed her.

She'd wanted to remember everything, but it

was already too much. The taste of him, the heat as their lips parted, the stroke of his tongue, the way his hands clutched her shoulders. He was touching her and she needed every moment, but the only thing her brain registered was pleasure and the hard pulse of her heart beating in every part of her body.

His tongue stroked hers, over and over. She couldn't draw enough oxygen to feed her pounding heart, but she didn't want to break away. She didn't want this to stop. It was their first kiss, their first taste, and it was already as deep and dark as sex. She moaned into him, tipping her head so she could take him deeper, but he finally gentled the kiss and tasted her more slowly. Her bottom lip, then her top, then a faint kiss on her jaw.

"God…Eve." His mouth was at her neck now, kissing, tasting. His shuddering breath chased over her. "You smell so good. Your skin… Christ."

Yes. He smelled good, too. Pressed tight against her so she could breathe him in the way she'd always wanted. She was practically panting, and her own frantic need embarrassed her, but she couldn't stop it. His hands were at her waist, sliding over her curves, and her own hands had finally found their place on his shoulders.

He was hot and solid, and she stroked him as his mouth set her nerves on fire.

Chemistry.

She was more turned-on than she'd been in years. Wet already, and aching and so desperate for more that she moaned when his teeth caught a sensitive spot on her neck.

His words whispered against her skin. "What the hell is this between us, Eve? You have no idea how many times I've imagined this. How many times I've gotten off to this. You feel so fucking good."

She'd thought her nerves were already awake, but her whole body lit up with new brightness at his raw words. He'd thought about her. He'd come to fantasies of her. Joy seemed too innocent a response to that revelation, but it felt that simple, and that good.

She reached for the top buttons of his shirt and tore them open so she could slide her hands against his bare skin. Joy. Yes. His breath went just as rough as hers.

He drew back then, just enough that he could look down and watch as she unfastened the rest of the buttons and tugged his shirt free of his jeans. She spread her fingers over his hot chest and his breath broke. She'd always thought his chest hair would be crisp and a little rough, but it was soft under her fingertips. She brushed her mouth over his chest and hummed her satisfaction.

Her own breath hitched when she felt him reach for the zipper at the nape of her neck. She stopped breathing altogether as he pulled it down and the air of the room touched her back.

Then his hands, sliding beneath the fabric. Oh, God. God. They were really doing this. Undressing each other. Being together.

She should have worn something more complicated, because it took only a few seconds and then he was sliding her dress down, just as she'd imagined. But suddenly it was so much. So fast. He was a photographer. He saw beauty every day. He worked with models. Artists. He examined every image with a critical eye. He'd see her the same way, and this moment meant so much that she couldn't do it.

But by the time she reached to hold on to her dress, it was already past her hips and falling to the floor.

He whispered her name and his hands were on her naked hips and he kissed her again, more urgently this time, more deeply. And then his hands slid beneath her panties to clutch her ass, and she forgot her stupid fears. She forgot them because he was hard against her, pressing his hips to hers as his mouth devoured her. When he reached to unfasten her bra, she wasn't nervous. She was eager and thrilled, because his hands were rough with excitement, and he groaned into her mouth as the bra dropped away and he cupped her breasts.

This wasn't about a fantasy for Brian any more than it was for Eve. This was about a need so deep that even fulfilling it hurt. An ache so overwhelming that his heart thundered beneath her hands. She didn't feel scared anymore. She felt glorious and needed. Triumphant.

Yes. Yes.

She unbuttoned his jeans as he pushed her panties down, but she didn't have a chance to do more. Before she could sneak her hand beneath his underwear, he'd slipped his fingers between her thighs.

"Jesus," he cursed as she bit back a cry. Even she was surprised at how wet she was, at how easily his fingers pushed deep inside her.

She threw her head back at the wild shock of holding him inside her. She tipped her hips toward him, eager for more. "Yes," she urged as he fucked her with his fingers. "Please."

She opened her eyes to find him looking down, watching as one hand teased her nipple and one worked at her pussy. She felt a distant shock at her own boldness as she arched her back and rocked her hips into his fingers, but it was worth it just to see him so undone. This cool, confident man transformed into a hungry animal, teeth bared, eyes narrowed and glinting, the sharp edges of his cheekbones flushed with need. For her. Just like she'd always wanted.

He caught her watching him and slid his hand up from her breast to cradle the base of her skull and pull her in for a deep kiss. He turned her in the same motion.

Eve gasped at the sudden vulnerability of not having the wall at her back. The air stirred across her skin, reminding her of how naked she was, but before she had time to adjust, Brian laid her on the bed. He kissed down her neck, over her chest, until his tongue circled her nipple. When he sucked, she cried out and grasped his hair to hold him close.

Every sensation was a revelation. The draw of his mouth at her nipple, the slide of his hands down her sides… It all felt better than it should. Better than should be possible. And it was still too much. She couldn't take it all in. The rough feel of his denim-clad legs between her knees, the slide of his hair between her fingers, even the faint scratch of his stubble against her breast. She wanted it all. She needed to remember it all.

Raising her head, she watched his tongue circle the tight bud of her nipple, then watched in tormented awe as his teeth scraped over her, so white against her pink flesh. He sucked again, harder this time, and Eve growled her approval at the small pain he drew out. His hands dug into her ribs as if he couldn't stop himself from holding too tight.

Yes, she wanted to say as he moved to torture her other nipple. Yes, more. *More.* More teeth. More sucking. More sweet, circling tongue. She twisted her fingers in his hair, so he could feel the bite of pain that his teeth pressed into her. His hand slid down to her hip and then between her legs.

Now the *yes* was pulled from her throat on a dark cry as she pushed her hips toward him. He stroked her clit, lightly at first, then more insistently as she rocked against him. "Brian," she moaned, as she had so many times in her solitary bed. "Brian, yes. Yes. That feels so good."

"I know," he whispered. "I know it does. You're so damn hot, Eve."

She whimpered when he pulled away from her, but then she realized he was standing between her knees to toe off his shoes and finish undressing, and she was happy to watch as his shoulders flexed and the muscles of his arms bunched. He slid his briefs off with his jeans and… Oh, God. Oh, God, his cock was thick and straight and hard for her, and she almost sobbed with need as he reached behind him to grab a condom from the dresser.

She wanted to taste him, smell him, feel him in her mouth, but he was already setting his knee between her thighs. She scooted higher on the bed as he opened the condom.

"Wait," she breathed. "Wait. I want to…" Reaching for him, she curled her fingers around his shaft, nearly groaning with relief as he jerked in her grasp. "I want to touch you, Brian."

"No. I can't….I can't hold out."

"Please," she whispered. "Let me touch you." She stroked him, thrilling at how thick he was. He'd push inside her soon. She wanted that so damn much. But first, she wanted to feel the silk-iness of his skin, the way it moved slightly with her stroking, the way he pushed toward her when she squeezed.

On his knees, he watched as she touched him. She slid her hand down to the base, then slipped her fingers lower to learn the shape of him, the weight of him.

His belly sucked in as she stroked up again. "I need to be inside you. Please. I've waited so long.

I have to feel you." But he still watched as her fist worked up and down. Up and down. Slowly. She could do this for hours. Forever. Explore his body. Please him with her hands.

"Please," he groaned one last time.

She finally let him go, loving the small, desperate sound he made as she released him from her tight grip. He slipped the condom on and lowered himself until he was poised just above her.

He met her gaze. She wanted to look away. She could handle everything tonight, but not the way he looked at her as he eased the head of his cock against her heat and pushed slowly in. He held her gaze as she gasped. As she spread her knees wider for his hips. As he stretched her and she took him in. He watched her face as he filled her, and she couldn't hide her emotions. She couldn't hide that his body sliding inside hers was everything she'd ever wanted.

In the end, she had to close her eyes so he couldn't see that this one night would never be enough. Nothing would ever be enough.

When he was as deep as he could get, he paused, his breath leaving him on a slow, deep sigh. He whispered her name then, and moved inside her, his cock pulling against the tight grip of her pussy.

She clutched his shoulders, digging her nails in at the shock of his thickness inside her body.

His cock filled her so thoroughly that she was caught between utter relief at having him inside her and the amazement of being invaded so completely. Tears of joy welled in her eyes. "Brian," she breathed, the only truth she could speak at that moment.

"Jesus, Eve. It's perfect. You're perfect. Tell me you need this."

"I need it," she answered immediately. "I need it so much."

"Yes. God, yes." He fucked her deeper. Harder. Pushing out all the loneliness and hurt. He filled her up with what she'd always wanted. His body and need and want. "Tell me," he urged again.

"I need you, Brian. I need you. I always have. Please. Please."

He whispered her name again, over and over, each time he buried himself inside her. Every stroke made her want to weep. Every thrust was an answer to all her needs and sorrows. Brian was inside her. Finally.

Just as she slid her hands down to his ass to pull him even tighter to her, he paused and shook his head. "Wait. I need a second."

Her eyes popped open. "Why?"

"Because if you keep being so hot, I'm going to come. So just…get your nails out of my ass and stop making those fucking gorgeous sounds."

Hard to believe she could go from tears to laughter in the span of a few minutes, but she could hear herself laughing in disbelief. "Are you serious?"

"Yes, I'm serious."

She let go of his ass.

"Just give me a second to…" He withdrew slightly and slipped his hand down her belly.

"Oh," she groaned, arching into his fingers as they teased her clit. "Oh, fuck."

"Shh. You have to be quiet, remember?" He thrust slowly inside her and she cried out. "Shh."

But she cried out again and again, and he urged her on, telling her how beautiful she looked, telling her how she drove him crazy. "I need to feel you come for me, Eve. I need to feel that. I need to see that. Come for me."

She couldn't believe Brian was saying these wicked things. Couldn't believe how rough and dark his voice was. He'd always been so careful with her. Always so circumspect. And now his voice was in her ear, telling her to come. *Come.*

He drove her crazy with the same slow thrusts, but his fingers stroked her clit faster and she was screaming now. Screaming as she felt everything in her body draw tight and heavy and huge. And then she broke apart with a wild cry, her hips bucking against him, forcing him to fuck her harder, faster.

"Yes," he growled. "Yes, Eve. Jesus...I can't..." His words ended on a strangled growl as he shuddered and pushed himself deep inside her body.

She slipped her hands down his slick back, thrilled that she'd made him sweat for her, thrilled at the way his breath tore from his throat. And thrilled with the unbelievable pleasure that had nearly broken her in two.

It was too much with him. Everything always had been. And though she'd told herself that he'd never live up to her fantasies, that it couldn't possibly be that good...God, it had been.

How the hell was she going to leave?

But she didn't have to think about that now. Not for a few minutes. He was still inside her, after all, still naked and pressed against her. He put his forehead to hers and opened his eyes. "You're beautiful when you come," he murmured.

"So are you," she said, meaning it despite the way he laughed and shook his head. When he rolled off her to grab a tissue, she blinked in shock.

He'd left her body too quickly. Didn't he know she'd never get to feel that again?

He lay back down with a sigh. "I didn't think that could feel better than I'd fantasized, but Jesus…"

She smiled despite her sadness. "Yeah. I know." When he tucked his arm behind her head, she turned toward him. It felt like the most natural thing in the world to lie naked against him, her knee on his thigh, her belly against his hip. How could it feel like resuming her normal place when she'd never done this before?

"Did you fantasize about this?" she asked as she laid her cheek against his warm chest.

"Yes. A thousand times. Did you?"

"Yes."

"I was never sure. Not until the very end."

She brushed her hand lightly across the dark hair of his chest. "I didn't want you to know."

He nodded. "I know. We were friends. It felt too important to risk, especially since…" He let the words die, and Eve didn't fill them in. "It got so bad I could barely be around you sometimes. And when I realized you felt the same, it made it better and worse all at the same time. I had to go."

She stroked her hand down until she could skim her fingers over his stomach. His muscles drew in.

She touched his hip bone, his thigh. She memorized the shape of him under her fingers. Because two years ago, he'd had to go. He'd had to leave her. And she couldn't forgive him for that.

"How long have you planned to come back?" she asked.

"When I left, I knew I'd come back if I could. And six months ago, Julia and I decided it was over. There were loose ends that needed tying up. Details to work out. But it was over."

"What if I'd met someone? What if I'd gotten married?" She tried to ask it lightly, but his chest rose beneath her cheek on a deep breath.

"I couldn't ask you to wait. Everything was up in the air. I knew I was taking a big chance, but I had to go back to Raleigh one more time."

She nodded, but she wanted to scream. She wanted to hit him and tell him he could stuff his morals where the sun didn't shine. Because what he meant was that it had been worth the risk. Worth the risk of giving her up forever. Worth never knowing if everything he'd wanted was right there in front of him. Worth breaking her heart.

She hadn't been able to talk to anyone. She'd had to carry on as if she were happy to have this new business, this new life.

"I had to remodel the gallery, you know." She

closed her eyes and listened to his heartbeat. "I had to spend money I didn't have to change everything, because I could see you there. Every day. In every corner."

His arm squeezed her closer. "I'm sorry."

"Everything I'd ever worked for, all those years in banking and finance, working with people who didn't understand anything about me… All those years of saving up and dreaming, and I finally had a place. My own place in the world. And it meant nothing without you."

"Eve—"

She pushed up and sat on the edge of the bed. She hadn't meant to say that. She shook her head. "You gave me up, Brian. You told yourself you *had* to, so you did. But I wasn't left here just to be scooped up when you wanted me back." She stood and pulled on her panties. "You took the chance of walking away, the risk of losing me forever, and you lost."

"I'm sorry. I know you're angry."

He sounded so calm. So steady and understanding. She wanted him angry and afraid, damn it.

"Don't go now," he whispered.

"I told you this was it, and I meant it."

"You said one night, not an hour."

She fastened her bra and pulled on her dress

before turning to smirk. "I have to go. There's really nothing I can do."

"Damn it, Eve. Don't be petty."

"Fuck you," she growled. "I'll be as petty as I want. What did being reasonable ever get me?" She could feel it inside her now, every time she moved. The way he'd stretched her and filled her and left his mark. Her body was sore. She'd feel him for a day, at least. Maybe more.

"All right." He sounded so calm as she tugged up the zipper of her dress. "Go. I hate it, if that's what you're looking for. I want to strip that dress off you and push you back on this bed and have you again." He stood, still naked in the face of her anger. "But go, if you need to. I can let you, because this isn't the end of us. It can't be. I can't live with that."

"I know exactly how you feel," she snapped, grabbing her purse and trying to get her heels on at the same time. "And I was wrong when I thought it, too. Goodbye, Brian."

She walked away from him, telling herself not to look back. Not to take him in or reach for him or change her mind. She walked out and her numb legs took her away from him for the last time.

CHAPTER FOUR

"YOU LOOK AMAZING!" Grace said after she'd downed half her coffee.

Eve ducked her head and stared harder at the proofs she was examining on her laptop. She'd expected to toss and turn all night. She'd expected to be racked with heartbreak. Instead, she'd fallen into bed and slept like a woman who... Well, a woman who'd just had the best sex of her life.

Christ, it had been so good. Everything else aside, how was she going to live without that for another fifty or sixty years? Knowing she'd had that and wouldn't again? She scowled.

"What is going on with you? Why are you growling at the proofs?"

"I'm not growling."

"Okay, tiger. I guess that's a perfectly normal photography-related sound."

"You get more annoying every day, you know that?"

"What's that red mark on your neck?"

Eve jumped so violently that the stool shifted under her and she had to grab the counter to keep from tumbling to the floor. She raised her head slowly to find Grace standing there, arms crossed and a huge grin spreading over her face. It was the most delighted she'd ever looked.

"I hate you," Eve whispered.

"Spill it."

"No."

Grace nodded. "You took that cute guy home from the party?"

"I did not! He was still there when I left."

"Booty call?"

"No!"

"That must be a hell of a new vibrator, then. I'll need the make and model, please."

An image of Brian, naked and boxed and wrapped in a bow, flashed through Eve's brain. "It's not... He's not..."

Grace raised an eyebrow, and Eve slumped in defeat.

"I don't know what I'm going to do," she whispered.

"Oh. Hey." Grace's grin disappeared and she stepped forward to put a careful hand on Eve's shoulder. "I'm sorry. I thought this was just about sex."

"It is," Eve insisted, but her voice was too desperate to fool even the dullest friend, and Grace was sharp as a razor.

"Eve," she scolded, but the word was mostly worry. "Are you okay?"

She wanted to say yes. She meant to say yes. But instead she told the truth. "No, actually. No, I'm not okay."

"All right." Grace scooted around the long counter and locked the door. Then she turned the sign to Closed.

"What if we have a customer?"

"It's March. The only customers are locals. We'll reopen in a few minutes and they'll come back."

"Fine." She followed Grace into the office and dropped resentfully into a chair.

"What's going on with you?" Grace demanded, then seemed to realize her tough-girl attitude was the wrong call and softened her voice. "I mean... What's wrong?"

Eve opened her mouth. And she closed it. She shouldn't have admitted anything. She should have kept quiet. But the words pushed at her from the inside. She'd never been able to say anything to anyone. He was married. People had known his wife. Eve's heart had been breaking, her dreams in turmoil, and all she'd ever done was keep working. Keep moving. Because if she'd ever stopped, it would have caught up with her.

But now she wanted it out.

"I fell in love with a married man," she blurted, then pressed her fingers to her mouth to stop the sob of shock that followed her words.

"Oh, sweetie, no." Grace wrapped a hand around Eve's elbow.

"I didn't mean to."

"Hey. Listen. Everybody screws up sometime, okay? It's going to be all right. I swear."

Tears spilled over Eve's cheeks and she ducked her head.

"Don't cry," Grace urged as she scooted closer to wrap her arm around Eve's shoulder. "Don't cry."

"I can't talk to anyone," Eve sobbed.

"You can talk to me. You know I won't judge you. You didn't judge me and that was one of the best gifts I ever got from anyone. You can talk to me, Eve. Please."

She shook her head, half because she was afraid to let it out and half because her throat was so tight she couldn't.

"Are you still seeing him or did you break it off?"

Eve shook her head again.

"Oh, Eve, you're not pregnant, are you?"

"God, no!" Eve yelped. "No! It's not like that. We never... That is... We never took it that far."

"Oh." Grace looked slightly disgruntled when she sat back.

"Oh, my God. Are you *disappointed?*"

"Of course not!" She cleared her throat. "But you know...if you're going to be all heartbreak and longing over the guy, you should at least get sex."

"You're terrible," Eve scolded. But she also indulged in a watery laugh.

Grace smiled. "I know. But you stopped crying. Now, tell me what happened with this married man you never had sex with."

So Eve did. Explaining how she'd left a lucrative, unsatisfying career in banking and moved to Jackson to take a year off. She'd skied and hiked and rediscovered her old love of photography. And then she'd met Brian. She'd worked for him in the gallery during the busy season. During the quiet months, he'd helped her relearn everything she'd forgotten about photography since college. Then he'd taught her more. And he'd become her best friend. Her companion. Her world.

"I never said anything. I never did anything. He was married, and I didn't want to be a mistake. I didn't want to hurt him or anyone he loved. But I did wonder if he felt the same. I fantasized. I hoped. He and his wife were separated. She'd gone back to their old home in Raleigh two years before. So...I hoped. And then he told me he was leaving."

"Her?"

"No. Me. He was going back to try with her again."

"God, Eve. I'm so sorry." Grace squeezed her hand.

"I tried to be supportive. I said the right things. But suddenly I was choked up and I couldn't stop the tears. I ran out. I didn't take his calls. I couldn't. Because I loved him and I hated that he didn't care. It hurt so much. And it was humiliating. So when I came back a few days later, I pretended nothing had happened. Nothing was wrong. And when he offered to sell me the gallery, I bought it, as if it were nothing but another business deal. A month later, he left. It was over."

"But that must have been years ago."

"Yes. Two years. He came back yesterday."

Grace leaned forward. "And?"

"He's divorced. He wants another chance. Or a first chance, I guess."

"And?" she repeated, her voice rising.

"I can't."

"Can't what?" Grace demanded.

Eve pulled her numb fingers from Grace's fist. "I can't do that. I can't feel that way again. It was too…"

"Too good?"

"No. Too much. Too hard. He overwhelms me, Grace. He makes me want everything. Makes me want to *give* everything. And that sounds romantic and lovely, but when he walked away, he took all of that everything with him. I can't forgive that. And I can't risk that again. I was so damn lost." She didn't cry. It wasn't much, but at least she kept it together in that moment. And it felt good to say it out loud.

"I understand. You know I do. But this guy… he came back. And as cruel as it sounds, you can't fault him for trying to make his marriage work."

"As cruel as it sounds…yes. That's the worst part. I hate him for that. And I hate myself for that ugliness. It was bad enough that I wanted someone else's husband. Jesus. Then I resented her, too?"

"You're human. And so is he. He probably didn't realize what he felt for you until he was gone."

"But that's the thing. He did. He left me a letter. He knew what there was between us. He knew what it could be. He was honest and up-front and honorable. It was beautiful to read. And so damn horrible, because I couldn't pretend he was just an oblivious man who didn't get it. He understood perfectly, Grace. And it still wasn't a good enough reason to stay." She swallowed and said the words out loud that she'd thought to herself so many times. "I wasn't enough reason to stay."

It hurt, hearing herself speak the truth. But it was a relief, too, like lancing a wound. And now that she'd said it, some of the fear left her.

Grace shook her head. "So you're just giving up? That's it?"

Eve closed her eyes. "I don't know."

Grace squeezed her fingers one last time. "Listen to me. It wasn't about you not being enough. He's a man. And he had it in his head that he needed to try to make his marriage work, right?"

"I guess."

"He had a plan, and he stuck to it, and he was doing what needed to be done. It had nothing to do with hurting you."

"I know," she said with a harsh laugh. "I was collateral damage."

Grace nodded. "Yes. Unfortunately. That hurts in its own way. I get that. You're hurt and pissed off, so…what? You just told him to go away?"

"Kind of. I told him I couldn't give him another chance."

"And?"

Eve squirmed. She picked at the rough edge of her thumbnail.

"Spill it."

"I told him we could have one night. That's it."

Grace slapped a hand over her mouth. "Oh, my God," she whispered past her fingers. "You dirty little slut. You *granted* him one night in your bed?"

"Not quite like that. And not in my bed. I went to his hotel."

"Okay, I'm sorry. I know this is serious, but just one second." Grace jumped from her chair and danced around the room with a frantic little step that didn't seem possible in her clunky black boots. "Oh, my God, I knew it. You look transformed." She dropped back into the chair. "Was it that good?"

"Oh, God. Grace. I don't even…" Eve let her head fall back and stared at the ceiling. "It was so damn good." She didn't realize she'd started crying again until she reached to scratch her temple and her hand came away wet. "It was the best. Another reason to hate him."

"For making it so good?"

"Yes. Exactly."

Grace's smile turned sympathetic. "Shit. I'm sorry. He's a bastard."

"He is," she said, not meaning it. She could hate him, but he wasn't mean or cruel or a liar. He'd hurt her with complete honesty.

She didn't want to talk about this anymore, so she cleared her throat and reached out to straighten a vivid blue strand of Grace's hair. "Will you let me take some shots of you this weekend?"

Grace groaned.

"Come on. I want to get it done before the spring colors start blooming. Your hair will be perfect in a grove of winter aspen. All that black and white and gray. And then you in the center of it."

Grace tried to shake off her hand. "Fine. Okay. But stop trying to change the topic. Is he leaving?"

"Brian?" she asked.

"Yes," Grace answered drily. "Unless there's more than one guy."

"I don't think he's leaving. Not yet."

"Good. You need to think carefully about this. You can't throw something like that away. Not even over a broken heart."

Eve crossed her arms. "I can."

"Well, you shouldn't."

"Why not?"

All the hard humor she normally showed fell away from Grace's face. She met Eve's gaze and she held it. "Because he makes you want everything, and you deserve that. You've earned it, Eve. Everything."

Everything. Oh, God. "I can't," she said, shaking her head, but something that had been sleeping inside her seemed to wake and raise its head. Something strong and proud. "I can't," she repeated, and that animal inside her growled.

Because…what if she could?

CHAPTER FIVE

BRIAN WALKED ALONG the boardwalk, watching his shadow stretch in front of him. He walked toward Eve. Toward what he wanted.

He didn't care that she'd tried to send him away. He'd already gone once. He wasn't going again. Especially not after last night.

Holy shit. That had been both the most natural thing he'd ever done, and the most breathtaking.

Everything. She was everything. What he wanted, what he needed, what was good for him. All of that in one woman.

He wasn't letting her go. Yesterday, he'd been uncertain, filled with guilt about hurting her. Unsure if she'd take him back. But today? Today he knew he wasn't going anywhere. That he'd never touch anyone else if Eve would have him. That this was it.

When he reached the gallery, he stopped at the front window. Though a large photo of Grand Teton was suspended in front of it, he could see past the edge of the frame to the long counter beyond. A girl with bright blue hair sat there, and beyond her stood Eve.

Yesterday Eve's hair had been down, a long brown curtain of silk that had slipped over his hands. But today it was pulled back in a careless ponytail, and his gut tightened at the familiar sight. How many hundreds of times had he seen her like that? Caught up in something, unaware he was watching, her head bent and brow drawn down with thought? How many times had he let his gaze drift to her neck and imagined kissing her there, at that tender spot just where her hair swept up?

He sighed as that old, dull ache beat in his chest. As much as he'd wanted to make love to her, it had been those small touches that had been the hardest to resist. His love for her had come so naturally that not acting on it had felt like blasphemy. It had killed him a little every day.

But last night had been a damned glorious resurrection.

He opened the door.

"Hi," said the blue-haired woman, still clicking away on her laptop. "How can I help you?"

Eve turned before he could answer. He didn't bother saying anything. She knew why he was here, and she didn't seem happy about it.

"Oh," the other woman said as she looked up. "Um."

He cleared his throat and reached out a hand. "Hi. I'm Brian."

She shook his hand. "I'm Grace. And I just realized it's almost closing time, so…" She glanced at Eve, who nodded. Grace scooted off her stool. "Nice to meet you, Brian. I'll see you later. Maybe. Or not. Um. Anyway, I'll go now."

Judging by the awkwardness, Eve must have spoken to this woman about him. He wasn't sure whether to be worried by that, but he couldn't deny the primal thrill he felt at the thought of Eve telling someone about him.

"What are you doing here?" she asked as soon as Grace had grabbed her bag and disappeared out the door.

"I came to see you. I thought you could give me a tour. Show me what you've done."

"I told you this was over."

"And I told you it wasn't."

She walked past him to lock the front door. "You don't get to dictate this, Brian. This time it isn't up to you."

He winced inside but kept his face blank. "I'll just have to convince you, then."

She shot him a cool, inscrutable look. It was

meant to keep him at a distance, he supposed, but he'd already been at a distance. He'd be damned if he'd go back.

Eve retreated behind the counter and started straightening things. Brochures. Business cards. It had always struck him as funny, this nervous habit of hers, because her living space was so chaotic, the difference being that when she was comfortable and happy, she didn't need things to be organized. He wanted her to be messy with him.

"Can I talk you into dinner?" he asked.

"Brian—"

"I'm not going away. I know you're hurt. I'm sorry. I'll apologize a thousand times, but I won't leave."

"So you're going to stalk me," she snapped.

"No." God, he didn't know how to say this without sounding psychotic. That he'd thought about her every single day. That she'd been everything to him, even when she shouldn't have been. "After last night, Eve, I'm not giving up."

Her jaw went tight. Her cheeks turned pink. She avoided his eyes and walked toward an office door to shut off the light.

Her phone rang and she seemed relieved to answer it. Brian was content with the chance to watch her move.

"Hello? Oh, hi, Mitch." Her gaze flew to Brian, then slid quickly away. "Good. Yes, it was good to see you, too. Of course."

He listened openly, not bothering to hide his interest.

"This Wednesday? I'm not sure I..." She looked up and flushed. "Maybe. I'll need to check my schedule, but I have a customer here right now. Can I call you tomorrow? Good. Thanks."

Brian raised an eyebrow as she ended the call. Eve just glared.

"A date?"

"Yes," she snapped. "Absolutely."

"I hope you'll let him down easy."

"I won't. I don't have any reason to. We've gone out a few times and we'll do it again."

"Yeah? Lots of chemistry?" He felt more than a small surge of satisfaction when she got flustered at that. No. She didn't have chemistry with that guy. At least not the kind she had with Brian. That was an impossibility, because it was too damn rare. He knew that from personal experience.

Everything about Eve made him want to sink into her. It had all been right...except the timing.

"You're jealous?" she finally snapped. She stalked to the far wall to turn off the exhibit lighting.

"No," he answered honestly. "Should I be?"

"You're kidding, right? Do you think I've been celibate for the past two years?"

She snapped off the last of the lights and plunged them into darkness, but the streetlamps leaked light through the window, and his eyes adjusted. She grabbed her bag, and he followed her out the front door.

"You think I just gave up when you left?" she pressed as she locked the door and stomped away from him. He followed. "You think I just pined for you?"

"No." No, he'd known she would see other men. He'd even known she might fall in love. He'd wanted that for her. Wanted her to be happy. Even if he'd also hoped she'd wait for him, if he were being honest. "I know you didn't. That's okay."

"That's okay," she repeated. She stopped halfway up the stairs to her apartment and shot him an inscrutable look over her shoulder. "Of course it's okay. It means nothing to you." She hurried up the rest of the stairs.

Brian shoved his hands into his pockets and followed her into her apartment. "What do you want me to say? That it's not okay? That'd be a little hypocritical of me, wouldn't it?"

She slammed the door. "I want you to say it

matters to you! That you're jealous. That you're hurt by it."

"Eve…" He dropped his head and studied his shoes, hoping that would make his mind work better. He didn't know what to say. Didn't know how to take her pain away or even mitigate it. "It matters to me."

"I had sex with him," she said coldly.

He hadn't wanted to know that. He didn't like it. It twisted inside him and tightened everything into pain. But if he was being honest… "After last night," he started, then paused as a memory washed over him, of Eve coming for him, her body squeezing his cock as she screamed his name. God. "If I'd known about it before, while I was away, it would have driven me crazy. Is that what you want to hear?"

"Yes."

"Fine. It would've tortured me to know. It would've killed me. But after last night, I don't care what you did with that guy. Because it wasn't anything like what we did, was it? Nothing has ever been like that."

The anger on her face melted into a vulnerability that stripped his nerves raw. She looked… scared. Of him. "Eve." He reached for her slowly, easing his fingers along her jaw. He traced her bottom lip with his thumb. "I don't care what you did with him, because after last night, you're never going to do it again."

"You can't—"

But he slid his hand behind her neck and eased her closer. Close enough that he could press his mouth to hers and stop her words. Her lips parted. He tasted her. His bruised heart pounded.

Her neck was warm against his fingers. That sweet, smooth skin he'd stolen so many glances of. The place he'd wanted to kiss for years. He rubbed his thumb up to her neckline and felt her shiver. "I love you," he whispered against her mouth.

She gasped and turned her head. "Stop it. You don't get to say that."

"Yes, I do. I love you. I loved you then, and I love you now. Nothing's changed."

"I've changed." She pressed her hands to his chest to push him away, but when he dragged his mouth to her neck, she arched into him.

"Fine," he said against her skin. "But I haven't. I still love you. I still want you. My hands still shake when I think about you. Your smile. Your laugh. That look on your face when you're working and you forget I'm there. And your skin. Jesus, Eve. Your skin. And the line of your back." He slipped a hand down her spine, closing his eyes at the way the small of her back curved into her ass. He pulled her against his body and kissed her neck again. "The scent of you. And the taste. I want to taste you, Eve. I want to spend hours tasting you. Days."

She wasn't pushing away anymore. Her hands slid around to his shoulders. Her nails dug into him. She pressed herself against his erection, and he groaned at the pleasure.

"I can't do this," she whispered. "I can't. You walked away. You tossed this aside like it was nothing, and it wasn't."

"I know. It was the hardest thing I've ever done. Even though I had to do it, I regretted it. I hated it."

"But *I* was the one who felt guilty. Who felt wrong. For wanting you at all, and then for not wanting you to try again with your wife."

"Is that why you're tossing it aside this time, Eve?"

She stiffened in his arms. "You can't just say it like that. Like it's easy. Like I'm just throwing something away."

He let her go and met her narrowed gaze. "You are. You're giving this up. Walking away. This time it's you. And you're doing it because of pride."

"It's not pride," she snapped, her voice breaking a little. "You *hurt* me."

He winced at the way her pain flashed through him.

"You made a decision that changed my life and you never even asked how I felt. Do you have any idea how lonely I was? And how eaten up inside? *I* knew that thing you didn't want to know. I knew you were with someone else, sharing a life, sharing a bed. I knew that every second of every day. So I had to give up everything I felt for you, because it was *killing* me."

Tears spilled over her eyes. She tried to wipe them away, but her face crumpled. "It hurt so much that it scared me. I didn't know how to make it go away."

"Eve." He wrapped her in his arms and she clung to him, sobbing against his chest. If he could take the past back, he would. He'd make a different decision. He'd do it all *right,* but he'd never had the chance. "I'm sorry. I'm so damn sorry. Nothing in the world would have made me walk away from you except that one thing. My obligation to my wife, yes, but I also didn't want it to start that way with you. My marriage felt over, but, Eve, it was still there in my life. I wasn't a clean slate for you. I didn't want it to feel wrong, because it's so fucking right between us. It's so easy and comfortable but there's need and lust, too, and...I've never felt that before. I didn't want it to be something either of us would regret. I'm sorry."

Her fists tightened in his shirt. Her back trembled under hands.

"I'm sorry," he repeated. "Please give me another chance. Please. I swear, I won't hurt you again. It's right this time, Eve. I swear it."

She drew in a shaky breath. And then another. But she didn't say a word.

"I know you built a life for yourself while I was gone. I just want to see if you can fit me into it. If you can't, if you decide it's not worth forgiving me, then..."

Then what? He had no idea. He breathed in her scent and tried to imagine what he'd do with himself if he had to let her go again. It would be so much harder this time. This time, he'd be chained by the memory of her body, of knowing how good it was between them. Knowing he'd never have that even one more time, and that he'd never find it with anyone else.

Her back rose against his hands as she took a deep breath, but she still didn't answer. Instead, she kissed his chest, his shoulder, his collarbone. Her mouth opened against his neck and pressed lust into his skin to mix up with the pain and regret and reckless hope inside him. "Just touch me," she breathed. "Please touch me. I don't want to think anymore, Brian. I can't do it."

He didn't know what that meant, what she was telling him, but his lust for her shoved doubt and good intentions aside, and he spread his hands over her back to pull her body tighter to him. It didn't matter what she meant. If this was what she needed, he'd give it to her. He'd touch her everywhere and show her. That she loved him. That she could forgive him. That he'd make all the hurt go away if only she'd let him.

He took her mouth in a kiss and slid his hands beneath her sweater. The heat of her skin made him gasp, and just like that, he was dying for her. Dying to feel her everywhere, and in awe that he actually could.

When he slipped her sweater up, she let him, and it seemed as much of a miracle as it had the night before. She was in his arms and they moved slowly to the bedroom. Then she lay down on her bed and let him follow.

He tugged down her jeans. Eased off her bra. "You're beautiful," he whispered as her hands reached to cover herself from the dim light that leaked in from the living room. She was beautiful.

She always had been. Soft and natural and sweet. He reached for her panties and pulled them down.

She tried to squeeze her thighs together, but Brian caught her knee.

"I need to see you, Eve."

She looked up at him, her hair spread across the bed, her body bared to him, a picture of everything he wanted for the rest of his life. His heart shook.

"And—" he slid a hand up her thigh "—I need to taste you. I've always needed it."

Her gaze softened and swept down his body. "Have you?"

"Yes."

She bit her lip. Her thighs relaxed and moved the tiniest bit farther apart.

He tightened his grip on her leg, and slowly, slowly eased her open.

He'd thought he was hard already, but now his cock was straining. She was so gorgeous and wet and pink.

"Yes," she finally whispered. "Do that."

He did.

The taste of her arousal filled his mouth and made his cock throb. He teased her and licked her, sucked at her clit and tongued her pussy, figuring out exactly what she liked by the way her hips bucked against him and her cries filled his ears.

She came with his fingers buried deep inside her. He wanted to insist on one more orgasm, wanted to do it all again, but he needed to be inside her. He needed it like he'd never needed anything.

When he slid his cock slowly into her wet heat, love got all mixed up with the tight pleasure and squeezed his heart until it hurt. His hands shook, and his heart beat so hard it scared him. By the time he came, muscles shaking and skin slick with sweat, he'd lost the will to hold back his words. "I love you," he rasped into her skin. "I love you, Eve." Her hand gripped his hair in a tight fist as he lost himself inside her.

He felt different afterward. When he lay down beside her, he felt dizzy and dazed and broken open. The sheets were cool on his back. Her limbs slippery and hot where they lay against his skin. Her body was deliciously heavy and languid against him, as though she'd melted into him. But Brian felt dangerously untethered, as if he'd drift away if she let go. As if he'd be nothing.

"You'll hurt me again," she said into the dim silence.

He took a breath so deep it stabbed through his chest. "I won't," he promised. "I—"

"Stop. You will." Her fingers spread over the skin above his heart. "Loving someone…that means feeling things that will hurt sometimes, in small ways, at least. And in big ways when things go wrong."

"Eve…" He shook his head.

"But I learned how to be strong when you left. Stronger than I thought I was. I got through it." Her fingertips traced the hollow beneath his throat. He felt the faint pressure when he swallowed.

"You're amazing. You always have been."

"I don't know. But now I know that even though it will hurt, I can get through it. Even if it ends. I don't need to be so scared."

Brian held his breath, waiting to see if his hope was justified.

"Yes," she finally whispered, face hidden against his chest.

"What?" he rasped.

"You're worth forgiving. You're worth the risk. And more than that…I'm worth taking the chance. I love you, Brian." The words broke, rough with tears. "Still. I never stopped. I tried, but I couldn't make it stop. I didn't know how."

He wasn't the kind of man who cried easily. In fact, he couldn't remember the last time he had. At his father's funeral, probably, five years before. But now his eyes burned, and he had to squeeze them shut to stop the tears.

"I love you," she said again, as if she were making herself face it.

"Thank God, Eve." He pushed up to his elbow and tipped her chin up. "Thank God. I've missed you so much." He leaned down and kissed her. He didn't stop kissing her until he was filled with the taste of her. He didn't realize how terrified he'd been until the relief washed over him and he felt whole and right.

"I can't promise more than a chance," she warned as she kissed his jaw. "I might be too mad. I might not be able to trust you."

"You can be as mad as you want. We'll get through it. I promise."

"Brian…" Her hand tightened in his hair and she pulled his head up until their eyes met. "You can't know that."

"I can know it. I do," he said, meeting her gaze without even a heartbeat of doubt. "You're my best friend, Eve."

She looked at him for a long moment. He let her see everything he felt for her. Finally, her mouth quirked up in a half smile, and he knew they'd be fine. It was the old Eve. "Best friends, huh?"

He smiled at the wry edge of her words, and her hand slipped down to rest on his jaw as he stole another kiss.

"Yes," he answered honestly. "Not to mention that you're the sexiest woman I've ever met."

"Oh, Jesus, Brian." She rolled her eyes. "You don't have to lie to me just because we're still naked."

"That's a good point. We are still naked. Thanks for reminding me." He reached past her to switch on the bedside lamp, and Eve squeaked.

"Turn that off!"

"Are you kidding me? I have to make up for all these years of not seeing my best friend naked."

She gave a huff of incredulous laughter and strained toward the light as her other hand tugged at the covers. "No way."

"Come on." He grabbed her wrist before she could reach the switch. "Give in gracefully. I want to see all of you. Over and over. Naked and turned-on and open to me."

She groaned and dropped her head to the pillow. "Why didn't you tell me you were coming back? I could have hired a personal trainer."

"Eve—"

"Brian, this is embarrassing! You've spent your entire career looking at perfect women. I'm just…"

He smiled at her. Then grinned down at her until she finally let go of the blanket to shove at his shoulder. "What?" she demanded, trying to hold back her own smile with a disgruntled pout.

"Perfect?"

"Yeah, right."

He laced his fingers into hers and kissed her thumb. "Eve, you're perfect. *This* is perfect. You're here and so naked under me. Nothing could be better. See?" He pressed his hips to hers and showed her he was already hardening for her again.

The smile that bloomed over her face filled him with a shock of joy. Was there anything better than a beautiful woman being happy about his cock? "That's perfection, huh?"

"Well," he murmured as he bent to taste her mouth, "if you say so."

Her laughter trembled through him, making his heart shake, but her quiet words set it right again. "I love you, Brian," she whispered against his mouth. And that was everything he needed.

CHAPTER SIX

"HOLD STILL!" EVE ordered, lining him up in her sights again. She watched his shoulders rise and fall on an impatient sigh as she snapped away.

"Come on, Eve."

"Just a few pictures."

She angled the camera so that he was at the corner of the frame, but still in focus, his own camera raised to his eye and trained on the herd of deer in a faraway field. Even as she clicked, she knew one of these photos would be her new favorite. Brian, and the mountains beyond him, and the first buds of bright green aspen leaves just braving the spring on the tree to his left.

"Okay," she said, but when he turned toward her, she snapped one last picture.

"Hey!"

She snorted with laughter at the outrage that creased his forehead. She didn't know even one photographer who liked being in front of the lens.

"Okay, we're done," he groused, dropping his camera to glare at her.

"Be nice, or I'll make you strip down and pose for me the way I really want you to."

"You wish." She saw the way pink crept over his cheekbones, and suddenly all she wanted was to be in bed with him, naked and sweaty and tangled in his limbs. She couldn't believe the way he turned her on with the barest of glances. As painful as that had been two years ago, now it was a wonder.

"You're so sexy," she murmured as she moved close to his body.

"I'm beginning to think the beauty of your favorite male model has damaged your corneas. You're half-blind."

"No." His arms snuck around her and she looked up at him, brushing her thumb over the line of his jaw. "You're gorgeous."

"Eve…"

She leaned up to taste the spot she'd just touched. "I want you all the time," she whispered. "It's embarrassing."

"It's a miracle," he responded.

He was right. It was a miracle. Not just the way their bodies fit together, but the way the loose edges of their lives had stitched together perfectly. He was managing the gallery now, and she'd expanded her studio space into a back room she'd been using for storage. She'd never been good at spotting new potential and bringing in outside work. Brian, on the other hand, had a passion for that. He sold her photography better than she could, and now the walls were filled with gorgeous work by local artists. Sales were already up, and the busy season hadn't even started yet.

But none of that mattered as much as the way he looked at her when she touched him. As if *she* were the miracle. God, he was ridiculous. And so wonderful it hurt.

She kissed him one last time. "Do you want to move in with me?" she asked.

Brian pulled his head back as his eyebrows rose. "Really?"

"Yes."

He smiled. "God, Eve. This is all moving a little fast."

She shoved him hard enough that he had to take two steps backward. "You've asked me three times already!" she complained. "Always after you've made me come, I notice."

"I know when you're at your weakest," he drawled. He reached for her and tugged her close again. "Yes, I want to move in with you. Now. Today. This minute."

"This minute?" she repeated, sliding her hands behind his neck and into his hair to tug him down for a kiss. She moaned as his tongue slid against hers.

"Well…" he murmured, breaking the kiss to taste her neck. "In thirty minutes, maybe." He backed her toward his truck, then growled when she dropped to her knees beside it. "Or ten. Ten minutes."

"I think you're overestimating your stamina, big guy."

"I think…you're right."

Five minutes later, they were speeding back toward town, windows open to the cold and her laughter chasing away on the breeze. But Brian was still complaining.

"Because," she answered his latest plea, "I'm pickier than you, and I'd rather come in a cozy bed than in a cold truck."

"I said I'd turn the heater on."

"I want to stretch out. I want you to kiss me. Everywhere. For an hour or so."

He shot her a scorching look. The truck surged forward as he pressed the pedal harder. "All right. Deal. I guess I'll just have to make it worth the wait."

She drew his hand up to her mouth and kissed his knuckles. "You always do," she whispered.

"What?" he asked over the wind.

But she just shook her head and turned to watch the trees slide by. The wind whipped her silly tears away. And Eve smiled.

* * * * *

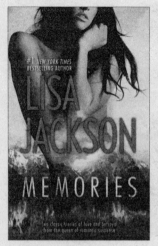

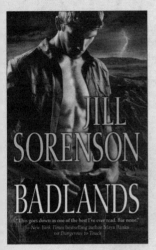

REQUEST YOUR FREE BOOKS!

2 FREE NOVELS
FROM THE ROMANCE COLLECTION
PLUS 2 FREE GIFTS!

YES! Please send me 2 FREE novels from the Romance Collection and my 2 FREE gifts (gifts are worth about $10). After receiving them, if I don't wish to receive any more books, I can return the shipping statement marked "cancel." If I don't cancel, I will receive 4 brand-new novels every month and be billed just $6.24 per book in the U.S. or $6.74 per book in Canada. That's a savings of at least 22% off the cover price. It's quite a bargain! Shipping and handling is just 50¢ per book in the U.S. and 75¢ per book in Canada.* I understand that accepting the 2 free books and gifts places me under no obligation to buy anything. I can always return a shipment and cancel at any time. Even if I never buy another book, the two free books and gifts are mine to keep forever.

194/394 MDN F4XY

Name _____ (PLEASE PRINT)

Address _____ Apt. #

City _____ State/Prov. _____ Zip/Postal Code

Signature (if under 18, a parent or guardian must sign)

Mail to the Harlequin® Reader Service:
IN U.S.A.: P.O. Box 1867, Buffalo, NY 14240-1867
IN CANADA: P.O. Box 609, Fort Erie, Ontario L2A 5X3

Want to try two free books from another line?
Call 1-800-873-8635 or visit www.ReaderService.com.

* Terms and prices subject to change without notice. Prices do not include applicable taxes. Sales tax applicable in N.Y. Canadian residents will be charged applicable taxes. Offer not valid in Quebec. This offer is limited to one order per household. Not valid for current subscribers to the Romance Collection or the Romance/Suspense Collection. All orders subject to credit approval. Credit or debit balances in a customer's account(s) may be offset by any other outstanding balance owed by or to the customer. Please allow 4 to 6 weeks for delivery. Offer available while quantities last.

Your Privacy—The Harlequin® Reader Service is committed to protecting your privacy. Our Privacy Policy is available online at www.ReaderService.com or upon request from the Harlequin Reader Service.

We make a portion of our mailing list available to reputable third parties that offer products we believe may interest you. If you prefer that we not exchange your name with third parties, or if you wish to clarify or modify your communication preferences, please visit us at www.ReaderService.com/consumerschoice or write to us at Harlequin Reader Service Preference Service, P.O. Box 9062, Buffalo, NY 14269. Include your complete name and address.

ROM13R

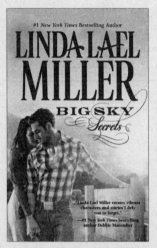